W9-CLN-791

Robert B. Parker's
Blood Feud

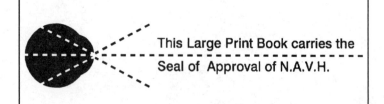

This Large Print Book carries the
Seal of Approval of N.A.V.H.

A SUNNY RANDALL NOVEL

Robert B. Parker's Blood Feud

Mike Lupica

THORNDIKE PRESS
A part of Gale, a Cengage Company

Farmington Hills, Mich • San Francisco • New York • Waterville, Maine
Meriden, Conn • Mason, Ohio • Chicago

Copyright © 2018 by The Estate of Robert B. Parker.
Thorndike Press, a part of Gale, a Cengage Company.

ALL RIGHTS RESERVED
This is a work of fiction. Names, characters, places, and incidents are either the product of the author's imagination or are used fictitiously, and any resemblance to actual persons, living or dead, businesses, companies, events, or locales is entirely coincidental.
Thorndike Press® Large Print Core.
The text of this Large Print edition is unabridged.
Other aspects of the book may vary from the original edition.
Set in 16 pt. Plantin.

> **LIBRARY OF CONGRESS CIP DATA ON FILE.**
> **CATALOGUING IN PUBLICATION FOR THIS BOOK**
> **IS AVAILABLE FROM THE LIBRARY OF CONGRESS**
>
> ISBN-13: 978-1-4328-5530-7 (hardcover)

Published in 2018 by arrangement with G.P. Putnam's Sons, an imprint of Penguin Publishing Group, a division of Penguin Random House LLC

Printed in the United States of America
1 2 3 4 5 6 7 22 21 20 19 18

This book is for my old pal, the great
Robert B. Parker,
who came into my life with
The Godwulf Manuscript
and has been in it ever since.

And for Esther Newberg,
keeper of the flame.

ONE

I said to Spike, "Do I look as if I'm getting older?"

"This is some kind of trap," he said.

"I'm being serious," I said. "The UPS kid ma'amed me the other day."

"I assume you shot him," Spike said.

"No," I said. "But I thought about it."

We were seated at one of the middle tables in the front room at his restaurant, Spike's, formerly known as Spike's Place, on Marshall Street near Quincy Market. It had started out as a sawdust-on-the-floor saloon, before there even was a Quincy Market. It was still a comedy club when Spike and two partners took it over. Then Spike bought out the two partners, reimagined the place as an upscale dining establishment — "Complete with flora and fauna," as he liked to say — and now he was making more money than he ever had in his life.

It was an hour or so before he would open

the door for what was usually a robust Sunday brunch crowd. We were both working on Bloody Marys even though it was only ten-thirty in the morning, being free, well past twenty-one, and willing to throw caution to the wind.

Spike took a bite of the celery stalk from his drink. I knew he was doing that only to buy time.

"Would you mind repeating the question?" he said.

"You heard me."

"I believe," he said, "that what you've asked is the age equivalent of asking if I think you look fat in those jeans."

I looked down at my favorite pair of Seven whites. Actually, I had no way of knowing if they were my favorites, since I had four pairs in my closet exactly like them. When any one of them started to feel too tight, I doubled down on yoga and gym time, and cut back on the wine.

"You're saying I'm fat, too?" I said.

"You know I'm not," he said. "And in answer to the original question, you always look younger than springtime to me."

"You're sweet," I said.

"That's what all the girls say. But, sadly, only about half the guys."

Spike was big, bearded, built like a bear

8

that did a lot of gym time, and able to beat up the Back Bay if necessary. He was also gay, and my best friend in the world.

"Only half?" I said.

"I'm the one who's getting old, sweetie," he said. "And probably starting to look fat in my own skinny-ass jeans."

My miniature English bull terrier, Rosie, was lounging on the floor in the puppy bed that Spike kept for her behind the bar, thinking food might be available at any moment, the way it usually was at Spike's. Spike called her Rosie Two. The original Rosie, the love of my life, had passed away the previous spring, far too soon. My father had always said that dogs were one of the few things that God got wrong, that they were the ones who ought to be able to live forever.

I'd asked Spike not to call her Rosie Two, telling him that it affected a girl's self-esteem.

"I love you," he'd say, "and by extension, that means I love your dog. But she's still a goddamn dog."

At which point I would shush him and tell him that now he was just being mean.

There was a sharp rap on the front window. Rosie immediately jumped to attention, growling, her default mechanism for strangers. There was a young couple peering in at us, the guy prettier than the woman he was with. They looked like J and Crew. Spike smiled brilliantly at them, pointed at his watch, shook his head. They moved on, their blondness intact.

"Where were we?" Spike said.

"Discussing my advancing age."

"We're not going to have one of those dreary conversations about your biological clock, are we?" he said. He trained his smile on me now. "It makes you sound *so* straight."

"Pretty sure I am, last time I checked."

"Well," Spike said, sighing theatrically. "You don't have to make a thing of it."

"You make it sound like we have these conversations all the time," I said.

"More lately now that you and your ex have started up again, or started over again, or whatever the hell it is you two are doing."

My ex-husband was Richie Burke, and had long since turned Kathryn Burke into his second ex-wife. He'd finally admitted to her that he not only had never gotten over me, he likely never would.

At the time Spike said it was shocking, Kathryn being a bad sport about something like that, and racing him to see who could file for divorce first.

Now Richie and I were dating, as much as I thought it was stupid to think of it that way. But "seeing each other" sounded even worse. When we did spend a night together, something we never did more than once a week, we always slept at my new apartment on River Street Place so I didn't have to get a sitter for Rosie. So far there had been hardly any talk about the two of us moving back in together, something I wasn't sure could ever happen again. It wasn't because of Richie. It was because of me.

The one time Richie had asked if I could ever see the two of us married again, I told him I'd rather run my hand through Trump's hair.

"I keep thinking that maybe this time you two crazy kids could live happily ever after," Spike said.

"I'm no good at either one," I said. "Happy. Or ever after."

"I thought you said you were happy with the way things were going?" Spike said.

"Not so much lately."

"Well, shitfuck," he said.

" 'Shitfuck'?"

"It's something an old baseball manager used to say," he said.

Spike was obsessed with baseball in general and the Boston Red Sox in particular.

11

He frequently reminded me of the old line that in Boston the Red Sox weren't a matter of life and death, because they were far more serious than that.

"You know baseball bores the hell out of me," I said.

"I can't believe they even allow you to live here," Spike said.

We both sipped our drinks, which were merely perfect. I used to tell friends all the time that they could call off the search for the best Bloody Mary on the planet once they got to Spike's.

"What's bothering you, really?" Spike said. "You only have to look in the mirror to see how beautiful you still are. And having been in the gym with you as often as I have, we both know you're as fit as a Navy SEAL."

"Remember when Richie told me it was officially over with Kathryn? He said it was because he wanted it all. And that 'all' meant me."

"I remember."

"But the problem," I continued, "is that I'm no better at figuring out what that means to me than I was when we were married. Or apart." I sighed. "Shitfuck," I said.

"You sound like the dog that caught the car," Spike said.

I smiled at him. "That's me," I said. "An old dog."

"I give up," he said.

"What you need to do is *open* up," I said, "and send me and my gorgeous dog politely and firmly on our way."

"You could stay for lunch," Spike said.

"And have Rosie scare off the decent people? Who needs that?"

"What *you* need," Spike said, "is a case. A private detective without clients is, like, what? Help me out here."

"You without a cute guy in your life?"

"Some of us don't need men to complete us," he said.

We both laughed and stood up. I kissed him on the cheek.

"Go home and paint," he said. "We both know that is something that actually does complete you. Then get up tomorrow and somehow find a way to get yourself a client."

"What if the phone doesn't ring?" I said.

Spike said, "It always has."

It did.

TWO

I'd loved the waterfront loft in Fort Point that I'd shared with the original Rosie.

I'd loved the light it gave me to paint in the late afternoon, when I felt as if I usually did my best work. I'd loved that it was completely mine after Richie and I broke up, and even remained mine after some very bad and very dangerous men had done their best to ruin it when I was once protecting a runaway girl. Mine and the original Rosie's, before and after the repairs. Ours.

But once Rosie died, there were simply too many memories for me to endure staying there. There was no place for me to turn without expecting to see her. She was supposed to be in the small bed next to where I painted, or sleeping at the foot of my real bed, or on the couch in the living room, or waiting at the door when Richie would come to get her for a weekend, back when the two of us shared custody of her.

14

So I'd moved, to a town house at the end of River Street, parallel to Charles, at the foot of Beacon Hill, a couple of blocks from the Public Garden and Boston Common, around the corner from the old Charles Street Meeting House. It was owned by my friend Melanie Joan Hall, an author for whom I'd once served as a bodyguard on a book tour, and then saved from a stalker who happened to be one of her ex-husbands.

Melanie Joan had bought the place not long after all that, falling in love with it the way she so frequently fell in and out of love with men. But now she had remarried again, to a Hollywood producer, and had moved Out There. When I'd mentioned the new Rosie and I were moving, she'd insisted that we make River Street Place our new home. At first she wanted to let me have it rent-free. I insisted that I couldn't do that. We'd finally agreed on a rent that was ridiculously low for the area, she'd put a lot of her stuff into storage, Rosie and I had moved in, with a lot of my stuff, but not all.

There were four floors. The place had been built in the nineteenth century, and legend had it that back then ship sails had been woven in the loft next door. It was all kind of funky and wonderful, built like an old railroad flat, not one of the floors more than twenty feet wide. Living room and kitchen on the first floor, master bedroom on the second, guest room on the third. The fourth floor became my art studio. I still thought of it all as Melanie Joan's house, as if it were a halfway house before I would find something more permanent eventually. But Rosie and I were still doing the best to make it ours. For now we were content, if in an impermanent way, in our twenty-by-fifteen rooms, and it was doing both of us just fine, Rosie more than me. As long as I was around, she didn't care if we lived in a shoe.

In the late afternoon she slept in a bed near the table where I was painting the small stone cottage Richie and I had come upon in the Concord woods last fall, when we had gone hiking up there. It was at the far end of a huge piece of property that belonged to a high school friend of Richie's who had gotten extremely wealthy in the real estate business.

"He's always telling me that there's a Thoreau inside me waiting to bust out," Richie said that day.

I told him that knowing what I knew about my city-boy ex-husband, busting out of a prison would be easier.

16

Richie's friend had told him about the cottage, which he said had been originally built in the early part of the twentieth century by a writer whose name Richie couldn't remember, and had gone empty for years. But I thought it was perfect, the masonry still beautiful, the place framed by autumn leaves and birch trees, and, beyond that, sky and God.

I had snapped some photographs with my iPhone but hadn't gotten around to finally painting the cottage until a month ago. I was still going slowly with it, still experimenting with which colors I wanted to dominate the background and which ones I wanted to mute, how dark I wanted the gray of the cottage to be setting off the leaves around it, how much contrast I needed between the stones of the cottage and the lone stone wall in front.

For the next few hours, I existed only in that world, trying to imagine what it must have been like to live in those woods nearly a hundred years ago, lost in the satisfied feeling of the work finally coming together, the shapes and color and proportion almost assembling themselves, as if exploring all of their own possibilities.

Over the years I had managed to sell a fair amount of my paintings. But it had never felt like a job to me, or work. It was nothing I would ever say out loud, not to Spike or to Richie or to anyone, but it was about the art in me. It had always been about the joy the feeling of a brush in my hand and then on the paper had always brought to me once I had gone back to working with watercolors.

There was also the sense of clarity and purpose it gave me, a completeness that my real job had never brought to my life, or my marriage.

"Rosie," I said when I finally put down my brush, pleased with the work I had done today, "why can't the whole world be like this?"

Rosie raised her head. Sometimes I thought that whatever I said to her always sounded the same, as if I were asking her if she wanted a treat.

I cleaned my brushes, put them away, took one last look at what I'd accomplished today. And smiled.

"Sunny Randall," I said, "you *may* be getting older. But this is one goddamn area where you're getting better."

I showered, changed into a T-shirt and new skinny denims, rewarded myself for a good day's work with a generous pour of pinot grigio. Then I inserted one of my favorite jazz CDs into Melanie Joan's player, John Coltrane and Thelonious Monk at Carnegie Hall.

It occurred to me that I hadn't thought about dinner until just now. It was, I decided, a good thing. Spike said another marker for getting older was when you started thinking about what you wanted to have for dinner as soon as you finished lunch.

"Once you're doing that," he said, "the next stop is the home."

I reviewed my takeout options in the neighborhood, finally settled on chowder and a Cobb salad from the Beacon Hill Hotel and Bistro.

I took Rosie with me when it was time to pick it up, brought the bag back to Melanie Joan's, and ate at the small kitchen table closest to the television in the downstairs living room. I stayed strong and didn't turn on the TV until I'd finished eating. I wasn't an animal.

When I finished cleaning up, I poured myself another glass of wine. There was no music now, just the sound of Rosie's snoring. And an aloneness, an aloneness that I had chosen for myself, that still swallowed me up sometimes in the night.

I thought about calling Spike, knowing he

would find a way to make me laugh and feel less alone. I could call Richie, but I knew better than doing that. You had to have a purpose for calling him; he was built less for small talk than anyone I had ever known.

Did I want him to come over? Did I want him to drink wine with me and make love later and share the ridiculously big bed upstairs? There was a part of me that did. But I knew that sometimes being with him that way made me feel even more alone afterward. As if there was an impermanence to that happiness, too.

I called Spike.

"Are you calling to tell me that since we parted you have somehow found gainful employment," he said, "even on a Sunday?"

"I am calling to tell you that I love you," I said.

"Red or white wine?" he said.

"White."

"I knew it!"

"How, might I ask?"

"White usually makes you sentimental," Spike said.

"What about a good bottle of red?"

"Melancholy," he said. "Or maybe it's horny."

Neither one of us spoke. He said he'd left the restaurant early.

"I'll die on the hill of you needing a client to make you feel better about things," Spike said. "But you'll never need a man to be fabulous."

"How come when you say 'fabulous' it doesn't sound gay?" I said.

"Because I'm fabulous!" he said, gaying it up as much as he possibly could.

I laughed.

"Now take two more slugs of wine and call Dr. Spike in the morning if you're not feeling better."

I didn't drink more wine, took Rosie out for one last walk, washed up, got Rosie settled in at the end of a bed that really did look large enough to be a helicopter pad, turned off the lights.

I slept until Richie's uncle Felix called me from Mass General a little after two in the morning to tell me that someone had shot Richie in the back.

I sat up in bed, feeling all of the air come out of me at once, instantly awake, knowing this wasn't a dream, knowing the nightmare was real, processing what I had just been told.

Richie.

Shot.

"Alive?" I said to Felix Burke, my voice loud and brittle.

I could see Rosie up and staring at me from the end of the bed.

"Alive."

I told him I would be there in twenty minutes, got dressed, blew up Storrow Drive, and parked at the Emergency entrance to the hospital, and realized I had made it in fifteen.

Richie.

Shot.

But alive.

THREE

To be any closer to Mass General when he was shot, Richie would have had to have taken a bullet at the front door.

The distance from his saloon to the hospital was less than a mile. Maybe a few minutes with no traffic and if you hit all the lights.

The doctors were still working on closing up the wounds, front and back, when I got there. Richie's father, Desmond, and his uncle Felix were in the ER's waiting area. They immediately walked me past the admittance desk and through some double doors, nobody saying anything to us, nobody making any attempt to stop us. It was as if the most famous hospital in Boston, one of the most famous in the world, was now being run by them.

"My son's wife," Desmond said to the first nurse he saw, as if somehow that explained everything.

The last thing Felix Burke had told me before we'd ended our phone call was "Through and through."

Meaning the bullet.

Now Felix said, "It was underneath his right shoulder. He was walking to where he'd parked his car after he closed up."

"Why was he even there on a Sunday night?" I said.

I was trying to process all of this at once. Why Richie was even at the saloon was a good enough place to start.

"Mickey, his regular weekend guy, called in sick. Richie knew he could watch the Sunday-night football game and thought it would be fun to work the stick."

We were about twenty feet down the hall from the room where Richie was.

"They cleaned him out with the kind of rod they use if the bullet doesn't stay in you," Felix Burke said.

"When the cops finished, they came over and asked if they could talk to Felix and me," Desmond Burke said. "I told them there was a better chance of Jesus stopping by tonight."

He was staring past me with his dark eyes, toward the room where his son was, or maybe past that, and into the darkness of his entire adult life, a life from which I knew

24

he had worked mightily to insulate his only son. I had always thought he looked like some pale Irish priest.

Felix Burke was different. Richie had shown me pictures of his father and Felix when they were teenagers, skinny, slicked-back black hair, all the brio in both of them staring out at you from the grainy black-and-white photographs. They could have passed for twins in those days. But that was a lifetime ago. While there was such an ascetic look to Desmond now, somehow Felix had grown broader as Desmond had become all hard angles and planes. He had been a heavyweight boxer in his youth, and you didn't have to look very closely to see the scarring around the eyes and that his nose was far more crooked than the one with which he had been born.

"One shot," Felix said. "Richie never heard him coming."

Desmond Burke said, "The shooter spoke to Richie after he put him down."

"The fucking fuck," Felix said.

I looked at Desmond. "What did he say?"

" 'Sins of the father,' " Desmond Burke said. "He didn't want to kill him. If he had, he would have put one in the back of his head. He wanted to send a message. To me. About my sins."

"Tell the fucking fuck to send an email next time," Felix said.

In a quiet voice Desmond Burke said, "Richard has never been a part of this."

"The family business," I said.

"Which has now brought him to this night and this place," Desmond said.

"Which will bring consequences," Felix said.

It went without saying. Felix had decided to say it anyway.

FOUR

"Fancy meeting you here," Richie said when we were finally alone.

He was in a room of his own. I didn't know how many private rooms were available in Emergency at Mass General at this time of night, but I assumed that even if it had been an issue, Desmond and Felix would have handled it. If they'd gotten it into their minds to put Richie's bed in the office of the chief of staff, I further assumed they would have made that happen, too.

By now I knew that the doctor who had cleaned out the wound and done the stitching preferred that Richie at least stay around for a couple hours. Richie had told him that wasn't happening and to please start the paperwork.

"Did you actually say 'please'?" I said.

"It was more an implied type of thing."

I had pulled a chair over near his bed and was holding his hand.

"They said you were lucky that the angle of the shot was up and not down," I said. "If he'd fired down, the damage could have been much worse."

"I gather luck had very little to do with this," Richie said.

"Meaning?"

"You know my meaning," he said. "If he'd wanted me dead I'd be dead."

We both let that settle until I smiled at him and said, "I thought we had an under-standing that I'm the one who gets shot at."

"Shot at," he said, "but never hit."

"Yet."

"You know how I like to be first," he said.

"Are we still talking about shooting bul-lets?" I said.

Richie offered a weak smile of his own.

"Tell me what happened," I said. "Your father and Uncle Felix told me what they know. Now you tell me."

"It's not a case, Sunny."

"Isn't it?" I said.

He started from the beginning, with Mickey Dunphy calling in sick. Richie said that because his social calendar happened to be wide open on a Sunday night, he decided it might be fun to cover for him. Sunday night was for regulars and, besides, he said, he still liked to bartend from time to time to keep himself in the game.

He had closed up, counted up, put the cash part of the evening's take in his office safe, set the alarm, and was walking to where he'd parked his car on Portland Street.

"And you heard nothing."

"Saw nothing," he said. "But I wasn't looking."

"And when you were on the ground he said what he said about the sins of the father."

Richie nodded.

"Is there any current trouble between your family and, uh, competing interests?" I asked.

"My father says no."

"But this was no random shooting," I said. "This was done with purpose, and planning."

"Evidently."

"He had to have followed you to the bar and waited," I said. "Because he had no way of knowing that you'd even be there on a Sunday night."

"Maybe he had been to the bar before," Richie said. "He picked a spot on the street with no cameras, according to the police. After I was hit, I tried to roll over to get a glimpse of him, or maybe a car. But he had just walked off into the night."

I leaned closer and said, "Who would do this? You've never been a part of that world."

"But I'm a part of their life," Richie said.

"You know what I mean."

"I do," Richie said. "My father always talked about boundaries. Now someone has decided to cross them."

"As a way of sending a message," I said.

"Evidently," Richie said.

"But about what?"

"Maybe that someone is coming for him," Richie said. "But we're not going to figure that out right now."

"Let me drive you home," I said.

"My father and my uncle have already insisted, I'm afraid."

Another weak smile.

"But feel free to engage them in a lively debate about that."

I squeezed his hand, in the quiet room in the quiet of the big hospital in the time before dawn. "Pass," I said.

"And you, always tough enough to charge at an automatic weapon," Richie said.

"There are boundaries that even I won't cross," I said.

"You should go," Richie said.

"When you go, big boy."

"Okay."

"Do you need anything?"

"As a matter of fact, I do."

"Name it," I said. "As long as it doesn't involve me locking the door and disrobing."

"Some Florence Nightingale you are," he said. "I'm just going to assume you dressing up like a candy striper is out of the question as well."

"Seriously," I said. "Is there anything you need?"

"For you to leave this alone," Richie said.

"You know I can't do that."

"I mean it," Richie said.

"Me, too," I said.

But the good news now that he was a client, I told him, is that he was looking at a whopping family discount.

FIVE

The last thing Richie had told me was that he wanted to sleep. So I didn't call him until late the next morning, to ask how he was feeling. He said that, all things considered, the biggest being that he'd been shot, he felt all right. I asked him if he was armed. He said that he was, with pain meds, and that he was going back to sleep.

An hour later I was sitting in Tony Marcus's back office at Buddy's Fox, his club in the South End. He had briefly changed the name to Ebony and Ivory. But now it was back to Buddy's Fox, and was as I remembered it, booths along both walls as you walked in, bar in the back. There were a handful of customers when I walked in, some in booths, some eating lunch, some seated at the bar. All of the customers were black. As always at Tony's place, I felt whiter than the Republican National Convention.

A new bodyguard of Tony's, who introduced himself as Tayshawn, was waiting for me at the bar. He did not ask to pat me down, just simply said, "Gun?" With the firepower on the premises, Tayshawn had clearly decided we could go with the honor system.

"Not to Tony's?" I said, and opened the Bottega Veneta bag that Richie had paid far too much for last Christmas to show him.

He walked me back to Tony's office. Tony's two main sidemen were back there with him. One was a small, jittery young guy of indeterminate age named Ty Bop. He was Tony's shooter. Today he was wearing a black baseball cap with a yellow *P* on the front, and the skinniest pair of skinny jeans I had ever seen on a man or woman. Even those hung down off his hips. His high-top sneakers were bright white. We had met plenty of times before, but he gave no sign of greeting or recognition, just leaned against the wall and swayed slightly from side to side, as if listening to music that only he could hear.

Ty Bop was to my right. To my left, opposite wall, was Junior, Tony's body man, one roughly the size of *Old Ironsides*. The threat from both of them was palpable. There had been a time, with two badass men in pursuit and fully intending to shoot

33

me dead, that I had come running into Buddy's Fox, where Tony's guys had dissuaded them.

Tony ran prostitution in Boston, and was involved with other criminal enterprises when they suited his interests, much like a street venture capitalist. He was as much of a badass as anybody in town, no matter how much he liked to present himself as a gent. He had always reminded me of what Billy Dee Williams looked like when he was young, a light-skinned black man with a thin mustache, bespoke tailoring at all times, day or night, a soft-spoken manner that was nothing more than a front.

Tony Marcus had his cut in Boston, and the Burke family had theirs, and the Italians, what was left of them, had theirs. Eddie Lee still controlled Chinatown. Two of the old bosses, Gino Fish and Joe Broz, were long gone. Joe had died of old age. Gino had not.

Tony and I were not friends. Tony didn't have friends, unless you counted Ty Bop and Junior. But we had managed to do favors for each other from time to time when our interests had coincided. I still trusted him about as far as either one of us would have been able to throw Junior. I was sure he felt the same about me.

He did not get up from behind his desk when I entered the office, just studied me up and down as if I were auditioning to be one of his girls.

"Sunny Randall," he purred. "You are still one fine-looking piece of ass, girl."

I sat down in the chair across from him and crossed my legs. The black skirt I was wearing was already short enough to show off my legs. Crossing them showed off more. Tony noticed, in full. But that had been the point.

"Don't make me file a complaint with Human Resources, Tony," I said.

It made him laugh.

"Girl, in my world, I *am* Human Resources," he said.

"How's business?" I said.

"Busier business than ever, Sunny Randall," he said. "Tryin' to keep up with the modern world. Lookin' to do some of that di-ver-si-fi-cation shit." Then proceeded to give me more information than I wanted or needed about how he planned to do that, with what he described as his "new fucking business model," and his plans for expansion out of state. As always, he went back and forth between talking street and trying to sound as if in training to become Warren Buffett.

35

He was wearing a gray pinstriped suit, a pale lavender shirt, a lavender tie just slightly darker than the shirt, and a pocket square that matched both. But he was looking older than he had the last time I saw him, softer underneath the chin, his face a lot puffier than I remembered, as if he had put on weight.

"So," he said, "to what do I owe the pleasure?"

"Somebody shot Richie Burke on Portland Street last night," I said.

"So I heard," Tony said. "Back-shot him, I heard."

"Before the shooter left him there," I said, "he told Richie it was about his father."

Tony nodded.

"I was wondering," I said to him, "if you know what might have precipitated such an event."

Tony chuckled. "I do love listening to you talk, Sunny Randall," he said.

"I'm just trying to get a handle on why somebody would not just make an aggressive move like this on the Burkes, but on the Burke who has nothing to do with the family business," I said.

"So ask them."

"I wanted to ask you," I said, and smiled. "Didn't you once tell me that you know

36

everything in Boston except why the Big Dig took so long?"

"Was just being modest," Tony said. "Knew that, too. The Italians just asked me not to tell."

He leaned back in his chair now, made a steeple with his fingers and placed them under his chin.

"Is this a professional matter with you," he said, "or personal?"

"Both," I said.

"But more personal."

"Yes."

He nodded. "And knowing what a hard people Desmond and Felix Burke are, even though they old as shit, we can assume that if there is some kind of dispute going on that they would prefer to a-ju-di-cate it theyselves, and for you to keep that fine ass of yours out of it."

"Listen to your own bad self," I said. "A-jud-i-cate."

He shrugged modestly. "Lot of layers to me, Sunny Randall, even the way I talk and all. You ought to know that by now."

"Lot of layers like an onion," I said. "But you haven't answered my question. *Is* there something going on that would make some-body ballsy enough to shoot Desmond Burke's son?"

Tony shook his head. There was still the faint smell of cigar in this room, even though Tony had told me the last time we were together that he had quit.

"Haven't heard anything, much as my ear is always to the ground," he said. "Got no idea why somebody would involve your ex. There's always been an understanding with the rest of us at the table, so to speak, that your man Richie had been granted diplomatic immunity. Not like in the past, when Whitey Bulger's crew didn't give a fuck who they took out. Sometimes it wasn't no more than Whitey waking up on the wrong side of the fucking bed."

"Until now," I said.

"But they didn't shoot to kill," Tony said.

"Guy knew what he was doing," I said.

"Even from point blank, you could make a mistake."

"He didn't," I said.

"If he wanted him gone, he'd be gone," Tony said.

"That's what everybody's saying," I said, "all over town."

I stood up.

"You'll ask around?" I said to Tony.

"What's in it for me?" he said.

"What about a good deed being its own reward?"

He laughed again, more heartily and full-throated than before, slapping a palm on his desk for emphasis.

"Gonna be like always," Tony said. "If I do for you, you do for me. Cost of doing business."

"Think of it this way, Tony," I said. "Maybe this time I'm the one pimping *your* ass out."

"I see what you did there," he said. "You ask me, it sounds like somebody wants old Desmond to know they coming for him, through people close to him."

"Nobody closer than Richie."

Tony nodded. "Best you be careful, too," he said.

"Always," I said.

" 'Fore you go," Tony said, "how's your boy Spike?"

"As you remember him."

"Toughest queer I ever met," he said.

I told him he was going to make Spike blush.

Then I told him not to get up. Tony said he had no fucking intention of getting up. At the door I turned to Ty Bop and grinned and pointed and pulled an imaginary trigger with my thumb.

In a blur, he had pulled back the front of the leather jacket he was wearing and showed me the .45 in the waistband of the skinny jeans, without changing expression.

Oh, Sunny, I thought to myself, *the places you'll go.*

Six

It turned into my version of Take a Crime Boss to Work Day.

After I left Tony Marcus I arranged to meet Desmond Burke at Durty Nelly's, an Irish pub on Blackstone Street in the North End that said "circa 1850" on the sign in front and "Old Time Traditions" on another sign behind the bar.

Richie had taken me there once, after a Celtics game.

"Being here makes me want to burst into 'Danny Boy,' " he'd said.

I'd offered to pick up the check if he promised not to.

Now his father and I were sitting at a table on the second floor. There was the last of the lunch crowd downstairs, all men, as white as Buddy's Fox had been black, eating hamburgers and hot dogs and egg sandwiches at the bar, watching a rugby game on the television sets above them.

41

There were, I'd also noticed, two men I always saw with my former father-in-law, and whom I'd seen standing near the entrance to Mass General about twelve hours before, whose names I knew were Buster and Colley. They took turns driving Desmond Burke around and acting as bodyguards. Richie had once told me that there was enough of an arsenal in the trunk of the black Town Car to invade New Hampshire.

"I've always liked it here," Desmond said. "Used to take Richie and his late mother here when he was a little boy for Sunday brunch."

"He told me."

I told him Richie and I had been here recently.

"Was there live music?" he said. "I've never been much for that."

He wore a blazer and a navy polo shirt underneath it buttoned all the way to the top and dark gray slacks and gray New Balance running shoes that he said eased the pain in his knees. His gray-white hair was cropped close to his head. It matched the color of his skin today. At the hospital and now here, he looked as old and tired as I'd ever seen him. I wondered if he'd slept at all.

"He's resting now," Desmond said.

"I spoke to him."

"You would."

"I assume you have people watching his apartment," I said.

"Of course," Desmond Burke said.

He was drinking Bewley's Irish Tea, plain. I was drinking coffee with cream and sugar. The cream and sugar made me feel soft. It wasn't the only thing about Richie's father that could make you feel that way.

We sat with the afternoon sun coming through the windows and on Desmond like a spotlight, and as we did I could recall only a handful of times when I'd ever been alone with him, when Richie and I were still married and then when we were not. Our relationship had been complicated from the start, because of my father being what Desmond still called a copper.

But we had always shared the bond created by our love for Richie, one that was not broken even after the divorce, especially when he could plainly see that Richie still loved me, and always would, even later, when he was married to someone else.

"I am sure you have spent the time since we were last together asking yourself who would do something like this," I said. "To him and to you."

43

He lifted his cup to his mouth and sipped some of his tea. It was not the first time it had occurred to me that his movements were as spare as the rest of him, the same as Richie's were.

"I have no answer," he said. "At least not yet."

He leaned back in his chair and folded his arms in front of him and closed his eyes, and then there was just silence between us, as if he were alone. I knew some of his history, from what Richie had told me and from what my father had told me, about how he came out of the Winter Hill Gang in Somerville, after he and his brothers had made their way to America from Dublin. It was before the gang had been taken over by Whitey Bulger.

By the time Whitey did take over the gang, Desmond and Felix Burke had gone off on their own, according to my father, and somehow Bulger had let them, partly out of respect for Desmond, and partly because of the Irish in him.

"I think it was the Irish Mob version of Verizon and AT&T," Phil Randall told me one time. "As batshit crazy as Whitey was, pardon my French, they thought there was enough of a market share for both of them."

Now, all this time later, Desmond and

Felix and the other Burke brothers had outlasted Whitey Bulger, and even the Feds who'd gone down with him. Desmond Burke had outlasted just about everybody with whom he'd come up, and his family was still the biggest player in our part of the world, still doing most of its business in loansharking and money-laundering. Lately, according to my father, he had made a modest move into the gun trade.

"Desmond has always fancied himself as some kind of gentleman pirate, and somehow separate from the other vulgarians," Phil Randall said. "He must think that the guns he brings up from the gun-loving states fire themselves."

So his specialty was all of that, my father had told me, and one other thing:

Settling old scores.

I quoted my father now to Desmond Burke and asked if this might have something to do with someone trying to settle an old score with him.

He opened his eyes, almost as if coming out of a deep sleep, and said, "How is your father?" He paused and offered a thin smile and added, "Not that I give a flying fig."

I told him he was aging both reluctantly and gracefully.

"Does he still, and even in retirement,

dream of seeing me behind bars?"

"I think he's let it go."

Desmond Burke offered another thin smile and said, "Not bloody likely."

He sipped more tea.

"The thing of it," he said, "is that most of my blood enemies are dead and gone."

There was still just a hint of Dublin in his speech. Sometimes "thing" came out "ting."

"I saw Tony Marcus before coming up here," I said.

"You think I don't know that?" he said.

"He said there was no current conflict that he knows of that would have brought Richie into the line of fire."

"There is not, at least not at the present time," he said. "What happened to my son, then, has to be something out of the past, perhaps before the boundaries were as well drawn as they are now. From a time when it took so little for shooting to start up."

"Could it be something from out of town?" I said. "Albert Antonioni, as I recall, wasn't exactly thrilled when you backed his people off Millicent Patton for me that time."

She was a teenage runaway I had rescued both from street prostitution and from her parents, even though it had been her parents who originally hired me to find her and bring her home. Antonioni, as it turned out, owned Millicent's father, whom he very much wanted to be governor of Massachusetts. That result was worth enough to him, or so he had decided, that he'd tried to kill both Millicent and me. At the time Antonioni saw having his own man in the governor's office as being the Mob equivalent of being able to print his own money, or winning the lottery, and merely saw Patton's daughter and me as collateral damage.

So it was two of Antonioni's men who had chased me all the way into Buddy's Fox. I told Richie about it. Richie told his father and his uncle Felix. There was eventually a sit-down involving all of us, something that I really did feel was out of a Mob movie, when Desmond Burke quietly and forcefully told Antonioni to call his men off. He did. It all reminded me of a line I'd once heard at a Bette Midler concert, when she was explaining why she called the other singers in her act backup girls.

Because, Bette said, *sometimes I have to tell them, "Back up, girls."*

"Albert is in Providence, I am here," Desmond said. "He manages to keep a hatred for me that began long ago under control now."

"Do you hate him in a similar way?" I said.

"He has never mattered enough to me to hate," Desmond Burke said.

He closed his eyes again. There was another silence between us. It was clear that he wasn't uncomfortable with it. Richie never was. If neither Desmond nor I said another word, it was already the longest conversation we had ever had.

"I will find out who did this," he said.

"Or I will."

"I would rather you stayed out of the way."

"With all due respect," I said, "that isn't your decision to make."

The dark eyes stared at me now, with both force and intense focus.

"You honestly think you can be better at the finding out than the army of people I can put on this?" he said.

"I do."

"I don't want us to be at cross-purposes," he said.

"No reason why we should be," I said, "except for the fact that we see a different end game, you and me."

"That being?"

"I want the person who did this to be arrested and put in jail," I said. "You want to issue a death penalty."

"After a fashion," Desmond Burke said.

There was nothing more to say. I thanked

him for seeing me, and for the coffee, and told him I would be in touch if and when I knew something.

"As I will be with you," he said.

"I love him, too," I said.

He nodded and squinted into the afternoon sun, and I left him there. The only time I slowed up as I walked through the downstairs room was to nod at Buster and Colley, Buster posted near the bar now, Colley near the front door.

I walked out onto the sidewalk and drank in some air.

Tony Marcus and Desmond Burke in the same afternoon.

I was living the dream.

SEVEN

I called Richie when I got back home and knew immediately from the thickness of his voice that I had awakened him.

"Not gonna lie," he said. "Getting shot isn't for sissies. I told myself I'd just close my eyes for a little while and slept until now."

"I won't tell Spike what you said about sissies," I said. "I think he could take you in a fair fight today."

"Maybe not just today," Richie said, "not that I'd ever admit that to him."

He told me that Danny Kiefer, the detective who'd caught the shooting, had called before he fell asleep to tell him that the whole thing was still clean, no cameras, no bullet, no witnesses. The neighbors who'd heard the shot thought it might be a tire backfiring. Kiefer, Richie said, seemed less interested in Richie getting shot than why he'd gotten shot, and kept bringing the conversation back to the Burke's family business.

"I told him," Richie said, "that it has always been my policy to mind my *own* business."

"Which," I said, "is not technically true," and I reminded him of the meeting he had brokered between his father and Albert Antonioni once.

"Didn't think that was any of *his* business," Richie said.

"Even if you might possibly know something that would help him identify the shooter?"

"I don't," Richie said, "even if."

"Kiefer is a good detective," I said.

"I know how tough a grader you are when it comes to detectives," Richie said. "It must mean he's great."

"Takes one to know one," I said.

"My father told me that he had asked you to stay out of this," Richie said. "But I told him that if you listened to me, we'd still be married."

I asked if he'd eaten anything, assuming that he had not. He told me he had not.

"Maybe later," he said.

I told him to check out the menu from Spike's and text me an order and I'd deliver.

"Are all of the good restaurants closed?"

51

Richie said.

"Would you like me to tell him that you said that?"

Richie said that if I was such a great detective I'd figure it out.

Spike and I sat at a table for two in his back room, at a little after seven. The chef was cooking up veal chops for Richie and me, and chopped salads. Spike insisted on adding two orders of apple pie.

I told him I was dieting. He told me to shut it.

"You lied when you said it was his idea to get takeout from here, didn't you?" Spike said.

"Absolutely not."

He raised an eyebrow. Not everyone could carry that off. Spike could.

"More likely," Spike said, "he made some kind of snippy remark about the cuisine at what *Boston* magazine recently called the hottest restaurant in the entire Quincy Market area."

"For me to say anything more would be a violation of client privilege," I said.

"So he *did* make a snippy remark."

"Totally."

Spike was wearing what I was sure was a Brioni suit that might have cost more than my car, with an open-necked white shirt. All in all, he looked good enough to take the big town for a whirl. Spike wasn't handsome in any sort of classic way. But the sum of him, the combination of looks and fun and physicality and danger, is what did make him attractive to men and to women.

No woman more than me.

"So he is a client," Spike said.

He made no attempt to make it sound like a question. Just a simple declarative sentence. A statement of fact.

"In theory," I said. "Just without any money changing hands."

"There is more than one way for him to pay you," Spike said, and raised the eyebrow again.

"Don't be coarse."

We each sipped some Whispering Angel, my favorite rosé and Spike's, too, as much for the name as for the taste.

"Play this out," Spike said. "Say this is some bill being presented to Desmond Burke because of something he did in the past. And say Richie is only the first in the family this guy's going to come after. What makes you think he won't come after you, too?"

"I can take care of myself."

"To a point, girlie. But if they can hit

Richie they can hit you."

"I am ever vigilant."

"But when you start poking around, you will eventually annoy this guy, or whomever sent him, if somebody sent him."

"That will involve finding out who the guy is, or the whomever."

"Sins of the father," Spike said. "I mean, what the fuck?"

"Excellent point."

"I'm not just eye candy," Spike said.

"It's amazing how often I manage to forget that," I said.

One of the waitresses had stopped by the table to tell us that the food was being bagged up. Spike and I talked a bit more about Desmond Burke. He asked how much I really knew about his past. Most of it, I said, had come from Richie, who I knew had never told me as much as *he* knew. As complicated as my relationship with his father had always been, I knew that theirs was far more complicated than I would ever possibly know. As much as Richie Burke was his own man and had forged his own path in life, with me and the saloon business and everything else, he was still Desmond Burke's son.

"You have to be aware that the detecting in this case is going to be more about

Richie's father than anything else," Spike said.

"Profoundly aware," I said.

"And that you will likely uncover inconvenient truths," Spike said.

"And not Al Gore's," I said.

"I'm being serious," Spike said.

"I know," I said.

"Richie may have spent a lot of his life compartmentalizing," Spike said. "You're not going to have that luxury."

"Aware of that, too."

"He's a fucking gangster," Spike said, "no matter what kind of manners he has. And will most likely not want you poking around in his affairs, even if it means finding out who shot his son."

I sipped more wine.

"The irony," I said to Spike, "is that Richie had been telling me that his father and Felix and Peter, the youngest brother, have basically been downsizing the past couple years, mostly because they're so goddamn old and so goddamn tired. He said that he'd heard his father say more than once that he had come to find the illegal gun trade as distasteful as he'd always found drugs."

"Hasn't made him quit it, from what I hear," Spike said.

I felt as if I raised a pretty saucy eyebrow

55

of my own.

"I know people," Spike said. "Who know people."

"Forgot."

"And probably forgot that one of the biggest gangsters in town was gayer than Greenwich Village."

"Gino Fish."

He nodded.

"I've always wanted to ask you," I said. "You never hit that, did you?"

"Don't be coarse," Spike said.

EIGHT

For the past six months Richie had been living in an apartment on Salem Street in the North End.

He hadn't stayed in one place for very long since our divorce, and had even moved once while still married to Kathryn. After they divorced, she kept their town house in Brookline and Richie had moved to Salem Street, at least partly to be closer to the saloon. The apartment was meticulously neat and sparsely furnished, and so fit him completely. The only photographs were of me and the two Rosies. There was one ancient black-and-white of his late mother, Theresa Clancy Burke.

There was a large living room, a large master bedroom, a smaller bedroom that served as Richie's office. When I'd arrived I'd seen a car parked across the street, and knew that at least two of Desmond Burke's men were inside.

I didn't think anyone would make a move on Richie here, or ever again, for that matter. But Desmond Burke hadn't survived as long as he had in the world he inhabited without being an extremely careful man.

Richie didn't eat much of the food Spike had sent over, saying he wasn't as hungry as he'd originally thought. As much as he said he'd slept across the day, he still looked and sounded tired.

"Tell Spike thanks, though," he said. "And that the food didn't suck."

"A review like that will probably make him want to kiss you," I said.

"Then maybe you better tell him that I thought it did suck," Richie said. "Can't take any chances."

We were sipping a pinot noir from Willamette Valley that he'd requested. I'd asked if that was wise, given the pain meds he was taking. Richie said that if I wouldn't squeal to the doctors, he was willing to risk it.

He was wearing a plain gray pocketed T-shirt and faded jeans, and was barefoot. There was more beard to him than usual, which meant he hadn't seen fit to shave a second time today. We were next to each other on a couch I'd helped him pick out when he'd moved in. There was a Red Sox game, muted, on the big screen mounted

58

on the wall across from us. I think he had the game on only for his own twisted amusement. We had many things in common, but he knew that baseball wasn't one of them. He just didn't think my indifference toward baseball was sick and depraved as Spike did.

"I think we can agree," Richie said, "that it was a shot that might of gone through me but was intended to go across my father's bow."

"We can," I said. "We think so, your family thinks so, Spike thinks so, as do the cops."

He grinned.

"You and Dad," he said, "chopping it up at Durty Nelly's. Would you mind terribly if I asked you to live-stream it next time?"

"I know I probably set a low bar where he's concerned," I said, "but it wasn't as awkward as I thought it might be."

"He never showed it very much," Richie said, "but he was always quite fond of you, even if you are Phil Randall's kid."

"I was looking through our wedding album before I went to Spike's," I said. "In the few pictures your father and my father were in together, they each looked like somebody had just pulled a knife on the two of them."

"I don't believe they've spoken since,"

Richie said.

"Oddly enough," I said, "they might be able to help each other on this."

"Might, but won't," he said. "The last person my father wants involved is you. Second-to-last would be Phil."

"Your father," I said, "has to understand that this isn't just about him, or what he wants."

"Why don't you tell him that?" Richie said.

He leaned forward, grimacing slightly, and reached for the bottle on the coffee table and poured each of us more wine. As he did, I looked past him and saw the painting of mine on the wall behind us, a sailboat in Boston Harbor that was one of my favorites.

"I might have to uncover secrets," I said to Richie.

"Well, he'll love that, won't he?"

"You know the writer Gabriel García Márquez?" I said.

"As a matter of fact I do," Richie said.

It shouldn't have surprised me. As much as I knew about him and we knew about each other, I was constantly making new discoveries.

I said, "He once wrote that we all have public lives, and private lives, and secret lives. I have this feeling that the answers we're looking for might come out of Desmond's secret life."

"Finding out secrets," Richie said. "Your best thing." He smiled. "Well, maybe not your *best* thing."

There was no indication that anything had changed in the quiet of the room, or the air between us. But it had, suddenly, the way it often did. We both sensed it. I turned so I was facing him more directly. I put my glass down. He did the same.

"I have a secret," he said.

"I don't think it would take a great detective to figure out what kind."

"I'm thinking of going public with it," Richie said.

"I'll bet you are," I said.

He stayed where he was and let me come to him. I fitted myself carefully against his left side. He put his arm around me. I leaned up and leaned in to him and kissed him. The kiss lasted a long time. The force of it seemed to have surprised us both when we finally pulled out of it.

"Are you sure you're up to this?" I said.

Richie brushed hair out of my eyes and gently kissed me on the forehead.

"You know what they say," he said. "What doesn't kill you only makes you stronger."

NINE

Richie was already asleep when I got out of bed, dressed, let myself out. Had I planned better for romantic possibilities, I would have arranged for Spike to take Rosie for the night. But I had not.

On my way back to River Street Place it had occurred to me that I hadn't asked Richie whether Kathryn knew that he had been shot. But there was nothing unusual about that. We discussed his most recent ex-wife about as often as we discussed the opera. As far as I was concerned, it was as if he hadn't as much divorced her as deleted her.

But I still didn't know with either clarity or certainty if I wanted Richie all to myself. All I had ever known is that I didn't want Kathryn to have him all to *her*self.

I got home a little before midnight. Rosie greeted me as joyfully and loudly as she always did, as if I'd just shipped home from a tour overseas. I put her on a leash, took her out, gave her a treat, put her on the small blanket at the end of my bed, and got ready for bed myself, this time alone.

But after I had washed and brushed and moisturized and hand-creamed, I fixed myself a glass of Jameson and took it over to the Eames armchair that I knew must have cost Melanie Joan thousands. It was situated underneath an antique reading light and at the corner of the wood-burning fireplace. Melanie Joan had told me it was her favorite chair in the whole place for reading.

"And," she had told me with a wink as theatrical as everything else about her, "it can be used in other creative ways."

"*That* chair?" I said.

"Oh, God, yes," she'd said in a husky voice.

I sat uncreatively in the chair now, in cotton sweatpants and a "Boston Strong" T-shirt I'd bought after the Boston Marathon bombing, feeling the warmth of the whiskey making its way through me. Who was it that had said that whiskey had done more for him than he had ever done for it? Someone. Spike would know. Or Richie, who read Gabriel García Márquez, would know.

63

Public lives, private lives, secret lives.

What was I going to find out about Desmond Burke's secret life, if I could find out anything? How many enemies were still alive, and still out there?

What kind of history was involved here, history about the Irish Mob that could not be learned from Google?

All these things I thought as I sipped Irish whiskey, moving up on twenty-four hours exactly when I had gotten the call from Felix Burke about Richie being shot, and I had been on my way to the hospital.

Who had done this?

And, far more important, why?

I finished the last of the Jameson. By now it was past one in the morning. Rosie barely stirred as I got under the covers. I had set the alarm for eight because I wanted to take a class at the Exhale Spa on Arlington Street. My Glock was in the top drawer of the bedside table to my right. I told myself I wasn't being paranoid, just extremely alert.

I slept, soundly, until I was awakened by the old-fashioned ringtone I used on my iPhone. At first I thought it was the alarm, then looked at the screen and saw that it was still only seven o'clock.

Caller ID said "Richie."

"Are you all right?" I said.

"Somebody just shot my uncle Peter in the back of the head," he said.

TEN

It was past eight by the time I met Richie in the little park set above the Chestnut Hill Reservoir, across from the football stadium at Boston College, on St. Thomas More Road. A little sign set in among the benches read "Chestnut Hill Driveway."

Richie told me that an early-morning jogger, a BC student, had discovered the body of Peter Burke on her way down to run the reservoir. By the time I got there, Peter's body was gone, and the cops had closed off both ends of St. Thomas More. Richie's father was with him, and his uncle Felix. So, too, was Lieutenant Frank Belson. Richie had told me over the phone that all of the uniforms at the scene had been told to let me pass.

Frank Belson was a friend of my father's and had once been a wingman for the great Martin Quirk, the most famous homicide cop in the history of the Boston Police

Department and now its assistant superintendent. Frank made no secret, at least to me, of his dislike for Quirk's replacement as his boss. The department knew her as Captain Glass. To Frank she was "her." Or worse. He smoked cheap cigars, even in the age of enlightenment about the evils of tobacco whether you inhaled or not, and almost always wore the same navy blue suit, no matter the season. But he was what my father called a righteous detective, no bullshit to him, eyes that took in everything at once, an ability to recall a crime scene after the fact as if he had photographs from the scene spread out on his desk.

When he saw me come walking up the path he took the unlit cigar out of his mouth and said, "Now I know it's my lucky day."

He looked tired, even this early. But then he always looked tired. He reminded me of the old Indiana Jones line, the one about how it's not the years, it's the mileage.

"I would've thought your uncle spent as much time in Chestnut Hill as he did on the fucking moon," Belson said to Richie.

"The shooter must have set up a meet," Richie said. "It's the only thing that makes sense. More privacy up here than the reservoir, even in the middle of the night."

"Could it have been someone who owed

him money?" Belson said.

"Someone like that would have come to Peter," Richie said, "not the other way around."

Peter Burke, I knew from Richie, had always run bookmaking in the family. His office, if you could call it that, was in the downstairs part of a two-bedroom flat on West Broadway in Southie. Richie had taken me by it once, after we'd had dinner at the L Street Tavern. It was when Richie was still living in Southie himself. His uncle's office had about as much charm as a holding cell. When I'd pointed that out to Richie he'd said, "And on a good day, they can clear as much money here as banks do on State Street."

I hadn't noticed Desmond Burke come up behind us.

"He was told not to go anywhere alone," he said. He shook his head fiercely and stared at the water. "A fucking cowboy until the end," he said.

It came out "fooking."

"He called me after midnight and told me he might have a lead on Richie's shooter," Felix Burke said. "I told him to stay where he was until he spoke to Desmond. He said he would. He lied. Peter did that. He was the youngest of us, and never much took to

68

being bossed around."

"Wasn't anybody with him?" I said.

"He sent them home," Felix Burke said. "Without telling Desmond or me."

"Anybody find a phone?" I asked.

"Shit," Belson said, slapping a hand to his forehead. "Why didn't I think of that. Good thing for me I've got a crime solver like you on the case."

"I'll take that as a no," I said. "Car?"

"Found it over there at the construction site where they're building some new fucking facility for the football team," Belson said.

"How would you possibly know that?" I said.

Belson jerked a head in the direction of the big uniformed cop standing with his arms crossed, facing in the general direction of Cleveland Circle. I'd spent a lot of college nights there drinking at a bar called Mary Ann's, where their policy on fake IDs was more liberal than Elizabeth Warren.

"Novak played tight end here until he blew out his knee with one of those injuries that has all the initials," Belson said.

"Weapon?" I said.

Richie answered before Belson could. "The lieutenant thinks it might be the same kind of .22 used on me."

"I'm surrounded by crime solvers this morning," Belson said. He looked at me and said, "Sometimes you run into them in the oddest places."

He turned now to face Desmond Burke. My own father might be out of the game. Frank Belson was not.

"You say you have no working theories about what happened to your son and what has now happened to your brother," Belson said.

"I do not," Desmond Burke said.

They were a few feet apart, eyes locked on each other. It reminded me of a playground stare-down.

"You're convinced this had nothing to do with some kind of grudge against your brothers."

"I am."

"You're likewise convinced it is only about you," Belson said.

"I am," Desmond Burke said.

"You need to leave this to professionals," Belson said.

"I have my own professionals," Desmond said.

Belson said, "How's that working out for you today, Desmond?"

I could see the tightness in Desmond's face, and saw him clench his fists, but Belson was already walking away from him, trying to relight his cigar, bending down to take another look at the exact spot where I assumed Peter Burke's body had been discovered.

When he stood up, he made a motion with his hand. Richie and I started to walk in his direction.

"Just her," Frank Belson said.

When I got to him he said, "I assume you're all the way into this."

"They shot Richie," I said. "You knew I wasn't going to sit this out even before they shot his uncle."

"Sadly, I do know that," he said. "But since you are the daughter of a great policeman, I also know that you know that if you in any way interfere with my homicide investigation, you can add the fact that you're Phil Randall's kid to the list of things about which I don't give a fuck."

"Understood," I said.

"I'll be in touch," he said, and walked past Desmond and Felix Burke and past the young cop Novak, in the general direction of where I could already see TV satellite trucks lining up on the side road that fed into St. Thomas More.

When he was about twenty yards away, I said, "Hey, Frank?"

71

He turned around.

"That list you just mentioned?" I said. "Is that an actual thing?"

ELEVEN

I'd met Wayne Cosgrove of *The Boston Globe* when I was still with the cops.

My father had always trusted him, which was about as much of an endorsement as Wayne could ever have expected from a member of the force. Like most Boston cops, Phil Randall had always viewed most reporters as a life form just slightly higher than the New York Yankees.

We stayed in touch after I got my PI license, and he'd occasionally helped me out on cases, mostly because of what was, in a simpler time, known as an encyclopedic knowledge of the city and its players, good guys and bad guys. Especially bad guys, from Desmond Burke and Joe Broz and Gino Fish and Eddie Lee and Tony Marcus and the DeMarco family all the way to the politicians in the State House. Eventually the newspaper had been smart enough to give him his own column.

Every time I would run into him, I would hear versions of the same complaints about what had happened to the newspaper business. But he was still at it, two days a week, appearing on local television as a talking head, and occasionally on MSNBC and CNN and even Fox News, where he said he felt safest, knowing they wouldn't use words that were too big for him.

He had looked like the last hippie when I first met him, dressing as if the sixties were still in full force. But by now he had cut his hair, telling me that guys his age who still wore their hair too long made him think of Howard Fucking Hughes. When I'd see him on TV, he'd be wearing blazers and a white shirt and skinny dark silk ties, like a real grown-up, even though I knew that below where the camera was shooting him he was still wearing jeans and beat-up Doc Martens boots.

In a world where you heard such an amazing amount of bullshit about Fake News, Wayne Cosgrove was as real as the dust on library books.

I was having a drink with him the night after Peter Burke had been shot. We were in the bar facing out to Arlington Street in the Taj Boston. My father still called the place the "old Ritz," even though it now had absolutely no connection to the much newer Ritz-Carlton on the other side of the Boston Common. The only connection here was to the past, because the bar remained unchanged, and one of the very best on the entire planet.

We had managed to score a table by the window. I had decided that it was a civilized enough hour in this civilized place to have a dirty martini, with extra olives. Wayne was nursing a glass of Pappy Van Winkle bourbon, which I knew was a rare and expensive brand only because of him. He had been coming here long enough that they kept one bottle of the stuff for him, and off the drink menu.

We were talking about Desmond Burke. Wayne had written a column published in that morning's *Globe* about Peter Burke's death. The headline read "Casualty of War We Thought Was Over."

Wayne told me he had missed me at the reservoir by about fifteen minutes.

"In the old days," I said, "you would have beaten me there."

"Operative word being *old,*" he said.

"Be happy you're in a game where it doesn't matter if your legs go," I said. "Because the words never do."

We clinked glasses.

"Problem is," he said, "words matter less and less and the game is more and more about page views and the president's last fucking tweet. Not the business I entered."

"You sound like a Burke talking about days gone by," I said.

He said, "But their business, as far as I can tell, is still lucrative, if less than it used to be."

His gray hair was still a bit on the longish side, but he carried it off. He was, I thought, still handsome in his sixties, in an aging-rock-star sort of way.

"It has occurred to me as I've done my reading over the past couple days," I said, "how little I really knew about Desmond's career over there on the dark side."

"I always wondered how much Richie really knew," Wayne said.

"Spike says Richie has always been able to compartmentalize."

"Got him good and shot anyway."

It had begun to rain, the first umbrellas appearing on Arlington Street, people waiting under the awning as Jesse and Ray, the two guys out front, hailed them cabs. I liked this bar anytime. I particularly liked it on rainy nights like this one, with good company right across the table from me and nowhere I needed to be.

"Richie was shot to scare Desmond," I said. "Hundred percent."

"Maybe the only thing that *would* scare the old bastard," Wayne said.

"First put one in his son, then kill one of his brothers," I said. "This is starting to feel like the Mobbed-up version of *Ten Little Indians.* Why I don't think Peter is the end of it."

"Fuck, no," Wayne Cosgrove said.

He gave me a tutorial about what he knew the Irish Mobs were like when Desmond and Felix and their brothers were first coming up. Some of it, the edges of it, I knew from my reading the night before. Wayne knew a lot more. I stopped him at one point and asked why he'd never written a book about any of it. He grinned at me and said, "Because it has always been my fervent hope not to write something that would have me end up like Uncle Peter."

"Point taken," I said, and we clinked glasses again.

He sat and took me through the old wars and grudges and all the blood that he said was once on the street as the rain came down harder. He told of the Charlestown Mob, run by the McLaughlin brothers, and about Winter Hill, before Whitey Bulger was in charge, when the bosses were Buddy

McLean and Howie Winter and a different McLaughlin than the ones from Charlestown.

"Wait," I said. "I think I know how the trouble is supposed to have started between Charlestown and Winter Hill. I read about it last night."

"Look at you," Wayne said, "still trying to be the smartest girl in class."

"Almost as smart as you in this subject," I said.

"Georgie McLaughlin," he said, "tried to make a move on Bobo Petricone's girl. Bobo was with Winter Hill. So Bobo and some of the other boys go over and beat the living shit out of Georgie. And his brother Bernie, as you can imagine, didn't take that so well. You can't imagine how much of this shit started with beefs about women."

"I'll bet," I said.

"So one thing led to another," Wayne said, "and poor Bernie ends up dead in the middle of Charlestown Square. And that was the beginning of the end of the Charlestown Mob as anybody knew it at the time. What was left of it was folded into Winter Hill."

Finally Whitey Bulger was in charge of consolidating Charlestown and the Killeens and the Mullens. And somehow Desmond

Burke ended up with a lot of the loansharking that had been run by the Killeen Gang, with Whitey's blessing, even though no one actually ever could figure out why.

"Every time I think about Whitey I think of Johnny Depp playing him in that movie," I said.

"Well, the reality of Whitey Bulger was much worse, of course," Wayne said. "But somehow he steered clear of Desmond. Maybe Desmond did him a solid at some point, and made that stand up until Whitey finally went on the run. No one was ever quite sure why. Maybe he decided he liked killing the Italians and the Chinese more than killing other Irish. Who the fuck knows? But somehow he allowed Desmond to start building his own empire, even though I'm sure your ex's father would be resistant to the notion that anybody ever *allowed* him to do shit."

"Then Whitey goes on the run and Desmond is the last Irishman standing," I said.

Wayne had his glass nearly to his lips. He stopped now and looked at me.

"Maybe not for long," he said.

"Manifestly," I said.

"I think I've mentioned before that you sound hardly anything like a private dick," he said.

"Watch your mouth," I said.

"Little late for that," he said, and grinned, and drank.

"You forget I was a fine arts major."

"Who now has a license to pack a gun."

"Fine arts majors with guns," I said. "Sounds like a pitch for a new TV series."

The bar was beginning to fill up. The rain continued to come down. The people moved faster on Arlington Street, with and without umbrellas. But I felt safe and warm in the bar at the Taj, even as we talked about Mob killings out of the past, and the killing of Peter Burke the day before.

"Maybe the answer is back there somewhere," I said.

"Maybe there's someone who worked with one of those Mobs who's not dead or in prison who still has a score to settle with old Desmond," Wayne said. "You know the joke about Irish Alzheimer's, right?"

"I thought it was Italians."

"Either way," Wayne said. "You forget everything except the grudges."

We drank to that. Wayne asked if we should have one more for the road, or old times' sake, or just for the fuck of it.

I said, "We'd be fools not to."

TWELVE

I was having my weekly session with Dr. Susan Silverman in the office at her home on Linnaean Street in Cambridge.

There had been times in my life when I had seen Dr. Silverman twice a week. Almost always, in the course of our fifty minutes together, the subject would involve Richie.

So it did today.

"At least," I said, "I feel as if my feelings about him are uncomplicated this time."

"Are they?" she said.

She was as beautiful as ever, in a way that was both ageless and timeless. And, if you were a woman, more than somewhat annoying. I had always thought it pointless to try guessing her actual age, though I knew it wouldn't take much crackerjack detecting to find out. I knew she would probably tell me if asked. When I sometimes did imagine myself asking, I could picture her smiling at me and saying, "How old do you think I am?" Or simply asking me why it mattered.

She had hair that was intensely dark, flawless skin, and an intelligence that felt almost kinetic in a room that today was splashed with sunlight. Often I really would leave this office feeling as if I knew myself better. Always, though, I wondered if I would ever have the sense of self that Susan Silverman clearly did.

Today she was wearing a navy suit with pants and a white shirt underneath and makeup and eyeliner that I knew required both time and effort and an almost professional expertise.

"Sunny," she said now, "I seem to have lost you there for a second. You had suggested that you felt a clarity to your response to Richie being shot."

"It was partially anger," I said, "and partially fear about how easily I could have lost him if the shooter had wanted him dead."

"Lost him in a random and violent and unexpected way," she said. "Even in a random world."

"It's ironic, if you think about it," I said.

She leaned forward, elbows on her desk, and made a tent with her fingers under her chin, her focus both calm and fierce at the same time.

"In what way?" she said.

"I've always known that Richie was raised within the structure of a violent family," I said. "But as far as I know, the violence of the world of his father and uncles had somehow never reached him."

These were things that I had been thinking about and discussing with Richie and Spike and others. Just not with Dr. Silverman. It was as if I had come here today looking for some sort of bottom line.

"But because of my work as a private detective," I said, "and even having been a cop before that, I've frequently encountered violence. It's kind of a weird duality, don't you think? At the very least, it's ironic."

Duality.

Look at you and your shrinky words, I thought.

Susan Silverman nodded.

"There's always a lot of that going on with Richie and you, though, isn't there? Duality *and* irony."

"Yes."

"What emotion was most powerful and present for you?" Susan Silverman asked. "The anger or the fear?"

I thought about that, because I hadn't until now.

"Fear, I suppose."

"Of losing him completely."

"Yes."

"After all the other different ways when you felt you lost him," she said. "When he was dating other women, and even married one of them."

"That was different."

"Was it?" she said, her eyes big.

"He was still in my life," I said, "even when he wasn't."

"But it was you," Susan Silverman said, "who initiated the dissolution of your marriage."

I said, "I could still see him when I wanted." I smiled at her. "We've spoken of this before. We even shared custody of the original Rosie."

I shifted in my chair. Recrossed my legs. There was no reason for me to feel as defensive in here as I sometimes did.

But I did.

"And you didn't feel as if some sort of order had been restored to the universe the two of you share until he was the one who ended his second marriage," she said.

I smiled. "Bastard finally came to his senses," I said.

She offered a smile in return.

"You've suggested that your feelings for

Richie are uncomplicated," she said, "even though there is no clear resolution to them, or commitment from either one of you about the future."

"I think I might have to table those issues," I said, "until I find the sonofabitch who shot him."

I snuck a look at my watch. I know she saw me do it. Only a few minutes left in the session.

"There might be one other thing to consider," Susan Silverman said. "Perhaps you feel the sense of purpose that you're feeling right now, and clarity, because you've decided that in this particular case he needs you more than you need him."

"Gotta admit," I said. "Didn't see that one coming."

She tilted her head just slightly and raised an eyebrow, though not as artfully as Spike could. She wasn't perfect.

"Kind of my thing," she said. "And something else for you to consider until next time."

She stood and smiled and said, "While you are occupied with the rat-bastard sonofabitch who shot your ex-husband."

The mouth on her.

And her such a lady.

THIRTEEN

On my way back from Cambridge I called my father and told him I was probably going to have to make a much deeper dive into Desmond Burke's past.

I had Phil Randall on speaker, and could hear him make a snorting noise.

"Good luck with that," he said.

I told him that I'd already met with Wayne Cosgrove.

"Good reporter," my father said, "for a reporter."

"He actually knows a lot about the history of the Irish Mob," I said.

"From the outside," Phil Randall said. "Doesn't make him an insider. It's like thinking you know how to play shortstop for the Red Sox because you've watched a lot of baseball from the Monster Seats."

I looked in the rearview mirror and saw myself smiling.

"You know how much I love you, Daddy,"

I said. "But you do know how I stop listening when you use baseball analogies, right?"

"What I'm saying," he said, "is that you're gonna need someone who actually is on the inside. Or was. And whose last name isn't Burke." There was a pause and then he said, "I'm assuming you would have mentioned it if any of them had been shot so far today."

"Still early," I said.

I had slowed on Storrow Drive, and could see flashing police lights up ahead near the exit onto David G. Mugar Way.

"Desmond Burke is the most fastidious criminal I have ever encountered, if there even is such a thing," my father said. "It is why I haven't locked him up and no one else has, either."

I never failed to notice that he still talked about his career as a cop in the present tense. And, I assumed, always would.

Traffic had now come to a complete stop.

"You got a minute?" he said.

"I've come to a complete stop on Storrow Drive," I said. "I've abandoned all hope that I will ever make it back to River Street Place."

"I think you're being dramatic," he said.

"I get that from mother," I said.

He let that one go.

"One thing about the Burkes that always

fascinated me is that as closely as Desmond and Felix have worked, and as much as they're connected, there's a wariness that exists between them," my father said. "Like they've been concerned one might make some kind of move on the other. I've always wondered if there might be some brotherly resentment that Desmond was the one in charge."

The traffic finally began to move again, and then I was off Storrow and onto Beacon and making my way toward Charles Street. It occurred to me that the geography of the area was starting to feel more and more normalized.

"So what are you saying?" I said.

"You need to talk to somebody who knows where all the bodies are buried."

"Literally or figuratively?" I said.

He snorted again. "Both."

Then he said to hold on, he wanted to check his phone contacts, a list that he had slowly transferred to the iPhone I had gotten him last Christmas, something that had taken some doing, since the list was only somewhat shorter than the Old Testament.

Finally he said, "Write this down. It's Vinnie Morris's new number and his address up on Concord Turnpike."

"I'm moving again, Daddy," I said. "Text me."

"You know I'm not much for texting," he said.

"Make an exception for your precious princess," I said, then told him I should have thought of Vinnie on my own.

"It's like I keep trying to tell you," my father said over the speaker, "I taught you everything you know, missy. Not everything I know."

I told him I was pretty sure he had stolen that line from a movie. He told me to prove it. And then he reminded me once again of another line, from an old boxing promoter friend of his.

"It's better to be stolen from than to have to steal," he said.

"But aren't you technically the one who did the stealing?"

"What is this," my father said, "a grand jury?"

I asked him what Vinnie was doing these days.

"He owns a bowling alley," Phil Randall said.

"No shit?" I said.

"The mouth on you," he said.

"Yeah," I said. "And me such a lady."

FOURTEEN

When I got home I walked Rosie, locked up, got back in the car, put Vinnie's address into Waze. I thought about calling in advance to tell him I was coming and decided to surprise him instead, even knowing that someone who'd begun his professional career as a trigger man for Joe Broz and then moved up to bodyguard Gino Fish probably liked surprises about as much as the Secret Service did.

When I was on my way back to Cambridge, my father called back.

"I should have mentioned that the bowling alley is just a front with Vinnie," he said.

I told him that I had come to that same conclusion on my own.

"I hear he's got his own crew now," Phil Randall said.

Who knew, I thought, *that Vinnie, of all people, had always wanted to direct?*

There was a solitary bowling pin outlined

against the sky, looking as if it belonged in another time, in a much older Boston. There was a guy behind the counter inside who looked as big as Tony Marcus's man Junior, just white, almost to the extreme, wearing a Hawaiian shirt and halfheartedly cleaning the outside of some bowling shoes. I wanted to suggest perhaps working on the insides of the shoes but thought better of it.

The man had a huge shaved head that somehow seemed perfectly proportional to the rest of him, or perhaps to the place, as if you could take it off his shoulder and roll it down the lane to convert a difficult split.

"Vinnie around?" I said to the man.

"Who wants to know?"

"Sunny Randall."

"He know you?"

"Do any of us ever really know anyone?" I said.

"Is that supposed to be funny?" he said.

"Apparently not," I said.

There was a phone and intercom set on the counter in front of him. Something else out of another time. I pointed at it. "Would you mind terribly telling him I'm here?" I said.

He picked up the phone, turned as he spoke, turned back around and said, "Upstairs."

Vinnie Morris, by both reputation and results, had always been known as the best shooter in Boston, though a record like Vinnie's wasn't something you could find the way my father loved to find baseball records. He had, as far as I knew, operated at various times on both sides of the law. There had even been times when he had acted as a sideman for an old boyfriend of mine — *Boyfriend, Sunny? How old* are *you?* — named Jesse Stone, the chief of police in Paradise.

Vinnie was waiting for me at the top of the stairs. He was as I remembered him, small and whippet thin, gray hair short and parted almost military-style on the side, looking as if he'd just stepped out of the Brooks Brothers on Newbury Street: blue blazer, gray slacks, white shirt with pinpoint collar, thin rep tie. As I made my way up the stairs, I could see the shine on his cap-toed black shoes. There was no sign of a gun interfering with the sleek lines of his clothes. But I knew at least one was on him somewhere, one that could be easily accessed if necessary.

He looked as out of place in a bowling alley as my mother would have at a rap concert.

"So," he said, walking behind me into his

small office.

"Nice to see you, too, Vinnie," I said.

"Yeah."

Then: "Have a seat."

There was a desk, a single chair across from it, a couch, a flat-screen television mounted on the wall, a small refrigerator. On one of the other walls was a shooting-range target, the outline of a man black against white, featuring a series of concentric circles with numbers inside ranging from 7's to 9's.

"A target, Vinnie?" I said. "Seriously?"

"Whatsa matter?" he said. "Got no sense of humor?"

"I do," I said. "I just didn't know you did."

"Yeah," he said.

Then: "You want a Coke? I got some of those small bottles in the fridge."

I said that sounded delicious, and that just the bottle would be fine, no ice.

He went and got two bottles, uncapped them, set one down in front of me on a coaster.

"Old school," he said. "Like me."

He went back around the desk, sat down, drank some Coke, put the bottle down carefully on the coaster in front of him. Calling Vinnie Morris a neat freak didn't even begin to tell the story.

We sat looking at each other until he said, "Richie and Peter, huh? Some fucking thing."

"Kind of why I'm here."

"Figured."

"What do you hear?" I said.

"I got nothing."

"You're being far too modest," I said.

"All due respect to your ex," Vinnie said. "But in what world do I care about Burkes getting shot? I'm out of that shit."

I tilted my head to the side and in a singsong voice said, "Are you?"

"I just said. In what world does this involve me?"

"Theirs," I said. "Yours. Mine. Ours."

Then I told him what the shooter had said to Richie about his father.

"Maybe I did hear something about that," Vinnie said.

"So you do have a bit more than nothing."

"Hearing things is not knowing things," he said.

I felt as if I were on the other side of Cambridge and back to sparring with Susan Silverman. I sipped some of my old-school Coca-Cola. It defied explanation that it had always tasted better in the small bottles. I placed the bottle carefully on the coaster, afraid that Vinnie might put one between my eyes if I left a ring on the surface of his desk.

"You really want to know what I know?" Vinnie said. "I know that I need the Burkes in my business or me in theirs like I need a fucking hole in my head."

"Words to live by."

"Operative word being *live*," he said.

"I hear that you've become a bit of an entrepreneur yourself," I said. "Criminally speaking."

"This business is legit," he said. "I'm legit now. Like I said, I got no time for the other."

"So you're saying you haven't become, uh, entrepreneurial?"

"Fuck that."

"Just making conversation."

"Same."

"Can't lie, Vinnie," I said. "But sometimes it's hard to tell with you."

We sat. There must have been customers downstairs, because I would occasionally hear the crash of pins. Despite the setting, I knew I was in the presence of a Boston legend, at least if you were looking for a better shot than Annie Oakley, and idly wondered when was the last time that Vinnie had shot somebody for hire.

"Who would come for Desmond?" I said.

95

If I asked the question often enough, maybe somebody would finally give me an answer I could use. It was a variation of one of Spike's fundamental theories of detecting: Annoy enough people and eventually something will turn up. More words to live by.

"Why am I even talking to you?" Vinnie said.

"You like me?" I said. "You like my father?"

"That frankly ain't enough."

"Because I'm eye candy?" I said.

Vinnie almost smiled.

"Listen," he said, "it ain't a big secret that Desmond is moving toward the door. Looking to get out once and for all. He's old and he's tired and he's made his."

"But his," I said, "is not exactly the kind of profession where you cash out on your 401(k) and then retire to Arizona or Florida."

"Why not?" Vinnie said. "Pretty much everybody Desmond came up with is either dead or in prison. He retires now, he retires with the fucking trophy."

"But for now he's still actively in the life," I said.

"People say he wants to make one last big score."

"People," I said.

He nodded.

"And in what realm would that big score be made?"

"Guns," Vinnie said. "If I heard anything, which I'm not saying I did, what I maybe might have heard is that Desmond has figured out a way to make some real money bringing guns up here. Which frankly ain't easy, just because of the volume you need to move."

Just get them talking, Phil Randall had always told me.

Vinnie shrugged. "All this is above my pay grade. As much gun work as I used to do, I never got involved in all that supply-and-demand. But since we're just talking here, if Desmond has figured out a way to make real money, it might piss off some people who haven't. Figured that out, I mean."

"Piss them off enough to start shooting Burkes?" I said.

"I didn't say that," Vinnie said. "And I got no idea what Peter would have to do with that. Peter has always run the book, nothing else."

Before I could say anything, Vinnie said, "Ask you something?"

"Anything."

"You can't ask your ex about this without

coming up here?"

"It's complicated."

"Tell me about it."

"What does that mean?"

"Something else for you to figure out," Vinnie said. "I just run a bowling alley."

"Has anyone ever told you how opaque you can be?" I said.

Vinnie shrugged. "Not my color," he said.

I stood up. I asked what he wanted me to do with the Coke bottle. He said he'd take care of it. I thanked him for seeing me. He said, "Yeah."

Then I said, "You'll be hearing from me."

"You think you can just come up here and threaten me like that?" he said.

I told him that was a good one. He said, see, he did have a sense of humor after all. I walked down the stairs and made sure not to make any sudden movements as I walked past the guy in the Hawaiian shirt, just to be on the safe side.

FIFTEEN

It was a verifiable fact, of both my life and Richie's, that the new Rosie didn't love him nearly as much as the original had.

The original Rosie had been as much Richie's as she'd been mine, of course. After our divorce our custody schedule had been as strict as it would have been with a child. But even when Rosie was no longer living with Richie on a full-time basis, the love they continued to share sometimes seemed to pass understanding. Even when they were apart for only a few days the dog would, as Richie loved to point out, lose her shit every single time she saw him again.

The relationship between him and the new Rosie, on the other hand, continued to be a work in progress. Much like our own. Except that the dog, bless her heart, didn't overthink her relationship with Richie nearly as much as I did. Or require a therapist to sort through it.

Today she had lapped his face when he'd arrived at Melanie Joan's and then sat next to him on the couch until arriving at the conclusion that no treats were in the offing.

"A little sugar never hurts with a girl," I said.

"I'm going to forget I heard that," Richie said, "especially in this time of enlightenment for men and women."

"Just sayin'."

"Paying her off makes me feel like a john."

"Are you calling our precious angel a treat whore?" I said.

"If the round heels fit," he said.

He was feeling well enough that we had made an actual dinner date for Davio's, our favorite Italian restaurant in this part of town, on Arlington. He had informed me that the family had decided there would be no wake for his uncle Peter, or funeral, just a brief memorial service at one of the Burke family's cemetery plots at St. Augustine's in South Boston. The church itself, on Dorchester Street, was the oldest Catholic Church building in the whole state.

"My mother's there, and now Peter." He smiled. "As always, the Church cares about as much where the money comes from as a lot of other people with whom my family has done business."

Richie asked if we had time for a glass of wine before Davio's. I told him I was way ahead of him, and had already opened a bottle of La Crema.

I went into the kitchen, came back with two glasses. I handed Richie his, turned and tried to discreetly slip Rosie a small biscuit.

When I turned back to him, he was shaking his head.

"Busted," he said.

"I have no idea what you're talking about," I said.

"Right."

"And besides, who are you going to believe, me or your own eyes?"

"Chico Marx," Richie said, clinking his glass with mine. *Duck Soup.*"

"You always seem to know things that I didn't know you knew," I said.

Rosie was between us on the couch. I asked if he was feeling any pain. He grinned and said not after two sips of pinot noir. I told him he knew what I meant. He said that he was feeling as good as new and thanked me for asking.

"Why were you spared and your uncle was not?" I said.

"You think I don't keep asking myself the same question?"

"You had no way of knowing who your

shooter was," I said. "Your uncle had to know."

"But maybe didn't know it was the shooter," Richie said.

"Until it was too late," I said.

"This can't possibly be over," he said.

"There's a pleasant thought," I said. I grinned at him. "I take it that you didn't arrive here unaccompanied."

"I did not."

"You think the boys will allow us to walk across the Public Garden to the restaurant?"

"At a respectful distance," Richie said. "I told them I had my date, they had to get their own."

He looked less tired than he had the first day after the shooting. But he still looked tired. And did not look as good as new, or even close.

"You sure you want to go out?" I said. "We could order in." I brightened. "And have the boys go pick it up!"

"I am going to buy the artist formerly known as Sonya Randall a proper dinner," he said.

He sipped the last of his red wine. I did the same. Like an old married couple, with the baby between us. And armed men somewhere outside.

He blew out some air.

"My father has asked me to ask you once again to leave this alone," Richie said.

I reached down and absently scratched Rosie behind an ear. She did not stir, which meant she would provide no assistance to me in the moment.

"We've gone over this," I said.

"Now we're going over it again."

"No one knows me better than you do," I said.

He nodded.

"He's my father," Richie said.

"Yup. And I'm me."

I thought: *The date is not starting off well. Not the first time.*

"I went to see Vinnie Morris today," I said.

"He told me."

"Vinnie told you?"

"My father."

"Sweet Jumping Jesus," I said. "Desmond is having me *followed*?"

"*Monitored* might be a better choice of words," Richie said.

"Yeah," I said, smiling at him. "Go with that."

"This is not easy," Richie said. "For any of us."

"I know that," I said. "Don't you think I know that? But how about if I ask you to ask your father to stay out of *my* business?"

"This may sound like an odd choice of words," Richie said. "But don't shoot the messenger."

"Vinnie thinks this all might somehow be connected to some gun deal your father is about to make," I said.

Richie put his glass down.

"I don't want to do this," he said.

"You'll have to be more specific."

"Talk about things in my father's business about which I know nothing," he said. "Get between you and my father's business. Or just between you and my father. I didn't want to do it when we first fell in love. I have far less interest in doing it now."

"I am not worried about your father," I said. "I am worried about you."

"I'm fine," he said.

"One gunshot wound later."

"I am fine and will *be* fine," he said.

"You think that they won't come for you again?" I said. "Maybe this is just the beginning of this guy torturing your father. Maybe Felix is next. It took exactly one day for things to get dialed up with Peter."

"My father is a survivor," Richie said.

"So was your uncle Peter until he wasn't."

"I don't want to fight with you."

"We're not fighting," I said.

"What you used to say when we were married."

I sighed. It came out louder than I had intended. "I don't need his permission to do some detecting," I said. "But I would very much like to have yours."

"And if not granted?"

I tried to give him a smile that once had done everything except cause his knees to buckle.

"I will have to find ways to persuade you," I said.

"Wouldn't that make me the treat whore?" Richie said.

There seemed to be nothing more to say at the moment. Richie finally looked at his watch.

"We should get going," he said.

"I haven't annoyed you to the point where you want to dump me?" I said.

"I keep trying," Richie said. "But it just never seems to goddamn take."

"Maybe we should agree to drop the subject of your father's current business interests for the rest of the evening," I said. "Unless, of course, you just can't help yourself."

"I'll try to maintain control."

"Never been much of an issue for you, big boy."

He suddenly looked even more tired to me, as if the conversation had come close to exhausting him. I told him we could Uber to Davio's, or have the boys drive us. Richie said he could use the air. He walked more slowly than usual up River Street and then Charles and then across Beacon, and into the Public Garden past the small duckling statues that actually made Rosie growl when we'd walk past them.

When we were finished with dinner, there seemed to be no thought, and certainly no conversation, about the two of us spending the night together at my place. Two of Desmond's men had walked behind us on our way to the restaurant. I had seen one of them at the bar while we ate. When we finished, the car was waiting out front. The man who had been at the bar opened the door to the backseat for Richie and me.

Richie didn't introduce me to the two men, neither of whom I recognized, which meant nothing. Desmond Burke likely employed a small army of Irish just like them.

When we got to the house, Richie kissed me softly on the cheek. I said I'd call him in the morning. He said not to make it too early.

I went inside, grabbed Rosie's leash, took

her for a quick walk so she could perform her last-walk-of-the-night obligations in the little fenced-in area around the corner that the other residents of River Street Place had sadly nicknamed the Poop Loop. Then we went back inside and I locked the front door and got ready for bed, alone.

At least nobody I knew had gotten shot today.

It might not have been progress. But as my father liked to say, it wasn't nothing.

Sixteen

Spike and I had finished a morning run on the Esplanade.

We had crossed over Storrow on the Arthur Fiedler Footbridge, run all the way down to Mass Ave, then back. I had read somewhere that if you were particularly ambitious, or training for the marathon, you could make a seventeen-mile run for yourself on the Esplanade. Spike and I had opted for a considerably shorter distance today.

It was a beautiful morning, enhanced by the sights on the river, boats and crew teams and the familiar skyline of Cambridge on the other side of the Charles, so many of the simple pleasures that the city and its geography and its landmarks and people and culture and history had always brought me.

Now we were making our way back across the Fiedler bridge. I asked Spike if he needed to be anywhere. He reminded me that he was his own boss and a single gay man and could be wherever the hell he wanted to be on a morning like this.

"The only difference between us," he said, "is that I will actually be making some money before this day has ended."

"Thank you for pointing that out, dear," I said. "But I'm willing to buy you coffee anyway."

"I accept," he said.

He was wearing a Foo Fighters T-shirt, baggy basketball shorts that hung to his knees, and some new Hoka running shoes that seemed to include most of the colors of the rainbow.

When we walked into Peet's Coffee the size of him and the outfit and the shoes commanded the attention of most of the other customers, and all of the people working behind the counter.

"Tell them they're all fine," he whispered to me, "as long as they don't do anything to spook me. If they do, I may burst into show tunes."

"That will only frighten them more," I said.

We managed to score a window table. We both had large lattes with extra shots of espresso. I told him about my dinner with

Richie and how it had been something less than a triumph, mostly because I felt as if his father had been a plus-one.

"Sounds as if Desmond got romance against the ropes and hammered it with body punches," Spike said.

"Oooh," I said. "A sports reference. You know how those make my blood race."

He was more interested in my meeting with Vinnie Morris, and what Vinnie had told me about Desmond and guns.

"Funny thing about guns," Spike said. "We've got gun laws here as tough as anybody's. But the illegal guns keep coming up from the South. Used to be if you wanted a gun without paper and were willing to walk around with an unregistered piece, you had to travel down to Bumfuck, Georgia, or Asshat, Virginia, to get one and bring it back. Or head up to Vermont."

"The Green Mountain State?" I said.

"Don't be fooled," Spike said. "There's always been gun money in them there hills."

"So you think it's what Vinnie said, a case of supply and demand?" I said. "And Desmond really has found a way to supply those demands in a more, shall we say, efficacious manner?"

"Efficacious," Spike said. "Have I told you how much I love you?"

"Not enough," I said. "I read somewhere that only half the handguns seized in crimes in Massachusetts could be traced back to legal owners."

"Makes you want to do the math on the unseized guns."

"Lot of gun money on them there streets," I said, "especially if you could corner the market, which is what Vinnie suggested my ex-father-in-law is attempting to do."

"So who might that piss off the most?" Spike said.

"Italians?" I said.

Spike said, "Except I'm not even sure who the big Italians are anymore in Boston. In fact, the biggest one isn't even *in* Boston. It's your friend from Providence."

"Albert Antonioni," I said.

Spike raised an eyebrow. Eat your heart out, Susan Silverman.

"Maybe Desmond is cutting in on his action," Spike said. "But I heard one time that if Albert really wanted business up here, he wanted it to be with Tony Marcus, and that they could make some accommodation on girls down in Providence if Tony could cut him in on something else up here."

"Wouldn't just be an odd couple," I said. "Would be the oddest."

"Didn't you tell me that Desmond and

Felix and old Albert had agreed to stay out of each other's businesses?" Spike said.

"Basically, Albert blinked first," I said. "He finally decided that as appealing as the notion was of having the governor of Massachusetts on full scholarship, he didn't want to go to war with Desmond Burke over the whole thing. 'Least not at the time."

"Maybe you need to have another talk with old Albert," Spike said.

"Me and what army?"

Spike grinned.

"I've always dreamed about being a man in uniform," he said.

"Yeah," I said. "Somewhat like the Village People."

"You want me to go with you?" he said.

"Who said I was going?"

"You did and you didn't."

I told him I would make some calls and try to set it up. Spike, who liked to brag that he knew more bad men than I did, said he would do the same.

"You starting to feel like you're in the middle of a Scorsese movie?" he said.

"Little bit," I said.

He finished his latte and asked which one it was where everybody died in the end.

"All of them," I said.

He said he was afraid of that.

SEVENTEEN

I called Frank Belson when I got home and asked if there were any leads on Peter Burke.

"What," he said, "you haven't already broken this thing wide open on your own?"

"Frank," I said, "stop trying to act as if you don't like me. Everybody knows that behind that gruff exterior —"

"Lies a complete asshole," he said. "No, there are no leads as of yet, and maybe not forever. And let's just say that my bosses, starting with her, haven't exactly ordered me to drop everything to track down the killer of an aging thug."

"So the only way we catch this guy is if he comes after someone else," I said.

"Before I get back to work," Frank Belson said, "let me leave you with one thought: The fuck do you mean by *'we'*?"

By noon the next day Spike and I were on our way to Providence to meet with Albert

Antonioni. Normally I would have asked Felix Burke to set it up, as he had the last time I had been across a table from Antonioni. But if I did that, he would tell Desmond. And I didn't want Desmond in my business today. So I had asked Wayne Cosgrove for help, and he had put me in touch with a columnist at *The Providence Journal* named Mike Stanton, who had once written a bestselling book about a colorful and often crooked former mayor of Providence named Buddy Cianci. Wayne said Stanton knew all the players in Providence. Mike called back within an hour with a number for somebody he said knew Antonioni well enough to set it up.

"You people from the big city sure know how to have fun," Stanton said.

I told him Albert and I went way back.

"Sunny?" he said. "Hardly anybody goes way back with Albert."

I wasn't sure if Desmond Burke really was monitoring me, as Richie had suggested. But I decided to take no chances. I told Spike that I was going to walk over to the Taj Boston, walk out the service entrance, and that he should pick me up in the Public Alley between the hotel and Commonwealth Ave. Which he did. At noon we were on our way to Providence.

We were meeting Antonioni at a restaurant called Joe Marzilli's Old Canteen, which was in the heart of the Federal Hill section of Providence. Mike Stanton had told me the setting was perfect, that in the old days an old boss named Raymond Patriarca would meet guys in an upstairs room there when they got off the train from New York City.

We parked at the Rhode Island Convention Center and walked from there underneath the gateway arch on Atwells Avenue to where the Old Canteen stood, at what looked to me to be the corner of Atwells and 1955.

"Richie is not going to like that you went to see Antonioni without telling him," Spike said. "As I recall, it wasn't just Uncle Felix who set up the meet last time. It was Richie who put the whole thing in motion."

"He did," I said.

"So you've eliminated the middlemen," Spike said.

"But if you look at it logically," I said, "I'm actually doing what he asked me to do, and not putting him between his father and me."

"I assume you don't actually believe that."

"Hell, no," I said. "But I keep telling myself that if I finally get an actual clue today, it will have been for the greater good."

115

"As you continue your tour of extremely bad guys," Spike said. "Next up being someone who might not just be *a* bad guy, but maybe the worst guy of all of them. And dangerous as shit."

"So are you, sweetcakes," I said.

I expected the place to be dark. It was the opposite of that, with white linen tablecloths and pink walls.

"Hi ho!" Spike said.

I told him to behave. After we were patted down, one of Antonioni's men showed us to his table. Albert sat alone in a corner, back to the wall. *Classic,* I thought. There were other tables in the room that were occupied. I assumed that some were occupied by men who worked for Antonioni. Or all. I appeared to be the only woman in the room. There were two younger guys in dark suits at the table closest to Albert Antonioni's. Two other guys were standing at the end of the bar, one thicker than the other and looking like a bodybuilder in a leather jacket that was too small for him and strained at the zipper. The other was a Richie type, dark and not bad-looking. The thicker one seemed to be working hardest on his tough-guy stare, eyeballing Spike as if he were supposed to go into a dead faint. The Richie type seemed more focused on me.

116

Albert had a small cup of espresso in front of him. There were two cups and saucers waiting for Spike and me.

Albert had aged considerably since we'd resolved the fate of Millicent Patton. He still had a lot of white hair, combed straight back, and a well-groomed beard. He wore a black suit with a gray shirt buttoned all the way to the top. No tie. He seemed to have shrunk inside himself, in the way old people did, in the years since I'd seen him.

Albert stood up as Spike and I approached the table. Courtly. I shook his hand and noted that he was just slightly taller than I was. But he was still a hard-looking man. I remembered when I had first met him, at a place in Taunton. Richie had told me beforehand not to go all feminist, that I was in the world of Desmond and Felix Burke and Albert Antonioni, and that it was not a day to impress them with my wit and attitude. I managed to keep myself under control. And planned to do the same today.

"Who's this?" Albert said, nodding at Spike.

"My name is Spike, Mr. Antonioni," Spike said.

It was all part of the dance. Albert Antonioni knew I was bringing Spike because I had told Mike Stanton to tell his people that

117

I was. And if he knew I was bringing Spike, he knew who he was and what he did and maybe even his password on Amazon.

"Oh, yes," Albert said. "The *strano.*"

I knew enough Italian to know that meant queer.

Spike smiled, brilliantly. "And proud of it!" he said.

The old man let it go. He pointed at the cups and said, "You want something?" I told him that what he was having would be lovely.

Antonioni made a brief wave of his hand. The bartender was at our table like a sprinter, collecting our cups, returning just as quickly with espresso. I decided to drink it straight. No girly girl, I.

"You cost me some money the last time we were together," the old man said. "And kept me from making a very big move into Boston."

"There was no point once it became clear that I was going to be governor before that moron Brock Patton was," I said.

He shrugged and took a sip of espresso. "He ever try anything with you?" he said. "Patton?"

"He did," I said, "until I pulled out my gun and threatened to shoot him."

He looked over at the guys at the next

118

table. "You hear that?" he said. "This is one tough cookie."

"As I recall," I said, "that isn't the first time you have made that observation about me."

I casually looked around the room. The other men seemed to have their eyes mostly fixed on Spike. Somehow Spike had his own eyes on all of them at once.

"So to what do I owe the honor?" Antonioni said.

"I am told that you still know about everything illegal from here to Canada and back," I said. "And because you do, I was wondering if you had any theories about who might be coming for the Burke family."

"For Desmond, you mean," he said.

"Yes," I said.

The old man said, "I am frankly confused by this, as I am sure you are, Miss Randall. Desmond is an old man, the way I am. I had just assumed that all old fights that needed to be fought had already been fought."

"But you both have business interests that are still quite active," I said.

"Ones that we have mostly managed to keep separate, Desmond and me," he said.

"In the interest of mutual profit," I said.

"And respect," he said. He smiled. "It always comes down to that in our world, does it not? Respect. Or lack of respect. Or earning respect. Or avenging the lack of respect."

He closed his eyes and shook his head.

"Sometimes I think we are all still children," he said.

"Would you tell me if you knew who has been doing the shooting?" I said.

"For mutual profit?" he said.

"I am told that Desmond is getting more into guns," I said, "and that such an action might have angered you."

"Angered me in what way?"

"Perhaps he beat you out of making a similar action."

The old man waved a hand.

"Maybe there was a time when Desmond Burke beat me to things," he said. "But not for a very long time."

"He says you have hated him for a very long time," I said. "Why is that?"

"We were both full of piss and vinegar once," he said. There was a small smile. "When we could still piss."

Spike made a brief snorting sound.

Antonioni nodded at the bartender, who came for his cup, went back over to the espresso machine behind the bar, refilled it, brought it back. Antonioni sipped and nodded. The bartender looked relieved, as if maybe that meant his family could live. Spike wasn't looking at the other men now. He was looking at Antonioni, fascinated.

"If I thought the risk was worth the reward with guns," Antonioni said, "that Iron Pipeline about which people speak would be running through me, and fuck Desmond Burke. But it does not."

"Okay, let's assume it's not about guns," I said. "Who out of Desmond's past would shoot his son and kill his brother?"

"At last an easy question," Albert Antonioni said. "Anybody Desmond ever fucked over."

I started to say something, but he held up an old, veiny hand.

"We're done here now," he said.

"Evidently," I said.

"You have obviously taken it upon yourself to find out who is doing this to Desmond and his family, and why."

"I have," I said.

Antonioni stood and nodded.

"Tough cookie," he said.

"All due respect, sir?" Spike said. "You have no fucking idea."

"One last thing, Miss Randall," the old man said. "It is my experience that the Irish

121

in Boston only forget grudges when they are dead."

"Is that a suggestion?" I said.

"More of an observation," he said. "The answers you seek are likely there, not here."

He gave me a long look, with dark eyes suddenly full of light.

"By the way?" he said. "Brock Patton might have gotten elected, as much of a *stunad* as he is. As you have probably noticed, just about anybody can in this country."

He and his men left the room first. They had all been his. Spike and I remained at the table until we were certain they were gone from the Old Canteen. When we were outside and walking back underneath the arch, Spike said, "Did Albert's boys scare you as much as they did me?"

"Not as much as Albert does," I said.

"Fuckin' ay," Spike said.

EIGHTEEN

Richie's mother had died in her thirties, from uterine cancer. Desmond had never remarried. If there had been women after his wife died, Richie knew nothing of it. Or it was just more of Desmond Burke's secret life.

Felix had never married, despite what Richie said had always been an extremely active romantic life for his uncle until he just stopped giving a shit about women. According to Richie, the only meaningful and enduring relationship of Felix Burke's adult life had been his marriage to the family business. Felix now lived in a condominium at the marina in Charlestown, Charlestown being the second-oldest neighborhood in Boston, and more Irish than St. Patrick's Day. But it had become gentrified over time. The city had not only expanded the residential life of the marina, it had developed the Navy Yard as well.

As much as Charlestown always had been, and always would be, associated with the Bunker Hill Monument, there were so many lovely parts of it, located as it was on the banks of Boston Harbor and the Mystic River. So it was both a historic Boston address and a fashionable one these days, particularly if your address was on the water. I remember how surprised Richie had been when he'd learned Felix was moving out of the home he had lived in for forty years to a newer and much trendier one.

"Next he's going to get an electric-powered car," Richie said.

That morning Felix had met Desmond, as always, for seven-o'clock Mass at St. Frances de Sales Church on Bunker Hill Street, before they would have breakfast at the Grasshopper Café, on the same street. Desmond and Felix each had two bodyguards with them, as they had since Richie was shot.

And sometime after the black Lincoln with Felix and his men inside had left for church, someone had walked up to Felix Burke's condominium on the water side and blown out the ground-floor windows with a shotgun. No one saw who did it. There was the thought that he might even have come by small boat. All the neighbors heard the blast, muted slightly by the loud wind and rain that was blowing off the water at the time.

When those with the same view as Felix's looked out their own windows to see what had caused the commotion, all they saw was the water.

Richie was the one who called me, saying over the phone, "You would've found out. And I wouldn't have been able to keep you away."

I told him I would meet him there, which I did forty-five minutes later. There were two police cruisers at the end of Felix's block. Another, lights flashing, was directly in front of the condominium. There were onlookers in the street, even in the rain, the crowd of them roped off by cops. Richie was waiting for me near the entrance to his uncle's place. By then the cops knew he was Felix Burke's nephew, and let us both pass. Richie didn't even take me inside, just walked me around to the back.

Desmond and Felix were both there, both wearing tan, half-raincoats and the same kind of scally caps I imagined them wearing on the boat that brought them to America in the first place.

Frank Belson was with them. No one had

died, but Felix was a Burke and his brother had already been shot dead this week, after Richie had been shot in the back. What had happened here was a part of all that, clearly. But the randomness of it all, I thought, continued. Richie had been wounded. Peter had been murdered. Now it was only a residence that had been hit. Felix's residence.

Belson, as he often did and without greeting or salutation, made it sound as if we were halfway into a conversation when I went walking over to him.

"Shotguns are good," he said, "even though you have to get close to do any good damage with them. Usually no rifling or markings that can be traced or give you anything consistent enough for a match. Maybe my guys will find something we can trace back to a manufacturer. But it won't do shit."

"Another warning shot," I said.

"More than one, from the looks of the place," Belson said.

He took a small cigar out of the corner of his mouth, both he and it oblivious to the rain. Or perhaps impervious.

"Somebody," Belson said, "wanted to make a big, loud fucking statement to get somebody's attention. As if they didn't have it already."

Felix had come up next to me, like a ghost appearing.

"They wanted me to know that they could come to my house," Felix said. "They wanted me to know and my brother to know."

Belson said, "You saw nothing before you and your men left for church?"

"Marty and Padraig take shifts in the night," he said. "A way to make sure the perimeter is secure. But once it's time to leave for Mass, they just walk me out and into the car."

Belson nodded. At the same time he was focused on what Felix was telling him he was taking in everything around him, even the water in the distance.

He turned to me.

"Drip, drip, drip," he said.

"I am assuming," I said, "that is not an assessment of the current weather."

"You miss nothing," he said.

He walked over to Desmond Burke. I walked with him. The rain came harder. I tried not to imagine what my hair looked like.

"I am going to ask you again if there is anything you wish to tell me, Desmond," Belson said. I had seen this before with him.

Nothing about his posture or tone had changed, and yet it had become more aggressive anyway. "For fuck's sake, is there anything that you know and I do not that might help me put an end to this?"

Desmond looked at him, his face impassive. I knew he wasn't used to people talking to him this way. But Frank Belson had because he could and Desmond knew that he could, whether he liked it or not. It was as if all the animosity that had always existed between Boston cops and the Burkes was now in the air between these two men, even in a moment like this, when their interests should have been aligned.

"If I knew," Desmond Burke said, in a voice that seemed to be made of razor blades, "I would have already ended this myself. For fuck's sake."

Felix was behind him. I saw him reach into the pocket of his khaki pants, the parts of them below the knee not covered by his coat splotched with rain.

He came out with his phone, brought it closer to his face, squinted as he stared at it. Then he wordlessly handed it to his brother.

Then Desmond handed it to Richie.

I looked at the text message on the screen as he did.

"Ask Desmond," it said, "how he likes it when it's ones he loves."

Belson reached over, without asking, took the phone from Richie, read the text himself, put the phone in the pocket of his raincoat, and told Felix he would return it after his people looked at it.

"Probably came from a burner," he said.

"The way to bet," I said.

"Gotta check anyway."

Belson turned to Desmond again.

"You got any idea what that means?" he said.

Desmond's answer was to simply walk away from Frank Belson and the rest of us toward the water.

"He seems to be having some difficulty processing the fact that we are on the same side here," Belson said.

"Gee," I said, "you think?"

Nineteen

"Talking to Desmond Burke and Tony Marcus and Albert Antonioni," my father said, "seems to be working out splendidly for you. The only people who haven't been shot at so far this week are riding Duck Boats."

"You left out Vinnie Morris," I said.

"He is a separate category," Phil Randall said. "Vinnie falls on the right side of things more often than not, despite some of the crum-bums for whom he has worked in the past. In addition to being a very natty dresser."

" 'Crum-bums'?" I said.

"It's an expression older and nattier dressers like myself still use," he said.

We were in my living room having coffee that I had made with a Keurig that I'd owned for a month but was just learning to operate properly, having finally figured out when to close the lid. My father was wearing a gray V-neck sweater over a Tattersall shirt, underneath a navy blazer. His gray pants were pressed and cuffed. Black tasseled loafers. Argyle socks. There was the faint whiff in the room of the sandalwood cologne he had been wearing for as long as I had been alive. I called it the dad scent.

It was the morning after someone shot up Felix Burke's condo. My father had stopped at the Flour Bakery and Café on Dalton Street, down near the Hynes Convention Center, for cranberry-orange scones.

As far as I could determine, he was giving Rosie a bite for every one he took. There was no point in telling him to stop, it was like trying to stop the ocean when the two of them were together.

"Where's my sainted mother this morning?" I said.

"Don't try to change the subject," he said. "But since you asked, it is her turn to host her bridge group."

My mother, who was resistant to just about everything new except chin tucks, had shocked us all recently by announcing that she was going to learn how to play bridge. My father, who had always been a wonderful bridge player, now lived in fear that she would eventually ask him to partner with her in a separate couples group. This from a man who wasn't afraid of ISIS.

131

"How's that working out for her?" I said.

He sighed and sipped some of his coffee. "Bridge too far," he said.

I giggled.

"Go ahead," he said. "Laugh."

Then he said, "You still haven't told me about your meeting with Albert."

We were supposed to have had coffee yesterday, until the shooting in Charlestown. I told him now. I told him about the Old Canteen and Albert suggesting that if this were an ancient grudge, it might be an Irish one.

"An Italian saying that," he said, grinning. "Old boy's got balls on him still."

"This whole thing," I said, "has become a *mishegoss.*"

He smiled. It always made his face young.

"I'm not sure I remember that particular expression from our old country," he said.

"My therapist is Jewish," I said.

My father fed Rosie again, saw me watch him do it, winked.

"I'm going to tell you things I know you've already thought about, and Belson has thought about, and I've thought about," he said. "The guy could have killed Richie, didn't. Then he only murders some windows and furniture at Felix's. But he does murder Peter in between."

"Peter wasn't as close to Desmond as Richie and Felix are," I said.

"But them he spares."

"Makes no sense," I said. "But then little about this does."

"Richie would prefer you stay out of it," my father said.

"But he knows I can take care of myself, Daddy," I said. "I actually think there's a part of him that doesn't want me poking around in his father's past. Like even now, even though he's all grown up, he doesn't want to know what he doesn't want to know about Desmond."

"Desmond and Felix," my father said, shaking his head. "Still acting like knockaround guys even when they should be sitting on the front porch at a retirement community."

"Old men operating off all the old codes," I said.

"You still don't want to piss off any of them," he said.

"May have already," I said.

"Desmond loves Richie," he said. "Richie loves you. These are immutable facts, and will always count for something."

"You sound like a Jewish therapist," I said.

"Imagine that," he said. "An old flatfoot like myself."

"All we know for sure is that someone is slowly squeezing Desmond," I said.

"What does that text message to Felix really mean?" Phil Randall said.

"Perhaps just another way of talking about sins of the father," I said. "Even though Felix is Desmond's brother."

"Maybe Albert Antonioni is right about the Irish," he said. "Maybe this is something whose reach makes it all the way back to Winter Hill."

"I've got it!" I said, slapping my thigh. "I'll just call Whitey Bulger and ask him."

"Tell me again who played him in that movie?"

"Johnny Depp."

"I liked him better as the gay pirate."

"That's what Spike calls him."

"Well," he said, "Spike ought to know."

"I feel as if most of the people I need to talk to might be dead or in jail," I said.

My father said, "Maybe not all."

He got up, picked up my plate and his, took them into the kitchen. I could hear the water running. My whole life, he had been neater than hospital corners. I knew he would rinse the cups before he left, too. And maybe vacuum the rugs.

"You know someone?" I said when he was back in the living room.

"I may," he said. "Let me make a few calls."

He picked up the cups now, went back into the kitchen. I could hear the water running again. If you were born round, he always said, you didn't die square.

He said that he was going to take a nice long walk in the park while he was waiting for the bridge party to clear out of his house.

"The problem with retirement," he said, "is that you can never take a day off."

I hugged him. He hugged me back. Neither one of us ever went through the motions with that. I felt as safe and happy in his embrace as I always had been, for as long as I could remember.

"Be careful," he said.

"Always."

"I mean it," he said. "It doesn't take much knowing or asking around to know that you and Richie are still together. If they came for the others, they might come for you."

"Not a Burke, Daddy."

"Not to me," he said. "But to them."

I pulled back from him, smiling.

"Mishegoss!" I said in a loud voice.

"God bless you," my father said.

TWENTY

I called Richie, and was sent straight to
voicemail. No shocker there. He frequently
had his phone turned off, even in times like
these. Richie Burke was not one of those
people who believed he risked seizure if he
didn't check his phone every five minutes.

I knew I could have gone on the Internet
to read more about the Winter Hill Gang
but took a walk over to the Boston Public
Library instead, having decided to go
through ancient copies of the *Globe.* It was
detective work out of the past, without
search engines, and had always seemed to
suit me. But I was often happier living in
the past, even when it involved murder and
general mayhem and more questions than I
was currently equipped to answer.

It was late afternoon by the time I left,
having learned a lot about the bad old days
without learning anything that really helped
me. After I'd gotten home and fed Rosie

and walked her, Spike called and asked if I wanted to come over and have dinner with him at the restaurant. I told him I just wanted to whip up one of my specialties in the space-age kitchen Melanie Joan had inherited, then curl up with a good book.

"This might sound mean," Spike said. "But you don't have any specialties."

"You take that back."

"Name one."

"Spaghetti and broccoli."

"That's not a specialty," Spike said. "That's spaghetti and broccoli."

"I wasn't aware that I was talking to a special counsel," I said.

I didn't make spaghetti and broccoli. Instead I heated up a pizza from Whole Foods that I'd been saving. That would show him. When I finished I took Rosie for another walk, up Charles and over to the Common tonight. The dog trainer I'd briefly hired told me to always have treats with me and then say "Leave it" as soon as she spotted another dog and commenced growling and barking.

Tonight had been another total breakdown in theory.

The first dog she saw was a chocolate Lab, up in the corner of the Common near the playground. I assumed that you could hear

Rosie's subsequent barking in Kenmore Square.

"Sorry," I said to the Lab's owner, a young guy in a Harvard hoodie.

"We never felt unsafe," he said, grinning. "Have you ever tried a trainer?"

When I got home I poured myself a glass of wine and read a book Wayne Cosgrove had recommended, *Citizen Somerville,* Bobby Martini's account of growing up in the Winter Hill Gang. It was about guys with names like Rico and Tony Blue, and about how somebody near the pizza stand always seemed to be watching as Bobby or Rico or Tony got themselves shot.

Somehow, the man who was my ex-husband's father had come out of that world. The father of someone I loved and always would love, perhaps as much as any man I would ever know.

Me, I thought.

Honorary Burke.

The doorbell rang. I wasn't expecting anyone. Richie never dropped in unannounced, nor did Spike. Nor did my father. As I walked across the living room I reached into the top drawer of my desk and grabbed a Beretta Pico my father had purchased for me. He'd asked me after the Spare Change case how many guns I had in my house. I told him two. The next day he brought over a couple new ones, including the Pico, and said, "Make it four."

Before I opened the door, I slid open the peephole.

Desmond Burke was standing there, Buster and Colley right behind him.

I palmed the gun as I opened the door.

"I'm sorry I didn't call first," he said.

"How'd you know I'd be here," I said.

"Intuition," he said.

He turned to the men behind him and said he wouldn't be long. I briefly wondered if he and Felix had been those young men once, working strong-arm, as foot soldiers, and dreaming of bigger things.

Somehow Rosie didn't make a sound in Desmond's presence. Perfect. Even dogs were afraid of him.

"Can I get you something to drink?" I said.

As he walked ahead of me I put the gun back into the open drawer and quietly shut it.

"A beer would do me fine," Desmond said.

I went to the refrigerator and came back with a bottle of Samuel Adams. I wasn't a beer girl. I stocked it for Richie and Spike. I asked Desmond if he wanted a glass. He said the bottle would do him fine as well.

"I'll get to the point," he said.

"When have you ever not?" I said.

I smiled at him. He did not smile back. But then he rarely did. Everything about him, his entire taut-coiled self, was all business.

His business.

"I have always treated you, after a fashion, as the daughter I never had," he said.

"And I have been grateful for that," I said.

"But I simply cannot have you interfering in this," he said. "This isn't about Richie or Peter or what happened at Felix's. I simply cannot have you challenging my authority."

I started to ask him what year he thought this was but restrained myself. It wouldn't get either one of us anywhere.

"I don't work for you, Desmond," I said. "I don't work for Felix. I don't even work for Richie. I work for me."

He took a long pull of his beer. Tonight he was a man in black himself, black sports jacket, black knit shirt. It made him look even more pale than he usually did.

"You saw Albert Antonioni day before yesterday," he said. "With your friend. The gay man who owns the restaurant."

"I know I wasn't followed to Providence,"

I said. "So how exactly do you know that?"

It was as if the question had gone unasked. He took another pull on his beer and quickly wiped his lips with the back of his hand.

"I know Richie asked you to stand down," he said. "Obviously it did no good. So tonight I came myself."

"Is your current situation somehow tied up with a gun deal so many think you are in the process of making?" I said.

Now he offered me the barest hint of smile.

"Generally, or specifically?"

"You know what I'm asking," I said.

He looked down at the coffee table, at Bobby Martini's book.

"Are you reading that?" he said.

"Are you changing the subject?"

"I am."

"Research," I said.

He nodded. "Funny kid, Bobby," he said.

"I know you don't want help from the cops," I said. "But let me help you, Desmond. I'm good at this kind of work."

"I have never needed anyone's help," he said. He nodded at the book. "Not theirs, not yours, not anyone's. Not ever."

He abruptly stood.

"Thank you for the beer," he said.

141

Then: "Richie told me I was wasting my time."

"We have to agree to disagree on this," I said.

"I am generally not one with whom to disagree," he said.

I told him I was well aware.

"You are either with me or against me," he said.

He walked out the front door without saying another word. Rosie and I watched him go. Neither one of us said anything. I walked across the room and locked the door behind him and bolted it.

"Leave it," I said.

Rosie and I both knew I wasn't talking to her this time.

TWENTY-ONE

My father and I were in front of a nursing and rehab facility called Sherrill House, on Huntington Avenue. He was explaining to me that it was one of the top places of its kind in Boston, providing both short- and long-term care.

"Long-term care, of course," Phil Randall said, "is the same as God's waiting room. Just without magazines."

He shook his head, as if delaying going inside for as long as possible. But then smiled, as if another private joke were being told by him, to him.

"Every time I ask your mother where we should go when we're no longer able to care for ourselves," he said, "she gives me the same stock answer."

"Let me guess," I said. "She tells you she doesn't want to discuss it."

"Bingo," he said. "Then she asks me to fix her another bourbon."

"Does bourbon fall into the category of short-term or long-term care?" I said.

"Both," my father said.

Then we were finally on our way inside and into the part of the place where people in what they called the Special Care Program lived, if you could call it living. It was where they put Alzheimer's patients, or those suffering from what were described as "related disorders."

"His son was reluctant to call it Alzheimer's," my father said. "But the way he described things, if the old man isn't officially there yet, his exit is coming up fairly rapidly."

"But you said he still has good days and bad days."

"So I was told by the son."

"So we hope this is one of the good days."

"If there really is such a thing." My father sighed. "When you reach my age," he said, "you'd rather stare down an AR-15 than a place like this."

"You don't have to go into the room with me if you'd rather not," I said.

"I'd rather not," he said. "But I shall."

We checked in at the front desk and were directed to the elevators that would take us up to the designated floor. Tim Leonard, the son, was waiting for us at the nurses'

144

station. He was slightly overweight and had thinning hair and a wide, Irish face and was a successful State Street lawyer, despite being the descendant of a strong-arm foot soldier himself.

"Like Richie, then," I'd said to my father. "The honest son of a profoundly dishonest man."

"Well," Phil Randall had said, "if you can call a lawyer honest."

Tim's father, Billy Leonard, had come up on the streets at the same time as Desmond and Felix Burke and their brothers. Somehow along the way Billy managed to leave Buddy McLean's crew and get with the Burkes without getting himself shot in Scollay Square, where my research told me a lot of old Mob guys had ended up extremely dead.

Billy is someone who had become an honorary Burke over time, mostly working as a body man for Felix, collecting for Desmond in their loansharking business, or doing the same for Peter when he was still making book. The legend was that he'd officially become part of the family when he took a bullet intended for Felix one night when they were coming out of the old Boston Garden after a fight card. Billy Leonard recovered. Desmond and Felix never forgot.

We were here because Phil Randall said Tim Leonard owed him a favor. I'd asked how big. My father said big enough that we were here.

"And you believe he might know some of Desmond's secrets," I said.

"*Knew* Desmond's secrets," he'd said.

Billy Leonard was in a wheelchair facing the window when we walked into the sunny room. He was still a big man and made the chair look small, hands folded in his lap. He wore a faded red flannel shirt and faded cords and the kind of sneakers that had Velcro on top.

If he heard us come in, he gave no sign.

It was Tim Leonard who spoke first.

"Dad," he said as he turned the wheelchair around so Billy Leonard was facing us. "You remember Phil Randall. This is his daughter, Sunny."

Billy stared at us, frowning, focused on my father.

"I know you," he said.

It was somewhere between question and answer.

My father smiled as if he were here to get a donation for the Police Benevolent Association.

"Only from all the times I tried to put you

146

away," Phil Randall said.

And then Billy smiled back at him.

"Phil Fucking Randall," he said.

"Not the middle name with which I was baptized," my father said. "But considering our history, I'll wear it, as the kids like to say these days."

Billy said, "You're not dead yet? Jesus."

"Mary and Joseph," my father said.

"You knew Phil was coming, Dad," Tim Leonard said. "I told you what he and Sunny wanted to talk to you about."

"Tell me again."

"They want to ask you some questions about Desmond Burke," Tim said.

"Is *he* dead?" Billy said.

"No," I said. "But someone seems to be trying."

Billy focused his rheumy eyes on me.

"Who are you?"

"Phil's daughter."

"Cop?"

"Was until I wasn't," I said. "I'm private now."

Billy nodded, as if the old man were trying to process new information.

"Ask you something?"

"Sure?"

"Your ass as good as your legs?"

"Dad!" Tim Leonard said.

147

"It's okay," I said. And to Billy I said, "The answer is an unqualified yes."

"I was always an ass man," Billy Leonard said. "Give me a good ass over big tits anytime."

Tim sighed, shook his head, told his father he'd be outside, and left us there. My father and I pulled up the two folding chairs in the room so that we were facing Billy.

"Somebody is shooting at the Burkes again, Billy," my father said, as if he were still the lead detective on the case. "First Desmond's son, Richie. He lived. Peter Burke was not as lucky."

"What about Felix?" Billy said. "I worked for Felix, mostly. Took a bullet for him that time. You remember that, Phil? Stepped right up there like a fucking champion."

"Everybody remembers," my father said.

"Showed them all some rope that night," Billy said.

"Somebody shot up Felix's house this time," I said. "Just without him in it."

"Always liked that house," Billy said. "We had some times there."

There was, I knew, no point in telling him that Felix had long since moved to the water. I remembered what my father had told me about people in Billy's state, that

148

you should talk to them like they were drunk.

"I didn't know Desmond had a daughter," Billy said to me.

"Only by marriage," I said. "To Richie."

"Billy," my father said, leaning forward, "what we're trying to determine is who might have a beef out of the past that might make them move on Desmond now."

Billy's eyes seemed to brighten suddenly. "Trouble was our business!" he said.

"Wasn't it, though," Phil Randall said.

"We used to joke, we did, that Desmond's real profession was pissing people off," Billy said.

"Tell me about it," my father said.

Billy shook his head but was smiling again. "Girls," he said.

"Desmond had a thing for the ladies?" my father said.

What began as a laugh with Billy Leonard quickly became a terrible-sounding cough.

"He was some cock hound back in the day, I'll tell you that," Billy said when he was able to speak. "You didn't know that? What the fuck kind of detective were you?"

Billy Leonard reached down now without embarrassment, grinning at my father as if I weren't there, as if this were just old boys being boys.

Then he grabbed his crotch.

"I used to tell him this business going to get him killed before our real business ever did," Billy said.

"While he was married?" my father said.

Another laugh. More coughing, even worse than before. When Billy was able to catch his breath again he said, "Before, during, after. They'll probably have trouble closing the casket someday, he'll probably have one last hard-on."

I knew little of Richie's mother other than what he'd told me. He always made her sound like a living saint, and her romance with his father something that could have been imagined only by Irish poets, before the cancer took her. Coupled with what I knew about Desmond Burke, I found it difficult to imagine him tomcatting around Boston as a much younger man.

But I also knew something else: how often men thought with what Billy had just called their "business."

"Those were the days," Billy said, as if he was much happier back there than he was here.

"Was there possibly one girl more than the others who might have gotten him into trouble?" my father said.

Billy closed his eyes, rubbed a big hand

over them, hard. But he was nodding.

"I forget her name." He took his hand away and looked at my father and said, "You forget things?"

"Every day, Billy," my father said. "Every goddamn day."

"What was that big musical back in the day," Billy said. "The one with the spics doing all that singing and dancing?"

"*West Side Story?*" Phil Randall said. "Sharks and the Jets and great to be in America."

"*West Side Story!*" Billy Leonard said, slapping his thigh with his right hand. "It was like that. Shit, I thought them fighting over her was going to start a fucking war."

"Desmond was fighting for this girl from another outfit?" my father said.

But Billy was no longer listening to him.

"So you're Desmond's daughter?" he said to me.

Before I had a chance to answer, he was suddenly shouting.

"Didn't you hear me?" he said. "I asked you a fucking question."

"Sure," I said, "I'm Desmond's daughter."

"Goddamn it!" Billy said, trying to get up out of the chair, fear in his eyes now or anger or both. "Both of you stop talking to me now!"

He was wringing his hands now, rocking in the wheelchair, eyes darting around the room, having turned into a different person.

Which I knew he had.

"Both of you get the fuck out of here and leave me alone!" he shouted.

The door opened and Tim Leonard came hurrying back in.

"Get them out of here!" he shouted at his son. "I don't know them!"

My father and I stood. I said to Tim, "I'm not sure what touched this off."

"Air," he said.

Neither one of us said anything in the elevator, or until we were back outside.

"You think the girl he was talking about is real?" I said to my father.

"I do," he said.

"Same," I said.

"He also said there were a lot of girls," he said.

"He didn't say the boys were fighting over a lot of girls," I said.

"How do you plan on finding out who she was?" my father said.

"I'll use all of my feminine wiles," I said. "Look how well it worked with Billy."

"I need a drink," my father said.

"Same," I said, and called Spike and told him we were on the way over.

TWENTY-TWO

I was still at Spike's, with Spike. My father had polished off a quick whiskey, neat, and left for home, saying my mother had prepared meat loaf for dinner and to wish him luck.

"So Desmond liked girls, that pervert," Spike said.

"Billy seemed pretty fixed on the notion," I said.

"Another old perv," Spike said.

It was between afternoon and evening. There was an older couple in the back room having an early dinner. A group of young guys, clearly biggies-on-the-go, were drinking and laughing at the bar, likely celebrating the money they'd moved today from one pocket to another.

Spike and I were sipping dirty martinis, extra olives.

"It's not as if you can now request a sit-down with Desmond so you can ask him how much he was getting back in the day," Spike said, "and with whom."

"At which point, incidentally, I would be operating off the ramblings of an old man in the throes of dementia," I said.

I sipped some of my martini. There were times when a perfect martini tasted so good it made me want to burst into tears. Or song.

This was one of them.

"The thing is," I said to Spike, "that Billy actually seemed pretty stuck on this one girl, even if he couldn't remember her name."

"You know it proves nothing," he said.

"It does not," I said. "But how much of everything in this crazy old world comes back to sex or money?"

"Much," Spike said.

"I want this to be a clue," I said.

"I can tell."

"Maybe the story isn't Desmond fucking around with a gun deal," I said. "Maybe it's just Desmond having fucked around on Richie's mother back in the day."

"There was probably a more elegant way to put that," Spike said.

"My father likes to tell people I'm where sailors go to learn to swear."

Spike said, "Tough to talk to Richie about

his father and other women."

"Gee," I said. "Ya *think*?"

I looked over at the bar. One of the young guys, with one of those haircuts shaved close on the sides but with a fade in front, extremely good-looking even if he might be trying too hard with the hair, was staring at me. Now that he'd finally caught my eye, he raised his glass and smiled. I raised mine and smiled back.

You still got it, kid.

"Who would you even talk to about Desmond's, ah, romantic endeavors?" Spike said.

"It would have to be Felix," I said.

Spike said, "Even the thought of a conversation like that makes me want another drink."

"Same," I said.

It was, after all, why God had invented Uber.

TWENTY-THREE

I met Felix Burke at 10:30 the next morning at the Warren Tavern on Pleasant Street in Charlestown.

I knew for a fact that the Warren Tavern, with its American flag hanging outside and cobblestone sidewalks in front of the place, didn't officially open until eleven. But this was Charlestown, and Felix was Desmond's No. 2 and I assumed that if he'd wanted to meet me there for breakfast, they would have opened as early as a Starbucks.

He had two young men with him, neither one of whom I recognized. Maybe there was just an endless supply of young, hard-looking gunnies, all of them wanting to grow up to be Desmond and Felix someday, provided they lived long enough.

We sat in the bar area. The two young men stood on either side of the entrance. I knew there was another young man outside in Felix's Escalade. Because of the shooting at

Felix's house, there might be more men outside, ready to invade Marblehead if Felix gave the word.

Felix and I both had coffee cups in front of us. He asked if I wanted to add anything besides milk and sugar, because he already had. I told him it was a little early in the day.

"I told Desmond I was coming to meet you," Felix said.

"Bet that put some extra pep in his step," I said.

"He told me he has given you more latitude than he would anyone else because of Richie," Felix said. "But his patience with you has clearly grown thin."

I smiled at Felix. "I've gotten that reaction from a Burke before."

"You have," Felix said. "But with Richie, it never really stuck."

His voice, raspy as ever, always made me think that he'd taken too many punches to the throat when he was still a boxer. But there was a salt to Felix Burke that I had always found endearing. I liked him and he liked me. He had done professional favors for me over the years, all of them with Richie's blessing, some at Richie's request. I had frankly always considered him more family than Desmond.

157

"I need to ask you questions about Desmond that I cannot ask him, or ask Richie," I said. "Questions that you might not feel comfortable answering. And I just want you to know that you won't insult me or hurt my feelings — or hurt our friendship — if you choose not to answer them."

He squinted at me. Or smiled. With Felix it was sometimes almost impossible to differentiate. I knew how dangerous he was, perhaps more dangerous than Desmond. But there had always been a humanity about him, at least when he was with me. I still found it amazing that he and Desmond had once looked as much alike as they had.

There was something else about him that I found appealing: I'd always thought he'd done more fathering to Richie than Richie's own father had.

"Sunny," Felix said, "you know how fond I am of you. But I've far more important things to worry about these days than your feelings."

"Duly noted," I said. "Will you relay everything about which we speak to your brother?"

He shrugged.

"I told Desmond you weren't gonna quit on this," Felix said. "I even told him he shouldn't expect you to quit after that gum-

158

ball shot Richie."

"What did he say?"

"He told me to mind my own fucking business," Felix said.

Sometimes it came out "fooking" with him, too, as if a breeze from the old country had blown into a room, the way it occasionally did with his brother.

"But," Felix continued, "I reminded my brother that this is everybody's business now. They hit Richie. They hit me in a different way. They murdered Peter. I told Desmond we should welcome all the goddamn help we can get."

I took a deep breath and told him about my visits to Vinnie Morris and Albert Antonioni, and finally about the one to Billy Leonard, and what Billy had told me about Desmond and women.

"Guns and women," Felix said. "Like turning the pages in a scrapbook."

"For the time being," I said, "I am going to proceed under the assumption that one or both has something to do with the shooting."

He nodded and sipped coffee. I did the same. It was good, strong coffee even without a shot of whiskey added to it.

I said, "Can you tell me anything about the gun deal that might be useful?"

"So you can tell your father?"

"Felix," I said.

It was an admonishment, my way of telling him that he knew me far better than that.

"Sorry," he said.

"So about the gun deal?"

"There's a gun deal, and it's a honey," he said. "All you need to know. With enough money involved it moves Desmond and me closer to closing things down for good."

I asked him then what I'd asked Vinnie Morris.

"Might this honey of a gun deal have pissed off one of your competitors enough to precipitate all this shooting?" I said.

"Any competitors of ours know that shooting Richie in the back would result in death penalties," Felix said. "Several."

My cup was empty. So was his. Felix simply looked at one of the boys at the door. He walked past the bar and into the kitchen and came back a few minutes later with a fresh pot of coffee. I had absolutely no doubt that he had watched whoever was in the kitchen brew the new coffee. It was perhaps overly cautious, because those at the Warren Tavern were as interested in Felix Burke's well-being as the boys at the door. But these had quickly become desperate times for the Burke family.

"What about Desmond's women?" I said.

Felix Burke folded thick, gnarled fingers on the table in front of him. Put his head back and closed his eyes. I had always thought of Felix as being the same age he'd been when I met him. But he was not. It was as if he were aging in front of my eyes over the last week, as if he were as old as Charlestown or the church he attended in the morning or the Bunker Hill Monument or the river or the ocean.

"We were all young once," he said.

"I'm aware."

"I had my day as well," he said, "back in the day."

"Aware of that, as well," I said. "But you weren't married."

He closed his eyes, and for a moment when he opened them, the old man looked young. And somehow sad at the same time.

"They were always Desmond's weakness," Felix said, almost sadly. "Mine, too. But not like him. I never saw my brother drunk. Never saw him touch any more of a drug than aspirin, and not even much of that. But women, Sweet Mother of God. They could make him lose his fucking mind."

It came out "fooking" again.

"Does Richie know?" I said.

161

Felix shook his head.

"Richie and me have always shared a lot," Felix said. "But he never gave me a hint that he knew what his father had been like when he was Richie's age. I think it would dim the light he's always shone on his late mother, and her marriage to his father."

"It's why I can't ask him," I said.

"He knows his old man wasn't perfect," Felix said. "But he believes his parents' union was."

"Only it wasn't."

"Desmond felt he was faithful when he was with her," Felix said.

"I've heard that defense before," I said. "It wouldn't even stand up in the court of one of those TV judges."

Felix shook his head.

"The lies we tell," he said, "starting with the ones we tell ourselves." He closed his eyes again and said, "As we're remembering things the way we wanted them to have been."

He reached into the side pocket of his windbreaker, pulled out a silver flask, and poured some of its contents into his coffee cup.

"The problem with Desmond in the old days," Felix said, "was that he didn't just stray out of his marriage, he strayed out of the faith, so to speak."

"Meaning with women from other crime families? Billy Leonard mentioned spics and *West Side Story,* for whatever that's worth."

Felix shrugged.

"That was the one about Romeo and Juliet, am I right?" he said. "Maybe my friend Billy was just talking about a girl from the wrong side of our tracks."

"Italians?" I said.

"Could have been anyone in those days," Felix said. "Desmond was never a reckless man, except when he'd see another skirt and all the blood would rush out of his brain and end up in his trousers."

"Was there ever one relationship that made you feel as if he were endangering the family business?"

He rubbed his mouth, hard, with his right hand.

"One?" he said.

"One he loved more than all the others," I said.

Something changed now in his eyes. I didn't know why. I didn't know what I saw in them. Something.

"No," he said finally.

"Can you give me as many names as you can remember?" I said.

He sounded almost in pain now as he

said, "I cannot. Because that would feel like a betrayal. And trust me on something: any kind of betrayal, especially with family, eats away at your soul."

He started to say something and stopped. He was holding back and he knew it, and perhaps knew that I knew it.

"Did he hurt someone?" I said.

"We all hurt people," Felix Burke said.

"I can help him," I said to Felix. "I can help you both before somebody else gets hurt."

"Don't you get hurt, Sunny," he said. "Or go to a place where we can't help *you*, because you've hurt people."

Felix stood up abruptly, nodded at the boys at the door, leaned down and kissed me on the cheek. When the old boys with whom I had been spending company were done, they were done, just like that.

"I've always loved you, Sunny," he said, and left.

He didn't make it sound like a good thing, all things considered.

Twenty-Four

I went home and spent the rest of the afternoon painting on the third floor, with Rosie at my feet.

I often had more than one piece going at a time. Today I was at work on a watercolor I had begun months ago before moving on to my stone cottage, one that had been inspired by a photograph I had taken last winter when Richie and I had decided to spend a weekend at an inn we both loved in Litchfield, Connecticut.

On the way there we had been blessed with a spectacular December sunset, the clouds a bright red, a sunset unlike any I had ever seen at that time of year. Richie had been driving. He had pulled the car over and I had gotten out and taken some shots with my phone. I started painting that spectacular red sky the next day when we returned to Boston, as much as I had always been more comfortable with old buildings.

But the other day there had been a similar sunset, though not as colorful or vivid, when Rosie and I had been walking along the Charles. I had come home and gone through old blocks stacked on the floor in the corner, in various stages of completion. There was my sunset, or ours, Richie's and mine. I had resumed working on it and was doing the same, happily, today.

This was one of the afternoons when I shut off the phone, took off my watch, purposefully lost myself in the work and the expanse and possibilities of the moment. It was twilight when I finally stopped.

I cleaned my brushes and put them away and fed Rosie and walked her over to the park and back. And decided to make spaghetti and broccoli, which *was* one of my specialties, goddamn it, whatever a cynical person like Spike said. I made just enough for one. I knew how much that was by now. I was used to cooking for one.

I cleaned the dishes and put them away and felt suddenly restless, as I frequently did these days, as if I were spinning my wheels, wondering if Desmond Burke was right, wondering whether or not I should just walk away from this and leave him to clean up his own mess, I hoped before someone else close to him ended up dead.

Desmond had strayed out of the faith, Felix had said.

Was it Romeo and Juliet, or more like the Hatfields and the McCoys?

But if the Burkes were the Hatfields, who the hell were the McCoys?

I'd noticed when walking Rosie that the temperature had dropped and I had seen rain in the sky and felt it. But I liked walking in the rain. If it ruined my hair tonight, so what? So I threw on a rain jacket, put a faded red Boston University ball cap on my head and a very stylish belt that doubled as a holster for the handgun I decided to bring with me.

I had no real destination in mind. I thought I might walk all the way to Joe's on Newbury Street for a drink, and screw what my hair looked like when I got there. I knew the bartender, and was not intimidated by being a single woman alone at a bar. Sometimes I went to places like Joe's for the sheer sport of it, just waiting to see and hear what the pick-up lines might be, if there were any. Pick-up lines? Was I dating myself even thinking about pick-up lines? Or should I think about it as hooking up, the way the kids did?

The last man I'd hooked up with seriously, other than Richie, was Jesse Stone, up in Paradise. We had finally drifted apart, mostly because of the force of his lingering feelings for his ex-wife and mine for Richie, even after both his ex-wife and Richie had remarried.

But it had been serious while it lasted, for both of us.

I took a right on Beacon and then a left on Arlington, and walked to Newbury and took a right. The rain started to come as I crossed Berkeley, and was coming much harder by the time I was passing Joe's. I revised my thinking about looking like a drowned rat at the bar. Kept going.

The rain came even harder.

This was usually a busy time of the night on Newbury, stores closed but bars and restaurants fully coming to life. Or nightlife. I'd stopped briefly in front of the long window at Joe's, noticed a pretty sizable bar crowd. For a moment, I thought I saw Richie looking over at me from across the street, but when I turned there was no one there. It wasn't the first time I thought I saw Richie, on the street or across a crowded room, and had been wrong.

Richie on the brain, I thought.

Along with all the other Burkes.

It was raining too hard now for me to continue walking away from home. I took a right on Exeter to head back, the sudden storm at full pitch and roar. If I'd had Rosie with me, the scene would have started to feel like something out of *The Wizard of Oz*. I was now wetter than Jacques Cousteau, and wondering if I should head back to Joe's and call an Uber to take me home.

I never heard him behind me, or sensed his presence.

Just felt the first hard blow to the side of my head, an openhanded slap that made me feel as if I'd been hit with a board. The punch didn't knock me out but would have been enough to put me down if he wasn't dragging me down the alley, halfway between Exeter and Dartmouth, and into a small, sheltered construction site, the concrete walls blocking us from anyone's view.

I had enough presence to try to reach down and clear my gun from the belt, but he had his arms around me and his lips close to my ear.

"Don't even fucking think about it," he said.

We were sheltered now from the rain, but it was still at full howl. I wondered if anyone would even hear me if I were able to scream, which I was not, with his hand clamped over my mouth. As I tried to break free, he hit me again, this one a blow to my kidneys that would have made me cry out in pain if it hadn't knocked all the air out of me.

He had me up against one of the walls now, just inside the wire fencing to the makeshift entrance to whatever this room was someday going to be. Even if someone were walking down the Public Alley, it was unlikely they'd be able to see us. Now he grabbed the ponytail coming out of the back of my cap and gave it a good yank. I could now feel the gun in my back.

"Try to turn around again," he said, "and I will shoot you."

There was nothing for me to say, his hand still over my mouth. I feebly tried to reach down again for my gun. As I did, he shoved me harder into the wall.

"You need to leave this alone," he said.

I felt my knees start to go, felt myself start to fall, but then he jerked me up.

He turned around then, perhaps to see if there might be someone in the alley, and his hand was briefly away from my mouth and I was able to say "Why didn't you kill Richie?"

To my great surprise in the moment, he answered me.

He said, "Because we're alike."

What the hell? I wanted to ask him what that meant, but then his hand was back over my mouth.

"I will kill him next time if you don't leave this the *fuck* alone," he said. "Now go tell them all how easy this was. Tell Desmond we keep fucking with him because we can."

Then I felt one last blow, *this* one to the top of my head. I went down but was still not out as I lay on the ground, feeling the intense pain in my head and in my side, thinking that the asshole had been right about one thing.

It *had* been easy.

When I finally managed to get into a sitting position, waiting for the wave of nausea that would mean I had been concussed, I got out my cell phone. I thought about calling Frank Belson or Lee Farrell, probably my best friend in the department. But I didn't want to talk to cops right now. Or even Richie. I didn't want to go to the hospital.

I called Spike and told him what had happened and where I was.

"Shit," he said.

I said, "My thoughts exactly."

"You don't want to call an ambulance?"

"No," I said. "But you know what a cockeyed optimist I am."

"Cockeyed, anyway."

He said he'd be there in five minutes if he

171

had to drive straight across the Public Fucking Garden.

"Don't hit the little ducklings," I said.

"Fuck the ducks," Spike said.

TWENTY-FIVE

He picked me up in the Town Car that he sometimes had on call for special patrons who lived nearby. I didn't recognize the driver. I was happy I could recognize Spike.

On the way to Melanie Joan's he said a doctor would meet us there.

"You know a doctor who makes house calls at this time of night?"

"Friend of the family."

"Whose family."

"Somebody's," he said.

He walked me into the house. I asked him to walk Rosie while I took a shower. He asked me again if I were feeling dizzy or nauseated. I told him I was not, that I was just sore as hell.

"Not as sore as I am," he said.

I went and undressed. Every movement was a rousing number from the Pops. But I dragged myself into the shower and made the water as hot as I could, happy that I was able to stand.

The guy, whoever the guy was, had said that he and Richie were alike.

He had said that it had been easy.

But what did it mean?

I got out and dried my hair with a towel, got into a Maroon 5 T-shirt and sweats. When I emerged, there was a man sitting next to Spike on the couch, petting Rosie. Close-cropped gray hair, stylishly cut. A bright red Ralph Lauren polo shirt and faded jeans and sneakers.

"This is Dr. Greg," Spike said.

"Thanks for coming," I said.

Dr. Greg grinned. "Spike," he said, as if that explained everything except quantum theory.

Then he told me to stand where I was in the middle of the room, asking me to show him exactly where the guy had hit me. I told him side of the head, top of the head, ribs. He gently probed my head, asking where it hurt.

"Everywhere," I said.

Then he asked me what Spike had asked, about dizziness or blurred vision or nausea or loss of consciousness. I told him, none of the above. It was then that I noticed a small machine standing at the end of the couch.

"Mind if I ask what that is?" I said.

174

"It's a little thing we call the TRX Dragon," he said. "Portable X-ray machine."

"You just happened to have one handy?" I said.

Spike said, "Is knowing where he got it going to make you feel any better?"

"Not so much," I said.

Dr. Greg plugged it in, used it to take pictures of my ribs, then asked if I had a laptop handy. I showed him where mine was on the desk. He attached a cord from the X-ray machine into the laptop, hit some keys, nodded.

"Contusion," he said. "No fracture, no breaks. You're actually in pretty good shape considering the beating you say you took."

"I feel like I'm being graded against the curve," I said.

"This really happened in one of those Public Alleys?" he said.

"It did."

"No shit," he said.

"No shit," I said.

"Ice for the ribs," he said. "What do you take for headaches?"

Advil, I told him.

"Take three or four now," he said, "and three or four more in a few hours."

"Isn't that a lot?"

He grinned again. "What is this, a Senate

hearing?"

As he wheeled the TRX Dragon toward the door he said, "Ice pack to the top of the head wouldn't be so bad, either. You can alternate."

"I have two."

"No shit," he said again.

"Be prepared," I said. "I would have made a great Boy Scout if they were taking girls back then."

As soon as he was gone, Spike went and got the Jameson from where he knew I kept it. Came back with the bottle and two glasses. Poured what we liked to call a Spike pour at his restaurant.

I drank some Jameson. It felt much better than it tasted as it ran through me like warm water.

"Just what the doctor ordered," I said.

"Dr. Spike knows you way better than Dr. Greg," he said.

Then he looked at me over his glass and said, "Why didn't you call Richie?"

"Because it wouldn't have gotten me anywhere tonight," I said. "And he would have had no viable outlet for the rage he would have felt."

Spike grinned. "You really have been shrinked, haven't you?"

I said, "He said that he didn't shoot to kill

with Richie because they were, quote, alike."

"Alike?"

"Yeah," I said.

"The only person Richie's going to want to kill is him," Spike said.

"Tell you something else," I said. "He seemed to enjoy the power he had over me."

"This asshat seems to be enjoying himself, period," Spike said. "But maybe getting a little more reckless as he goes in light of tonight's festivities."

"Makes him more likely to make a mistake."

I took a healthy pull on the Jameson. My head no longer throbbed as badly as it had. I wasn't sure if it was the Advil or the whiskey or both.

"Pretty bold move on Exeter Street," Spike said. "All in all."

"I think the conditions might have emboldened him somewhat," I said.

"At least he didn't shoot you."

"There's that."

"Small blessings," Spike said. "Painful as they may be."

"I think we've established that this guy, whomever he is, wants to make Desmond Burke suffer," I said.

"And he obviously knows enough about you, missy, to be threatened by you."

"You think he plans to kill him if he can?" I said.

"Is that a rhetorical question?" Spike said.

"But he's gonna want Desmond to know why."

"What happened tonight doesn't sound as if it's about some gun deal gone sideways," Spike said.

I shook my head.

"This wasn't an old guy," I said.

"Doesn't mean an old guy didn't send him," Spike said. "Which gives you a leg up."

"In what way?"

"Old guys are like your thing these days," he said.

He said he was sleeping on the couch, and there wasn't going to be any debate or smart talk about that. I told him I was too tired for either, and that he had Rosie, the two of them could battle it out for space.

I finished my Jameson, decided against taking more Advil, and went to bed, where I finally managed to sleep, dreaming about drowning because a hand kept holding my head underneath the water and not letting it up.

Twenty-Six

The pain, in both my side and my head, wasn't nearly as bad as I expected it to be when I awakened.

There was bruising in the rib-cage area, I noticed when I took another hot shower. No bruising on the side of my face, though it felt tender near my right ear. It was official that I'd lost the fight. But the bastard hadn't knocked me out. Spike left after I came out of the shower. He told me that if I didn't check in with him every couple hours, he planned to call a cop. Preferably a cute one.

The guy had said what he'd said to me last night. In the text message to Felix, the guy had told him to ask Desmond how it felt when it was someone he loved. He had not mentioned a gun deal. It didn't mean that the deal wasn't a part of this.

What if it wasn't just about one thing?

What if it was somehow about love, in

some way I still couldn't begin to understand, *and* money?

I considered that as I walked Rosie up
Charles Street, gun in one pocket of my
hoodie, a taser in the other pocket. As ever:
Not being paranoid. Just alert.

"What if it really is about both?" I said to
Rosie on Charles Street. "What if, as they
used to say in the old movies, it's heaters
and a broad?"

Rosie looked up at me, always optimistic
herself, as if a treat might be forthcoming.
Which it was. When we got home I called
Frank Belson and told him what had happened to me, and asked if anybody in the
department could tell me more about a possible gun deal with the Burkes than Albert
Antonioni had.

"First off, you're all right?" he said.

"Is that concern I hear from you, you big
lug?"

"I'll take that as a yes," he said.

"I'll live," I said.

"Shit," he said. "I was afraid of that."

"I'm trying to assemble the pieces to a
puzzle here," I said, "but I'm starting to
think it might be more than one puzzle."

"I'll call Quirk," Belson said. "He still
knows everybody. Including guys from
ATF."

"I would be most grateful," I said.

"Yeah, yeah, yeah," he said. "Our relationship continues to be give and take. I give. You take."

Said he would get back to me and hung up.

I made myself coffee and sat there at the kitchen table drinking it, still nagged by the feeling that I had missed something the night before.

It only made my head start to hurt all over again.

I reviewed everything he'd said to me one more time, including the part about telling Desmond he was fucking with him because he could. And made a promise, to myself, that I would do the same to him, first chance I got, the sonofabitch.

Twenty-Seven

I met Charlie Whitaker, retired ATF, at George Lane Beach in Weymouth, on Boston's South Shore, once known as the Irish Riviera. Charlie said he'd rather meet me at the beach, a short walk from his home.

"Mrs. Whitaker," he'd said on the phone, "prefers I no longer discuss firearms in the house."

We sat on a bench, two coffee cups he'd brought with him from Panera between us. He was a tall, thin man who still had a lot of wavy white hair and still looked fit enough to be on the job.

"Thanks for seeing me," I said.

"Belson called Quirk," he said. "Quirk called me. Felt like the old days."

"I assume Frank told you what I've been hearing about the Burkes," I said.

"Wasn't surprised," he said.

"Why so?"

"Because there's something going on

lately, up and down the coast, even if we haven't yet been able to get our arms around it, or our hands on the bad guys," Whitaker said. "You probably know this, but used to be there wasn't enough volume, no matter how steady the flow of guns was from down south, to make big enough money to get the big guys fully engaged. But over the last few months, we've heard about shipments disappearing. One here, one there. At first our guys thought it might be random. Couple trucks that simply went missing. Not front-page stuff, just noteworthy if you're in the game. It's as if someone is stockpiling. But the guys on my crew don't believe those guns simply vanished. They're somewhere."

I grinned and said, "Stop, Charlie. You're going too fast for me."

"My old crew is on this, believe me," he said. "But so far they've come up with nothing."

I thought about my conversation with Albert Antonioni, who'd acted about as interested in the gun business as he was in lawn bowling.

Whitaker gave me a brief tutorial then about the Iron Pipeline, the name given to I-95 by various bad guys, from biker gangs to gunrunners. The people in charge, Whitaker said, send straw buyers with clean records to states like Virginia, where restrictions on gun sales are generally softer than soft ice cream. Then they bring the guns back, in whatever bulk they can manage, and sell them on the street in places like Providence, and before long the guns are on their way to Boston and various gang members.

"Any particular ethnicity?" I said.

"Yeah," he said. "The country of mutts."

He sipped some coffee and stared at the boats on the water.

"What they're basically doing is trafficking in legal illegal guns that were originally purchased legally in fucking Gun Show America," he said. "Then they start passing through one pair of hands and another — and another — until somebody's using one of them to shoot somebody in the head."

He smiled. "You can see why Mrs. Whitaker doesn't want such talk in her kitchen?"

"Discretion," I said.

"Better part of all that valor shit."

"So it really could be worth it to Desmond and Felix Burke to get big into the gun business this late in their lives?"

"Especially if they've figured out a way to become one-stop shopping for all of New England," he said. "Listen, guys like them have taken a big hit because of online gambling the way everybody else has, something that was always their bread and butter. Now, that hasn't dried up completely, mind you. But the online stuff has created a drag. And they were never into girls the way Albert always has been, though I keep hearing that Tony Marcus might want to expand his interests down here. You know him, right?"

"Far better than I would prefer."

"On top of everything else we're talking about, it's even been a while since the Burkes had the loansharking business to themselves in Boston," Charlie Whitaker said, still staring out at the water. "So in a world where the fucking NRA becomes like an unindicted coconspirator if you want to buy and move guns, maybe switching lanes is just a practical matter for Desmond."

"How much volume would there have to be?" I said.

"Most people just do it twenty to thirty guns at a time," he said. "Most popular item, even after all this time, is still a nine-millimeter. But if Desmond has a way to expand that to bigger guns, like that AR-15, and trade in really big numbers, the old man could do very well for himself."

"Albert Antonioni wanted me to think he

185

himself isn't particularly interested in the gun business," I said.

"Since when?" Whitaker said. "It was always a secondary business for him. But if Albert thinks there's money in it, he'd open a chain of lemonade stands."

"So it might anger him off if he heard that Desmond was poking around at the edges of a big gun deal," I said.

"Royally," Charlie Whitaker said.

"Would you be interested in keeping your ears open for me on this?" I said, smiling at him.

Turning on the charm with another old guy.

"Royally," he said.

We both stared at the boats on the water now.

"Just don't tell my wife," he said finally.

"Mum's the word," I said. "So to speak."

"She'd probably shoot me," Charlie Whitaker said and grinned. "Be ironic, if you think about it."

TWENTY-EIGHT

As far as I knew, Charlie Whitaker's wife didn't shoot him after I left and neither did anyone else.

But somebody did shoot Buster Doogan, Desmond Burke's top trooper, outside of Touchie's Shamrock Pub in Southie, just after last call, early the next morning.

Belson called me right before Richie did to tell me what had happened.

"You might as well come on over here," Belson said. "Maybe you can bring some ideas with you on how to keep this out of the papers that we maybe have a serial killer on our hands."

"Serial shooter, to be precise, Frank," I said.

"What is this," he said, "one of those fucking debate shows on cable TV?"

I threw on a sweater and jeans and jacket, threw my short-barrel .38 into my shoulder bag, drove over to Pearl Street. There was the usual small army of crime scene people already in place and at work. Desmond Burke was there, too, and Felix, and Richie. So was Colley, Buster's wingman, a tough young guy who looked to be in a state of shock.

When Belson saw me he waved me through the uniforms on the perimeter, and walked me up 8th Street, away from the crush. He always looked the same, day or night, always needing a shave, always slightly pissed off, never missing anything in his range of vision. Always with a cigar in his hand, sometimes lit, sometimes not.

"He lives over on Marine Road," Belson said. "Or lived. The guy, Buster Doogan. His shift bird-dogging Desmond was over. Desmond has them working eight-hour shifts now. Doogan is walking home when he gets popped."

"Witnesses?" I said.

"People heard," Belson said. "Nobody saw."

"Guy could have taken out anybody in Desmond's crew," I said. "But he takes out Buster, who's been with him the longest. Means our guy has been doing his homework."

"Richie, Peter, Felix, you, now Buster," Belson said. "Like the asshole is tightening a noose."

I looked past him. Desmond and Felix and Richie were watching us from their side of the yellow tape, faces lit by flashing lights.

Belson said, "What haven't you told me?"

"Very little."

"But something," he said. "Just because there always is."

"Why my clients trust me the way they do," I said.

He stuck the cigar in his mouth, took it out without inhaling.

"Might I remind you that you *have* no client here," Belson said. "From what I gather, what you mostly got is people, including your ex, who don't *want* to be your clients."

"Well, there is that," I said.

"So talk to me."

"It would mean telling you things that I haven't yet told Richie," I said. "Things to which I'm not sure how he'll react. And things that might cause him pain."

"You know what causes pain?" Belson said. "Getting shot. And you know what causes me pain? People getting shot and killed. So if you've got a theory you'd like to share, I am all fucking ears."

So I told him more than I had already about what the guy who'd put me down in the alley had told me before he did. I told him about what Billy Leonard had said about Desmond and women and what Felix Burke, who seemed to be in some pain of his own, seemed unwilling to say about Desmond and women. Belson let me tell it at my own pace, as if we had all night, which I suppose we did.

"Was about twenty minutes ago," he said, "that you thought this was about some kind of gun deal going wrong."

"Maybe it still is," I said. "But then this guy was right in my ear. And as much as he seems to be enjoying himself tightening the noose, what I really heard was rage."

"So this might have something to do with a woman from the old man's past," Belson said. "And the shooter's connection to her."

"Brother, husband, son, friend," I said. "Could be any of the above."

"Or none of."

"Frank," I said, "this runs deep, whatever it is. If this was just about business, the guy could hit Desmond no matter how well protected he thinks he is, and be done with it."

"Guy wants it made clear that nobody is safe," Belson said.

"Kind of the definition of a terrorist," I said.

"Ain't it, though?" he said.

He said the conversation he wanted to have with Desmond could wait, if Desmond would even agree to have it at all.

"We're on the same page here," I said to him.

"Be still my heart," Frank Belson said.

Twenty-Nine

Richie said we needed to talk. I asked him if it could wait until morning. He said, "You seemed to make time for Frank Belson." I told him that I was just being a good citizen, and that right now I wanted to sleep more than talk.

"Used to be the other way around, as I recall," Richie said.

I smiled and told him I'd see him at Melanie Joan's at about nine. Of course the doorbell rang at nine sharp. I had been up since eight, had walked Rosie, done my makeup as if performing major surgery, spent way too much time on my hair, put on a new pair of skinny jeans and a white cotton sweater that Richie had given me. Vanity, thy name is Sunny Randall.

Rosie was gradually becoming more excited when Richie would suddenly appear.

"At least she didn't pee on the floor the way she did last time," I said.

"As women so often do in my presence," he said.

I went into the kitchen, knowing how he liked his coffee, which was the same way I liked my coffee, and brought two mugs to the couch. Rosie sat between us.

"I'm really sorry about Buster," I said.

"Was with us a long time," Richie said. "Can't remember a time in my life when he wasn't with us."

He looked as if he'd slept very little, but he was still put together in a Richie way: white shirt, black jeans, black penny loafers with a nice shine to them.

"Buster always said he'd take a bullet for my father," Richie said. "Finally did."

"You said we needed to talk," I said.

"Actually, that was bullshit," Richie said. "I sensed that you needed to talk."

"Because you know me so well," I said.

"More than you know," he said. "Or will ever."

He sat. I sat. As comfortable as we could both be with silence, the silence between us was sometimes a tactile thing. I took a deep breath and let it out and said, "I need to broach an uncomfortable subject about Desmond."

"Broach away."

"It's about him and women," I said.

193

"I assume you mean women other than my mother," Richie said.

"Yes," I said.

"You're telling me that he was involved with women other than my mother," Richie said.

"Yes," I said again.

And Richie said, "Tell me something I don't know."

I came back from refilling our coffee cups and said, "You knew."

"I did."

"For how long?"

"For my whole fucking life," he said.

His face had not changed expression. Nor had his tone. He was as self-contained and composed as ever, as if the subject were no more serious than where we ought to have lunch. It meant he was Richie. If there was sadness in him because of this, or anger, or regret, or some combination of those emotions, he did not show it.

He was Richie. It was part of what drew me to him, and so often pushed me away, the sense that he was holding back so much of himself, whether he actually was or not. Jesse Stone had often exhibited many of the same qualities. He was gone from my life, other than an occasional phone call. Richie was not, not now and perhaps not ever.

"What does that mean, your whole life?" I said.

"A slight exaggeration," he said. "I was a kid when I found some letters. Back when people still wrote letters."

"Your mother was still alive?" I said.

"She had died the previous summer," he said. "But it was clear from the letters that what had been going on between my father and the woman who had written these letters had predated my mother's death." Richie paused and said, "Considerably."

Rosie had rolled over on her back to let Richie rub her belly, which he did.

"Did your mother know?" I said.

Richie sighed now. "There was some indication in one of the letters that they'd been found out, past tense, and had been forced to briefly end their relationship." He paused again and said, "Before it resumed."

"While your mother was dying?" I said.

"Yes," Richie said.

"So who was she?" I said.

"She didn't sign her letters with a name," Richie said. "Just the letter *M.*"

From across the room I could hear my cell phone buzzing. I ignored it. There was just Richie and me and the air between us. And perhaps the shared knowledge that when we had been man and wife, I had never cheated on him during our marriage and he had never cheated on me. Even though the other men in my life since had made me feel as if I were cheating, more than somewhat.

"Did you ask him about the letters?" I said.

"I did."

"What happened?"

"He slapped me," Richie said, "for the one and only time in my life."

Now there was hurt on his face, as if it had just happened.

"Then he told me that he had confessed his sins to his priest but was under no obligation to do the same to his own son."

"And that was it?"

"He demanded that I hand over the letters," Richie said. "Which I did."

"Because you were a good son."

"Because I didn't want him to hit me again," Richie said. "And I wasn't yet big enough or strong enough to hit him back."

"That woman could be the key to this," I said, and then told him what had happened to me in the alley, and what the man had said to me.

"Why have you waited this long to tell me?" Richie said.

"You had enough to deal with," I said.

"Not any part of it more important than you," he said.

"You would have wanted to do something about it," I said, "only there was nothing to be done. Then somebody did Buster."

We sat there. Rosie was still on her back.

"I thought it could have been any of his women," I said. "But perhaps it was this woman."

"We have no proof," Richie said.

"Call it a hunch," I said.

"You've always been big on those."

"Haven't I."

"We need to know who M was."

"Do you recall anything from what she wrote to him that might help?"

"She was Italian," Richie said. "There was something in one of the letters about the hatred between Italians and Irish and how it was almost as deep as the blacks against the whites. So there was that. And how much she had herself come to hate living in what she called their world. And how tired she was of all the death and dying."

"You remember a lot."

"There was a time when I had them committed to memory," he said. "She said she wanted them to get away, from his family and hers, and go somewhere and have a life of their own."

"Maybe if we can find her, or find out who she was, we can stop the death and dying now," I said.

"Only one way to find out," Richie said.

"Ask him," I said.

"He won't hit me this time," Richie said.

THIRTY

Desmond Burke now lived on Flagship Wharf in Charlestown, part of the old Navy Yard, with views of both the Bunker Hill Monument and the USS *Constitution.*

We were seated in the large, bright, airy front room. Colley was outside, posted by the front door. There were two other troopers, neither of whom I knew, sitting in a Town Car on the street.

The room, I'd noticed, was full of photographs, on the mantel of his fireplace and the walls and spread across an antique bureau that might have been as old as the *Constitution.* There were pictures of Desmond Burke's late wife and of Richie at different ages, all the way through our wedding. There was even one of Desmond and me from the wedding, one in which I looked far happier than I felt right now.

I looked younger. Much.

I was more fixed on the ones of Richie as

a boy, wondering about all the things that made him the man he had become, one I knew I would love more than I would ever love another, whether we ended up together, fully together, or not.

Richie and I were on a long white couch. Desmond was across from us, once again dressed all in black today.

"I've not much time," he said. He looked at me and said, "I've already told your friend Belson that I did not choose to speak with him."

I smiled. "Never talk to a cop," I said.

"Words to live by," Desmond said.

"Then we should get right to it," Richie said. "The woman who wrote you the letters I found — who is she?"

Richie establishing himself as the one in charge, even in his father's home.

"I thought we had agreed never to discuss her again," Desmond said.

"We're past that, Dad," Richie said. "Way past. Sunny has now been assaulted by the one doing the shooting. Sunny and I believe it might very well involve the one who wrote you those letters."

"And she knows of these letters . . . how?"

"Because I fucking well told her," Richie said.

Now it was as if Desmond had been

slapped.

"You talk to me in such a way?" Desmond said to Richie.

"I was taught that what matters most is often what is most necessary," Richie said. "Or something along those lines. I don't remember every one of your codes."

"I don't appreciate your tone," Desmond said.

"I didn't much appreciate finding out that you cheated on my mother," Richie said.

"I told you then," his father said. "I don't have to explain myself to you."

But you could see the fight beginning to leak out of him. It was as if the words died a few feet from his mouth.

Richie said, "If we don't stop this man, he is going to kill us all."

"Maria Cataldo," Desmond Burke said.

Boom.

THIRTY-ONE

In Desmond's telling, in a flat, almost beaten voice, it all had begun after the Winter Hill Gang had consolidated its power, including with the Italians.

"You hear in politics about gerrymandering," Desmond Burke said. "There was a lot of that going on in those days, across ethnic lines. It was around the time when a man named Bobo Petricone got himself into trouble because of a girl going around with one of the McLaughlins."

"George," I said.

He looked at me.

"I'm a reader," I said.

I watched Desmond Burke, fascinated, wondering how much he was willing to tell. It was somewhat like watching the old man begin to pull on a thread.

"Bobo was a cousin of Vincent Cataldo," Desmond said. "Maria was Vincent's daughter."

202

Richie said, "Uncle Felix told me once that Vincent Cataldo had something on Whitey Bulger, but no one ever knew what."

"To this day we don't know what," Desmond said. "But Vincent ended up running his own gerrymandered district, as I ended up with my own." He shook his head. "I always thought that it amused Whitey," he said, "pitting Vincent and I against each other."

"And you took up with Vincent Cataldo's daughter?" Richie said.

"I did," his father said. "For the first time in my life, I had power. Including, as I discovered, power over women."

"How lucky for you," Richie said.

"I am asking you again not to judge," Desmond said.

"You're allowed to ask," Richie said. "And I'm asking you if Mom knew."

Desmond nodded. "I finally admitted the affair to her. And she accepted."

"Easy for you to say," Richie said.

"No," his father said. "It is not. And was not."

He gave a quick shake to his head.

"It was around that same time that Vincent discovered that his daughter and I had been seeing each other," Desmond said. "And let everyone know that his solution to this particular problem was to have me killed. But Maria told him that if he did that, she would kill herself."

"So how was it resolved?" I said.

"There was finally a sit-down with Vincent and me," Desmond said. "He said I was lucky that his daughter had interceded on my behalf, or he would have commenced killing those close to me one by one. But he told me that I had to be the one to break it off with her, without telling her that I had met with her father."

"Did you?" I said.

"I did. I told her I was Catholic and could never be divorced and that it had been foolhardy of both of us to think that we ever could run away together," Desmond said. "I think she knew I was lying. But she accepted."

"The way mom did," Richie said.

There was something in Desmond's eyes, like a match being lit suddenly. But he let it go.

"What happened then?" I said.

"A few months after we stopped seeing each other, Maria left Boston," Desmond said. "On her own. Or was sent away. I never knew which. I was not told where she went, and never saw her again."

"Where is she now?"

"I swear to you I don't know," he said.

"So you don't know if she's dead or alive?" I said.

He shook his head. "I always assumed that somehow or someday I would see her again. I never did."

"You didn't attempt to find her."

He gave me a long look. "Nor did she attempt to find me."

"But now it appears someone is coming for you and those close to you much as her father once threatened to do the same," I said.

"Perhaps someone who wants to hurt you as he apparently believes you hurt her," Richie said. "And then kill you."

"Blood feuds," his father said. "As mean as brass knuckles."

"How did Vincent Cataldo die?" I said to Desmond.

"The theory at the time was Albert Antonioni," he said. "Who had become his partner by then."

I looked at Richie. He looked at me. We both looked at his father.

"Small world," Richie said.

"One full of coincidence suddenly," I said.

"Do you believe in coincidence?" Richie said to me.

"Not even a little bit."

"Is that all of it?" Richie said to his father.

"As much as is relevant," Desmond said.

"Even if holding back might keep us all in danger," Richie said.

"Even if."

There was one last, interminable stare-down between father and son, two pairs of dark eyes locked on each other.

"Please go now," Desmond Burke said.

We went.

THIRTY-TWO

We drove back to Melanie Joan's in Richie's Jeep. Two of Desmond's troopers were in a car right behind us.

Richie found a parking spot on River Street. He'd always had great parking karma, there was simply no explaining it. The troopers double-parked halfway up the block and shut off the engine. I tried to imagine the fun that might ensue if one of the good ladies from the neighborhood told them to move it.

We went inside. Richie immediately sat on the floor and Rosie jumped into his lap and began lapping his face. Whatever reservations she'd once had about Richie were clearly melting away, at an increasingly rapid rate. I asked Richie to take her out and he did. When he came back he locked the door behind him, gave Rosie a bone, walked across the living room and kissed me, hard and for a long time, with absolutely no resistance from me. When we finally pulled back, our faces were still very close.

"Lost love seems to be the theme of the day," Richie said.

"Not here," I said.

"Meaning you don't want us to do it in the middle of the living room?" he said.

"No," I said. "Not here and not in front of Rosie."

"Where to?" Richie said. "Place is full of possibilities, according to Melanie Joan."

"Bedroom," I said.

"I could carry you up the stairs," Richie said.

"Would be a bad time to lose you," I said.

"You will never lose me," he said.

We headed for the bedroom, both of us resisting the urge to run. I asked him to undress me. He did. There had been multiple times in our life together when Richie had struggled, and mightily, getting my bra off. Not today.

"Have you been practicing on the bras of others?" I said.

"Please stop talking," he said.

I did.

And somehow this time, even after all the other times, was like the first time, with the room in shadows, as if day had suddenly been transformed into night, at least in here, with the shades drawn and door locked and the two of us as together as two people could be, with a coupling informed by fierceness and gentleness and want and need. And love. Eventually I exploded and then he did. Or perhaps it was the other way around, in a moment where it was impossible to know where I ended and he began, in the big bed that Melanie Joan said had seen more traffic than the T.

It was Richie who finally spoke.

"I think you might have scared the baby," he said.

We were on our backs, on top of covers that had not been pulled back or down. The throw pillows from the bed were scattered around the room as if the place had been tossed.

Which, in point of fact, it had been.

My breathing had not yet returned to normal. Richie's had. I often joked with him that his standard resting pulse rate was just slightly north of dead.

Then Richie said, "Holy fucking fuck."

"An apt description," I said. "If not a terribly poetic one."

"Either way," he said.

He turned and reached his head over enough to kiss me above an eye. When I turned back, I saw him smiling.

"Did you know this would happen after we left your father's house?" I said.

"Ever hopeful," Richie said.

"Do you think the boys outside are concerned that I may be holding you hostage?" I said.

"They'll figure it out."

"You think they may have heard me in the car?"

He smiled again.

"Pretty sure," Richie said, "that they could hear you in Braintree."

I punched him in the arm.

We remained side by side in the big bed, in the dark room. Neither of us made any attempt to cover ourselves.

"Do you think I'm starting to look older?" I said.

Richie propped himself up on an elbow and made a big show of turning his head, as if inspecting every inch of me.

"Hey," I said. "This isn't a show."

"Speak for yourself, blondie."

Then we commenced to do our level best to toss the place again.

Later, much, I said to Richie, "We have behaved like horny teenagers."

"Redundant," he said.

He was in a Dropkick Murphys T-shirt

210

that he kept here for sleepovers, and a pair of black Boston Bruins sweatpants with gold trim. I was in jeans and a long-sleeved T-shirt. We had made our way out of the bedroom, at long last. It was, after all, the cocktail hour. Richie had made us both martinis.

"How much do you think your father held back?" I said.

"No way to know," Richie said.

"I need to find out a lot more about Maria Cataldo."

"Like working a cold case," Richie said.

"I have before," I said.

"Where do you suppose she went?"

"For me to find out," I said.

"A lot trickier for me," Richie said.

"Tricky *being* you right now."

"What do you mean right now?" he said.

The martini was perfect. I couldn't tell whether or not Richie had actually added vermouth, or just opened the bottle so our glasses could catch a whiff.

I said, "He said the Cataldos are all gone."

"Doesn't mean they are."

"You're saying your father lies?"

"Only to stay in practice," Richie said.

Richie said he'd cook dinner. I told him that was fine with me, we both knew he was a far better cook than I. And had more

211

specialties than just spaghetti and broccoli. He checked the freezer and refrigerator for possibilities. Found a steak I had bought the day before at DeLuca's and some mushrooms and a package of onion rings.

"Steak O'Shrum it is," Richie said.

"Yippee," I said.

I fed Rosie and took her out for a walk while he cooked. Outside I gave a smile and one-fingered salute to the boys in the car.

Richie and I ate steak and mushrooms and onion rings at the kitchen counter and drank a Chianti Classico we both liked. When we were finished and had cleared the plates, because Richie Burke never left plates unclean the way my father never did, we both took Rosie out for her last walk. When we came back, Richie and I made love again.

"I feel like a sailor on leave," he said.

"Don't leave, sailor," I said.

"Not tonight," he said.

In the morning Frank Belson called and said he might have found the shooter.

"Shot," he said.

"Dead?" I said.

"Oh, my, yes," Belson said, and told me where I could find him.

THIRTY-THREE

The body had been found between the Murphy Rink in South Boston and the park next to it on William Day Boulevard, not far from the Castle Island lagoon.

A man had been walking his dog at about seven in the morning, according to Frank Belson. The dog had suddenly become agitated and started barking. The man found the body, facedown, near a small clump of trees. The man with the dog called 911. I knew the drill about "body found" from my days as a cop as well as I knew the code to unlock my iPhone. Car dispatched. Patrol supervisor alerted. Full notification to the operations center. Call to the on-duty homicide officer, who called Belson.

He now stood with me about fifty yards from the perimeter of the crime scene. Body was already gone, pictures had already been taken, a handful of cops inside the perimeter looking for anything Belson might have missed in his own inspection of the scene. By now I knew there was as much a chance of them finding something Frank Belson had missed as there was of them becoming astronauts.

"We never close," he said.

"Fighting crime, reducing fear," I said from memory.

"What about improving the quality of life in our neighborhoods?" Belson said.

"Might have fallen a little short this morning on that one," I said. " 'Least in this neighborhood."

He made a snorting noise.

"One to the back of the head," he said. "Guy's own gun in the side pocket of his windbreaker. Looks like he never got the chance to clear it."

"What kind of gun?"

"One that killed him or one in his pocket?"

"Pocket?"

"A .22," Belson said.

"Was it not a .22 that shot Richie and killed Peter and Buster?"

Belson said, "Fuckin' ay."

"ID?" I said.

"Wallet in the back pocket of his jeans, intact," Belson said. "Rhode Island driver's license, credit cards, Dunkin' Donuts card, all in the name of Dominic Carbone, a resident of Cranston until a couple hours or so ago."

"I assume he wasn't moonlighting with the Cranston Chamber of Commerce," I said.

"We've already run his name through the NCIC," Belson said. "National Crime Information Center."

"I know what it means, Frank."

With the morning light hitting his face the way it did, he might have grinned.

"Dominic, as it turns out, was not what you might call an Eagle Scout. Did two falls for assault as a younger man. A third, according to the Providence cops my guys have already talked to, was tossed on account of a bad arrest."

I waited. I knew him and knew there was more.

"Which is not the most interesting part of Dominic's portfolio."

"Don't make me beg," I said.

"According to the Providence cops, Dominic grew up to be a button man for Albert Antonioni," Belson said. "Oh, wait. I meant to say alleged button man."

"You PC bastard."

"His gun is already back at the lab," Belson said.

"Because you want to know if it might be

the same gun somebody has been pointing at the Burkes," I said.

"How did we ever let a Crimestopper like you get away?" Belson said.

"And if it is a match," I said, "does that close the books on our recent crime spree?"

Belson snorted again.

"Fuck, no," he said.

"Would be an awfully tidy package," I said.

"Wouldn't it, though?"

"This work has made you cynical," I said.

"Hasn't it, though?" Belson said. "If there is a ballistics match, then what?"

"Then officially I've only got one stiff to worry about," Belson said.

"And unofficially?"

"Unofficially, and because I *am* a cynical-type person, I start to think how convenient it is that we put a bow around everything with a Mobbed-up guy from Rhode Island who somehow gets himself shot to death from close range outside an MDC skating rink in South Boston," Belson said.

"You think Desmond and Felix could have had this done?"

"Could have? Sure," he said. "But that means they got the guy out here and somebody got close enough to shoot him, the way somebody shot Peter Burke."

"It was done here?"

"ME says yes."

Being somebody who really did consider herself a good citizen, I thought about telling Belson about Maria Cataldo and what Dominic Carbone, if it was Dominic Carbone, had said to me while holding me down in that alley in the rain. I thought about possible connections between the late Dominic Carbone and the Cataldo family, once run by a man that Desmond Burke said Albert Antonioni had killed, or had ordered killed. Unless Desmond Burke had lied to me, always a distinct possibility.

If Peter and Felix Burke thought that Dominic Carbone, who worked for Albert Antonioni, was their shooter, how long would it take for them to go after Antonioni himself?

But I didn't share any of that with Frank Belson, at least for now.

Belson looked at me the way I knew he looked at crime scenes, as if he somehow saw something on my face. Or was reading my mind.

"I like you, Sunny," he said. "I love your old man. But you know me well enough to know that if you are holding back from me and I find out about it, I am prepared to harass the shit out of you."

"It's all the rage," I said. "Harassment."

"I didn't mean that kind," Belson said.

"I know."

Now Belson grinned. "Me, too," he said.

He really could be a funny bastard when he wanted to be.

THIRTY-FOUR

I spent the rest of the morning, and most of the afternoon, trying to find out anything I could about Maria Cataldo, whom Desmond Burke said he had loved and then lost.

And proceeded to get lucky, because of my father's assistance and contacts.

He was able to track down a birth certificate, which informed us that Maria had been born at Mass General in May of 1958. Good to know, I thought. But the information did nothing to help me find out what had happened to her after Boston, where she had gone, what she had done with her life. It wasn't until several hours later that a cop friend of my father's from Providence, Pete Colapietro, one who owed him a favor, just because somehow everybody in my father's orbit seemed to owe him a favor, emailed him a photograph of a death certificate from Rhode Island Hospital in Providence, which Phil Randall forwarded to me.

It was dated two months previously, and had the name Maria Theresa Cataldo on it. There was no next of kin listed. The cause of death was listed as complications from Parkinson's disease.

"Desmond said he didn't know whether she was dead or alive," I said. "But now I know."

"You going to tell him?"

"Yes," I said. "Just not today."

"There could be a husband or son or a daughter somewhere," Phil Randall said on the phone.

"But the name on the death certificate," I said, "is the same as the one on her birth certificate. Maria Cataldo. Daughter of Vincent and Bettina."

"Could have gotten married after Boston and never bothered to change it," my father said.

"Like you always tell me," I said. "Blood is blood."

"Interesting how much of this story runs through Rhode Island suddenly," he said.

"You *think*?"

"Might I make a fatherly suggestion?"

"Have you ever had to ask permission?"

"See if you can find out if there was a wake and a funeral for her down there," he said. "If there was, find out who paid. Not hard to check. Find out where she's buried, and who paid for the plot, and paid for a stone if there is one."

I smiled to myself. The guy Desmond Burke called an old copper. Still doing his copper thing.

"I would have thought of all these things, you know," I said. Still smiling. "It's in my genetic code."

"Still don't know why the Red Sox aren't," he said.

I got on my laptop and got as comprehensive a list as I could of all the funeral homes anywhere near Providence, Rhode Island, and simply started cold-calling them.

Finally found myself speaking to a man who identified himself as Mr. Otero Senior, at the Otero and Son Memorial Chapel, in Pawtucket.

I told Mr. Otero Senior that I was from the Boston Police Department, which was technically true. Invoking the spirit of the law, if not the letter of the law.

I inquired about funeral arrangements made for Maria Theresa Cataldo, if there had been any.

"Why, yes, there were," he said.

"And you handled them?" I said.

"We did."

"Was she buried or cremated?"

"You said you were with the police," he said. "Might I ask to what this is in reference?"

"A homicide investigation," I said.

Whole truth, nothing but.

"She was buried," he said.

"In Rhode Island?" I said.

"No, as a matter of fact," he said. "Up in your neck of the woods."

"Boston?"

"St. Augustine's," he said. "It's on Dorchester Street."

"In South Boston," I said. "I know where it is."

I knew where it was because Peter Burke had just been buried there. I could hear my own breathing, and wondered if Mr. Otero Senior could as well.

Down, girl.

"Ms. Randall? Are you still there?"

"I am," I said.

"Thought I'd lost you," Mr. Otero Senior said, and chuckled at his own joke.

"Was a headstone purchased?" I said.

"A tasteful granite one, actually," he said.

"By whom?" I said.

Now he was the one who paused on the other end of the line.

"To be clear," he said. "This is a police matter, is it not?"

"Three people who may have had a connection to Maria Cataldo have now been shot to death," I said. "So we can do this over the phone or in person."

"Just give me a moment," he said, perhaps needing to consult with Mr. Otero Junior.

When he came back on the line he said, "The headstone, and plot, were paid for by Mr. Albert Antonioni." He chuckled again. "I assume, you being a law enforcement professional, that you are aware of who he is."

"He's an acquaintance of mine," I said to Mr. Otero Senior.

"I'll bet!" Mr. Otero Senior said.

THIRTY-FIVE

In the late afternoon I went for a long run along the Charles, my short-barrel .38 Velcroed above my ankle and beneath baggier running pants than I usually wore.

I went past the Charles River Bistro after I crossed the footbridge, said hello to the bust of Arthur Fiedler, took a left at the small dock facing Cambridge, and headed toward Mass Ave, a light, pleasant breeze in my face.

Normally I liked listening to music on long runs. Just not today. I wanted my head clear, a blank board, hoping the quiet and solitude of the run would help sort out the information overload inside my brain, so much of it having to do with an old knockaround guy named Albert Antonioni, and whether or not he had been the puppetmaster here all along; whether whatever was happening here wasn't just about a woman out of the past, his and Desmond Burke's,

or part of a much deeper blood feud between him and Desmond that neither one
of them wanted to talk about, at least not
with me.

I kept coming back to the same thing: Was
it only about Maria Cataldo, or was it about
something more?

I thought back to all the times when I was
at BU and I had gone with either dates or
friends to the Brattle Theatre to watch *Casa-
blanca,* all of us bringing cheap wine and
glasses, everybody in the theater toasting
the screen by saying "Here's looking at you,
kid" when Humphrey Bogart said the same
thing to Ingrid Bergman, not long after Sam
had broken one of Bogey's rules by singing
about hearts full of passion, jealousy, and
hate.

How much of this might simply be about
jealousy and hate?

Before I got into the shower Frank Belson
called and told me that the casings found at
the scenes of the shootings of Richie, Peter,
and Buster did match the gun found in
Dominic Carbone's pocket.

"You think Carbone was the shooter?" I
said.

"No," Belson said.

"Why?"

"Because I don't," he said. "Because I

think this is some kind of head fake." And promptly hung up.

After my shower I fed Rosie and thought about fixing myself a martini, and decided that the cocktail hour was always better when it included Spike.

I called him and told him I was on my way over.

"And to what do I owe the impending pleasure of your company?" Spike said.

"I am hopeful that you can help me bring order to the world of objective facts," I said.

"Boy," he said, "I wish I had a dollar for every time somebody has asked me to do *that.*"

I asked if I could bring Rosie.

"Absolutely," he said.

"You know she bothers the customers sometimes," I said, "especially when they bother her."

"We can only hope," Spike said. "Objectively or otherwise."

Spike was waiting for me at a table he'd held for us near the bar. He was wearing a gray blazer over a gray shirt of almost exactly the same color. Tonight he had a diamond stud in his ear, an accessory that came and went.

"Any particular reason for when you wear

the earring and when you don't?" I said.

"I'm feeling kind of awesome," he said.

"Any particular reason for that?"

"Look around," he said. "Business is fucking awesome."

We sat down at the table, Rosie on the chair Spike had provided for her between us. As much as she would sometimes bark at strangers and other dogs when we were out on a walk, a crowded, noisy room did not seem to bother her as much. She was a complicated girl. Like her mommy.

"I got tired of being inside my own head," I said to Spike, and he said it had to happen eventually, and told our waitress that he wanted two filthy martinis, extra olives, and to tell the bartender not to get crazy with the vermouth.

I said, "Why do we even bother with vermouth? Have you ever asked yourself that?"

"It would diminish us," Spike said, "to order vodka with olives."

Our drinks came promptly, along with a calamari appetizer Spike knew was my favorite, and some chopped-up chicken for Rosie. Spike fed Rosie some chicken. He and I clinked glasses and drank.

"So where are we?" Spike said.

"Settle in," I said.

"Happily," Spike said. "The night is young and there's no telling how many vodka-with-olives we might drink before we're through."

It was not a linear presentation. Spike was used to that. He knew about the body at the skating rink, didn't know that the gun found on Dominic Carbone had turned out to be the one used on Richie, Peter, Buster. I told him that I knew hardly anything yet about Carbone, other than the fact that he had worked for Albert Antonioni. I told him about how Albert had made sure Maria Cataldo had a proper burial, and where Maria had been born and where she'd died. I told him that Desmond Burke thought it had been Albert who'd capped Maria's old man. But may have lied about that. Because he could.

"Albert sure do get around, do he not?" Spike said.

"Be interesting," I said, "to know more about what he was doing when Desmond was sowing his wild oats, so to speak, before Maria got sent away by her father."

"Could Albert have had a thing with Maria before Desmond came along?" Spike said.

"Worth knowing."

"Think Desmond would know?" Spike

said. "And if he did know, would he tell?"

"Knowing Desmond," I said, "I might have to extract the information surgically."

"Would explain a lot, though," Spike said.

"Wouldn't it," I said.

"Got another question," Spike said. "You think that Richie would know if Desmond and Felix decided this Carbone guy was the shooter and had him taken out?"

"No," I said.

"Even though him getting shot was the thing that started this?"

"Even though."

We reached down for our glasses at the same moment. Synchronized martini drinking. Maybe it should be an Olympic event. Why not? I thought. I knew badminton was.

"Belson thinks Carbone is too good to be true," I said.

"You think it's him?"

I shook my head. "Desmond and Felix find out it's him and manage to lure him to a skating rink in Southie? Makes no sense."

"What in this thing does?" Spike said.

Rosie growled suddenly, first time all night, at an older woman suddenly standing over our table, closer to Spike than to me. Pointing at Rosie.

"I wasn't aware pets are allowed here," the woman said.

"Actually," Spike said, "they're not."

He gave her his most brilliant smile now, one that he usually reserved only for dudes. And one I was convinced could turn straight ones gay.

"But he's sitting right there between the two of you," the woman said.

"He's a she," I said. "Her name is Rosie."

"Whatever," the woman said, exasperated.

"Rosie doesn't see herself as a dog," Spike said. "Per se."

"Are you trying to be amusing?" the woman said.

Spike looked at me, then shook his head sadly. "If they have to ask," he said.

I knew it was bitchy, but I reached over and fed Rosie some chicken.

"Well, if the dog stays, I'm leaving," the woman said.

Spike smiled at her. I smiled at her. Rosie growled. The woman turned and left. I had never actually seen someone turn on their heel. But I was pretty sure she just had.

Spike said, "So what's your next move? Finding out more about this Carbone guy?"

"I think it might be easier just to speak to Albert again."

"Fuck," Spike said. "I was afraid of that."

"If it's any consolation to you," I said, "I feel the exact same way."

THIRTY-SIX

There was no way of knowing, and might never be a way of proving, if the Burkes had ordered a hit on Dominic Carbone. Or if they had even determined that he was the man who had been stalking them. No way to know, at least not yet, if Carbone had some kind of relationship with the Cataldo family, or what was left of it, and had any real skin in this game.

And if it had been someone other than Desmond or Felix Burke who had ordered a hit on Carbone, who had? And why?

I also had absolutely no idea what was going to happen when Desmond found out that Maria had died in Providence, and that Albert Antonioni had been the one to make sure she got a proper burial.

Other than all that, the gods were smiling on me.

What I mostly knew, at least in the world of objective facts, was that Albert Antonioni's name kept popping up more regularly than old girlfriends did with the president, even though he'd led me to believe he had hardly anything to do with Desmond Burke anymore, whether the subject was guns or anything else.

"He's probably had more guys killed than Vladimir Putin," Spike said before I left the restaurant. "But he might have enough of a heart to have done right by Maria Cataldo."

"I still need to know why he was the one to whom it was left to have her buried," I said. "And why she died at Rhode Island Hospital."

"Why would he tell you that?"

"Sucker for a pretty face?"

"Okay," Spike said. "You've obviously been overserved."

"I'd like to find a way to head off a war between him and the Burkes, if that is what's looming," I said. "But it's not as if I can ask Felix to set up a meeting."

"Richie doesn't even want you to cross the state line," Spike said.

"I might have already asked Mike Stanton to call the guy we used last time," I said. "But he said the guy's number was no longer in service."

"So how do we get back to see him?"

"We'll think of something," I said.

"Is that the literary *we*?" Spike said. "Or does that mean me?"

I smiled at him.

"Had a feeling that's where this was headed," he said.

It was time to go. Spike said that just because somebody had shot a guy from Rhode Island didn't mean that I should suddenly stop looking over my shoulder. He insisted on standing with Rosie and me on the street in front of the restaurant until we were not only in the Uber I'd ordered, but also verifying that it was in fact that Uber I'd ordered before I gave the driver my name.

When Rosie and I got to Melanie Joan's, I saw nothing suspicious on the street, waited until Rosie performed her last ablution of the night, went inside, locked the front door, set the alarm, decided to take a hot bath before I went to bed.

When I got out of the bath, I checked my naked self out in front of the full-length mirror in the bathroom. Front first. Then, looking over my shoulder, back.

"Older my ass," I said out loud, winking at myself. "And I do mean ass."

It had been over an hour since I'd finished nursing the second martini I'd had at Spike's. I went to the kitchen and fixed

233

myself a Jameson, neat, and got into bed with a ballpoint pen and a yellow legal pad and wrote down everything that had happened, both everything I thought and everything I knew. Trying to make things linear this time.

Lists always help me. I never wrote them up on a laptop. I wrote them out in longhand, in my Catholic school handwriting. I thought better with a pen in my hand, the way I did with a brush in my hand.

I wished it were easy to make things take shape now.

I wrote and occasionally sipped whiskey.

It was late. I knew I should be tired, and just slightly overserved. I was neither. Maybe I could hold my liquor better as I got older. I thought of an old line from Winston Churchill, the one about how he liked to drink alcohol before and during and after meals, and often in the intervals.

It had never bothered me to drink alone. I never drank in excess when drinking alone, which meant alone with Rosie. This Rosie and the one before her. It was past midnight now. Another old line came to me, though I couldn't remember who'd written it or said it, about this being the hour when people told each other the truth. If I were with Desmond Burke right now, would he tell me the truth? Would Albert Antonioni?

Would they tell me truths about themselves, or each other?

If Richie were here with me right now, in Melanie Joan's big bed, and asked for the truth about us, what would I tell him?

Maybe I had been overserved after all.

Would I tell Richie that I preferred being alone? Maybe that was the real truth, from me, to me, at this time of night. I had been unable to work for others and with others when I was still a cop. Now I worked alone. I had been unable to succeed as a wife. So now I lived alone.

The most stable relationships of my adult life, other than the one with my father, had been with two miniature English bull terriers, both female, and a gay man.

My relationship with Richie, I knew in my heart, was both stable and unstable at the same time.

I checked what I had written one more time, still found more questions than answers, finished my drink, turned out the lights.

At least I *did* have Spike and Rosie.

Yeah, girl, I thought, before sleep came far more quickly than it usually did.

Who's got it better than you?

THIRTY-SEVEN

I left the Albert Antonioni negotiations to Spike and tried to find out everything there was to know about Dominic Carbone.

He had been born in Cranston, as it turned out, dropped out of high school there, been raised, according to a couple classmates I was able to track down, by a single mother who worked as a cocktail waitress at various local establishments that were never confused with the bar at the Four Seasons.

The father, according to Pete Colapietro, had been a midlevel thug in Antonioni's operation until he was found dead one night, shot in the head, in the front seat of a car parked at the Red Sox's minor-league ballpark in Pawtucket. Despite having been estranged from his father for most of his hardscrabble life, by then Dominic Junior had already gone into the family business.

I called Richie about Carbone. Richie said

his father had assured him he had nothing to do with the guy ending up the way Dominic Senior had. I asked if Desmond had bought into the notion that Carbone had been the one shooting at the Burke family.

"He's like you, and Belson," Richie said. "Suspicious of how insanely neat it all seems."

"But might there now be an escalation of the bad blood between him and Albert?" I said.

"My father says no," Richie said.

"Do you believe him?"

"I do not," he said. "But if there is the kind of escalation you're talking about, I'd sort of like you to stay out of the crossfire."

"You know I can't," I said, "even if your father is having a difficult time accepting that fact."

"He doesn't think you can't," Richie said. "He thinks you won't."

"All part of getting to know me," I said. "Just not as well as you do."

"And what a lucky boy I am for that," Richie said.

"Neither your father nor Albert Antonioni is the type to let bygones be bygones," I said. "I just find it counterintuitive to believe that this is over just because a stiff in Boston had the right gun in his possession when he died. I frankly think someone planted it on him."

"Counterintuitive," Richie said. "You continue to sound remarkably unlike a private cop."

"And you," I said, "sound remarkably unlike a child of the Boston Mob."

The second morning after they had discovered the body of Dominic Carbone, Spike called before my run and told me that, almost like a Christmas miracle, Albert Antonioni had agreed to once again meet with us.

"I think you and Albert are kind of in the same place," Spike said. "You want him to show you his, and he wants you to show him yours. So to speak."

"Where is this happening?"

"Joe Marzilli's Old Canteen," Spike said.

"It's practically become our place," I said.

Spike was dressed in what he called gangster chic for the occasion: black pinstriped suit with wide chalk stripes and wider lapels than I'd ever seen on him, white shirt, silver tie, ankle boots with zippers on the sides.

"You do look like a gangster," I said. "Unfortunately, it's Sky Masterson in *Guys and Dolls*."

"I see what you did there," he said, as I

slid into the front seat next to him. "Played the Broadway-musical card on the gay guy."

"Stereotypes are ugly," I said. "Just not as ugly as that suit."

"You no longer seem concerned about being followed," Spike said.

"I look at it this way," I said. "Desmond gonna be Desmond."

"Did you just say that?"

I giggled.

We hit little traffic on I-95 and ended up with a parking spot about a block away from the Old Canteen. I left my gun in the glove compartment. So did Spike. Our operating theory was that we would once again be patted down. A larger theory was that if Albert wanted to shoot both of us today, he could, but likely would not.

It was the same table as before, with what looked to be the same lineup of sidemen posted around the room.

There were no coffee cups on the table, no offer of anything to drink, nothing social about the gathering, which had all the charm of a parole board hearing.

"I don't have a lot of time," Albert Antonioni said when Spike and I were seated.

He sounded like Desmond.

"Maria Cataldo," I said.

"What about her?"

"Why did you pay to have her buried?" I said.

"Who says I did?"

"Albert," I said. "You said you didn't have a lot of time. Let's not either one of us waste it."

He leaned back in his chair, clasped his hands across a truly ugly polka-dot shirt.

"Why're we talking about her?" he said.

"Because she was Desmond Burke's great lost love," I said. "Because she was sent away in her youth, or left on her own, thus ending her illicit affair with Desmond. And at the other end of her life, when she dies, you are the one who pays for her final resting place."

"I promised her father I'd be there for her if she needed me, whenever she needed me," he said. "I kept the promise even after she died."

"Desmond says you were the one who had her father killed as a way of assuming full control of the business," I said.

"Desmond Burke is a liar," he said. "I wasn't the one who capped Vincent. *He* was. And you can fucking well tell him that I said that."

Antonioni started coughing then, making him sound like a lung patient. Or sounding the way Billy Leonard had that day at

240

Sherrill House. The young handsome guy I remembered from our last meeting was at the table in a flash with a glass of water. Antonioni drank enough to stop the coughing.

"We done here?" he said.

"Not quite," I said.

"What else?"

"Who's Dominic Carbone?" I said.

"Guy used to do some things for me," Antonioni said, "before he went off on his own." Antonioni shrugged. "I heard what happened to him," he said. "Life's hard. Then somebody shoots you."

"Did you send Carbone after the Burkes?" I said.

"Fuck, no," he said.

I said, "The gun they found on Dominic happened to be the same one used to shoot my ex-husband and kill Peter Burke and Desmond's bodyguard."

"I got nothing to do with any of that shit."

"You do have to admit that it's a bit of a coincidence, somebody who you say used to work with you ending up with that particular gun in his pocket," I said.

"Your problem," he said. "Not mine."

I smiled a killer smile at him. He managed to keep himself under control.

"How well did you know Maria Cataldo when she was a young woman?" I said.

He said, "We were friends, nothing more, nothing less. I had too much respect for her father. And too much fear of the old man."

"You're sure?"

"Listen to me," he said. "You know who wanted Maria in those days? Everybody did. Irish, Italians, everyfuckingbody. But the rest of us were smart enough to do our wanting of Vincent's little girl from a distance. Just not Desmond."

He leaned forward now in his chair.

"Can I give you a piece of advice?"

"Am I obligated to take it?"

"Walk away from this," he said. "I'm telling you for the last time. Go tell Desmond I got no problems with him anymore except if he makes problems for me. Then we all live out however many days we got left. But you stay with this, you're going to get into things you don't want to get into. And something could happen you don't want to happen."

I had more questions but knew they weren't going to get me where I wanted to go with Albert Antonioni, not now and probably not ever.

I stood up. So did Spike. Albert Antonioni watched both of us with the malevolent indifference of a snake.

"Stay out of my business," he said.

242

"What business?" I said.

"All of it," he said. He waved a dismissive hand at us. "Now go," he said.

Spike and I walked out of the Old Canteen and into the sunlight of Federal Hill. Neither one of us spoke until Spike's car was in sight. We both resisted the temptation, once outside, to look over our shoulders.

"He's hiding something," I said. "Or lying his ass off. Or both."

"I'm thinking he might have had a bigger thing for Maria than he's letting on," Spike said.

"He said everybody wanted her," I said.

Spike pressed his key, unlocked the car doors. We both got in.

"He did kind of blow your theory about him being a sucker for a pretty face all to hell," Spike said.

I said, "Albert didn't last this long without having an iron will."

Then Spike put the car into gear. We then got the hell out of Rhode Island.

THIRTY-EIGHT

Charlie Whitaker called the next morning.

"Did you read in the *Globe* about what happened at Logan two nights ago?"

I told him I was behind on my reading, even with my hometown paper.

"A big shipment of guns got stolen," he said, "from Smith & Wesson, on their way to Australia. Or maybe it was New Zealand, those countries all look alike to me."

I told him I would look up the story online when we got off the phone.

"So there's that," Charlie said, "which is in the news. But here is something that is not: Two days before that, a lot of guns went missing at Fort Devens."

"I thought that was some kind of base for the reserves these days," I said.

"It is," Charlie said. "Army Reserve and National Guard and Marines. Nearly eight hundred military vehicles. And a lot of guns never get fired."

"Sounds like they're going to get fired now," I said.

"Uh-huh," Charlie said.

"Stolen guns at Logan and missing guns at Fort Devens," I said.

"Sounds to me," Charlie said, "as if somebody might be trying to build up to a big finish on that granddaddy of all gun deals we talked about."

"You think it's the same people," I said.

"Doesn't matter what I think," he said. "ATF does."

"Be a pretty ballsy move to make," I said.

"I told you that volume is the key if somebody wanted to make real money selling guns illegally," he said.

"You think Desmond Burke or Albert Antonioni has the manpower to make a ballsy move like this?" I said.

"Whoever did it might have had to outsource some of the labor," Charlie said. "But, yeah, it's doable."

"And would involve enough money to have a fight over."

"You need to remember something about guys like Desmond and Albert," Charlie said. "They'd fight over dirt."

"If Desmond wants it, Albert wants it," I said. "And vice versa."

"Heavy on the vice," Charlie said.

"It might not even be as much about the money," I said, "as about one of them wanting to beat the other."

"It doesn't have to be one of them," Charlie said.

"I know."

"But you want it to be."

"I want this to be over," I said. "That's what I want."

"Welcome to my world," he said. "Or at least my former one."

"How's Mrs. Whitaker, by the way?" I said.

"Visiting her sister in Florida."

"If you hear anything else, let me know," I said. "I can use all the help I can get."

"Just remember something," Charlie Whitaker said. "If figuring shit like this out were easy, everybody'd do it."

I told him I would hold the thought.

Thirty-Nine

I met my father for lunch at the Legal Sea Foods at Park Plaza. Every time we went there he would give me a brief tutorial about the history of Legal, from the first one opening in Inman Square in Cambridge in the 1950s, and give me the most up-to-date count on how many there were in the chain now, including one at Logan Airport.

But this one was our favorite. They still served the best seafood in town, the service was terrific. It also wasn't too loud, even when crowded at lunchtime the way it was now. We both had chowder as an appetizer and fried clams as a main course. By the time the clams were in front of us, I had gone over as much of the conversation with Albert Antonioni the day before as I could remember.

"On a bet," he said, "you do not want to be in the middle of this any longer."

"I'm still not sure what *this* is," I said.

"Irrelevant," he said.

"I got into it because of Richie, and if I am in the middle of it, it's still because of Richie."

"Or because, and I say this with love, you are more stubborn than a tick."

"A tick," I said. "Really, Daddy?"

He shrugged.

"Come on," I said. "You think Antonioni is going to kill me for being nosy?"

He gave me a long look but said nothing. But we both knew it was his way of answering my question in the affirmative.

"So you're saying he *would* kill me for being nosy?" I said.

"I didn't say that," he said. "But clearly there is bad blood between those two old men that might be deeper than the kind you get in the Middle East."

He picked up a fried clam and dipped it in tartar sauce and ate it.

"But maybe if I can figure this all out," I said, "I can take everybody out of danger once and for all. Including me."

"My stubborn, darling daughter," he said. He grinned. "You think it's too late for med school?"

I had stuck my yellow legal pad in my purse. I used it as a study aid and told him everything that I knew and everything I thought and everything that had happened. I told him about my conversation with Charlie Whitaker.

"This continues to be a hairball, without question," he said.

"I can't let somebody like Antonioni scare me off the case," I said.

"It's never *been* your case," my father said.

"But if I do let him scare me off, what does that make me?"

"Alive," he said.

"If Desmond thinks Albert is after him," I said, "why hasn't he gone after Albert?"

"Just because he hasn't doesn't mean he won't."

He had finished with his clams. I'd eaten only half of mine, if that. He looked at the pile of them still on my plate, then looked at me, raised his eyebrows.

"Have at it," I said.

It had always been a wonder to me that for my entire life I had watched Phil Randall eat like a horse and never put on a pound. And, by his own account, he had cholesterol levels so low his doctors wanted to carry him around the room on their shoulders.

"I know this is important to you because Richie is," my father said. "It is why I have helped you as much as I can. But it becomes more clear by the moment that the only

249

person who still wants you in this is you."

I started to say something. He reached across the table and patted my hand to stop me.

"Desmond would never harm you," he said. "Likewise, I do not believe he would let anyone else harm you if he could stop it. But that does not mean he can stop this thing if it becomes a runaway train. And Albert Antonioni, from the sound of things, has issued his last warning to you."

"You're telling me I'm beating a dead horse here," I said. "Right?"

My father smiled his answer, and he was the one who looked younger than springtime. And made me feel safe, even as I knew I was not.

FORTY

"When you first came to see me," Dr. Susan Silverman said, "you said that you felt as if you lacked self-worth and purpose because Richie was about to marry someone else."

"As I recall," I said, "I did a lot of blubbering that day about the one whose name must not be mentioned."

She smiled a smile that made Mona Lisa look as if she were in the midst of a laugh riot.

"Kathryn," she said.

"Her," I said.

It occurred to me I sounded like Frank Belson talking about his new boss Captain Glass.

"And if there has been one consistent thread since that time," she said, "it has been your desire to understand both the depth and complexity of your feelings for Richie."

She was right, of course. I had been trying to deal with that in this room, as well as the daddy issues that she had made me confront for the first time in my life. And was doing better with it all. I knew there were qualities, especially ones involving strength and confidence, that both Richie and Phil Randall shared. I knew that as quick and funny as Richie could be, my father was quicker, and funnier. I knew I relied on both for their strength and confidence, even as I felt that challenged my own confidence and made me feel weak, almost as if I were existing on a fault line.

Susan Silverman had once asked me what she said would sound like a simple question, and was not.

"Is Richie your type?" she said.

I told her I had never thought about it, what my type was. The best I could do that particular day, and in many of the days since, was admit that someone I considered the love of my life might only partially be my type. And that I hated his strength as much as I loved it.

At least I did far less blubbering these days.

So there was that.

She wore a white sweater today and a black leather skirt and her skin looked as flawless as ever, and so did her thick, gleaming black hair. Her necklace was a freshwater pearl with small gold bands crisscrossed in front of it. Her fingernails were crimson. Susan Silverman, as usual, made me think of an old David Letterman line: She looked like a million damn dollars.

I wore a gray Michael Kors sweater dress I had bought on sale, with shoes to match. I always dressed up for her, every single time, as if we weren't just therapist and patient but having an ongoing fashion-off, even though I knew the competition existed only in my mind.

"We've come a long way since then," she said.

"Have we?" I said.

She didn't respond. She rarely did when I was the one asking a question. I had called her the day before upon returning from Providence and asked when her soonest opening was. It turned out to be late in the afternoon today. I had spent the hours between lunch with my father and my appointment trying in vain to find out anything about where Maria Cataldo had lived her life after leaving Boston, and had run into one dead end after another. The best I could do was her last residence, in Providence, not far from Federal Hill, the address listed on her death certificate. I had not yet been able to find out who owned the house because the tax assessor's office in Providence had closed early today. But I planned to take a ride down there myself tomorrow and talk to her neighbors. You just keep poking around and hope that eventually something will fly up at you.

For now here the two of us were, in the office on Linnaean Street, with the last of the afternoon sun coming through the blinds behind her. There was the soft scent of perfume in the room, hers or mine, or both.

"On some basic, practical level, I know my father is right and Richie is right, and even the old gangsters are right, and I should let this go," I said.

"But you remain resistant to the notion of quitting," she said.

"It all started with Richie," I said.

"It often does," she said.

"Man of my dreams," I said.

"Is it still about him, or has it become more about you?" she said.

She was completely still and self-contained, not taking notes in this moment. But as always, I still had the sense that she was in motion somehow and that I was trying to keep up with her. There were many times when I left this office feeling better than I had when I'd entered, but I often left feeling exhausted as well.

"There is a part of me pushing back against powerful men telling me to do something I myself have not chosen to do," I said.

"The old men are powerful," Susan said. "Your father has always held a position of power in your life. As has Richie."

"This isn't a me-too moment," I said. "But they have no right to impose their will on mine."

"Nor should they."

"You want to know the truth?" I said.

There might have been another slight upturn to the corners of her mouth.

She said, "My experience is that the truth serves everyone best in here."

"I get angry when they treat me like a little girl," I said.

"Angry or less empowered."

A statement of fact more than a question, as if she were answering for both of us.

"Both," I said.

"But are you more empowered to solve the mystery," she said, "or to prove a point that you will not be cowed or told to stand down, even by men who care about you?"

"Both," I said again.

Her dark eyes were alive, alight, and

completely focused on me.

"May I say something that might sound less than politically correct?"

"Of course."

"I can't let some old *goombah* threaten me," I said.

She nodded.

"And I always *have* hated being told what to do," I said.

"Only by the men in your life?"

"Not just them. But yes."

"What about Richie?"

"We've discussed this," I said. "This is my chance to protect him."

"And in the past, you have always felt, especially when going to him for help, that he was protecting you."

"Yes."

"But you will allow your friend Spike to assist you, and even protect you if need be."

"Spike asks nothing in return."

"But Richie does?"

"He wants *me* in return."

"Something you are unwilling to give."

"At least not in total."

"To go back to the beginning," Susan Silverman said, "you were shattered when you thought you had lost him to another woman."

"I felt my own sense of loss defining me,"

I said. "Even consuming me."

"And making you feel powerless."

"Yes," I said.

"Loss is a defining and consuming thing," she said.

"Oh, baby," I said.

Susan Silverman smiled fully now, eyes and face and teeth. A rare thing from her. It was as if one more light had suddenly been turned on in the room, or the sunlight outside her window.

"Oh, ha!" she said.

" 'Oh, *ha*'?" I said.

"It's a combination of 'oh, ho' and 'aha,' " she said, still smiling.

"Is that an expression you learned at Harvard?" I said.

"Actually," Susan Silverman said, "I got it from the man of *my* dreams."

FORTY-ONE

I had the feeling that my car was being followed on the way back from Susan Silverman's office.

There was a black car making the turns that I made off Linnaean to Humboldt to Mass Ave. I wasn't good on car makes but thought it might be a Taurus.

The car stayed with me to 2A to Eliot Street to John F. Kennedy. It was gone when I got to North Harvard, and then to Cambridge, but it meant little if whoever was following me, if somebody was following me, knew where I lived.

So instead of taking Soldiers Field Road and then Storrow Drive to my usual exit, I headed down Commonwealth Ave toward Chestnut Hill, before circling around to the entrance to the Mass Pike in West Newton. By then there was no black car behind me. I had called Spike and put him on speaker before I got on the Pike, and he told me to drive straight to his place if I thought the tail was still with me. I told him I would. He told me that even if I didn't spot anybody, he was going to meet me at Melanie Joan's, and bring food with him, and wasn't going to take no for an answer.

"Who says no to you?" I said.

"Gary," he said.

"May I ask who Gary is?"

"No you may not," he said.

By the time I had gotten off the Pike at the exit for Copley Square and the Prudential, I had lost the tail, if it had even been a tail in the first place.

I took Rosie out when I got back, fed her, changed into jeans and a sweater, and opened a bottle of wine and thought about Maria Cataldo, and how little I still knew of her life. I did not know if she had ever married, I did not know if she had had children, I did not know where she had gone after her father had sent her away, or if she had simply left on her own. Tomorrow I would call Wayne Cosgrove, who liked to brag that he was better at finding out things than I was, and never had to point a gun at anybody to get information.

But Maria Cataldo was dead, that was now part of the world of objective facts. So was Dominic Carbone. And Peter Burke.

And poor Buster. Somebody had shot at Richie, and shot up Felix's house, and beat me up. Somebody was coming for Desmond, that much remained clear. It could have been Dominic Carbone who did all the shooting, but it if had been, what grudge had he been settling?

And if it wasn't the late Dominic Carbone, then we were right back where we started, with a gun still pointed at the Burkes.

And what did any of this, or all of this, have to do with guns suddenly going missing?

I looked at Rosie at the other end of the couch and said, "Rosebud, maybe it's *not* too late for med school."

She picked up her head, quickly ascertained that there was no food anywhere in the area, put her head back down, and was soon snoring. Some sidekick.

The wine was in the ice bucket next to the dining room table, which I had set. I had already lighted the candles. Romantic dinner for two, just without the romance.

Spike arrived a few minutes later with a big bag full of food: Caesar salads with extra anchovies, veal Milanese, which he assured me traveled extremely well, a side order of french fries. I told him I didn't recall french fries being served with veal Milanese at Spike's and he said, "Have you ever turned down my french fries?"

I said I had not, nor would I ever.

"Didn't think so," he said.

When we were finished eating and on the couch drinking coffee laced with Jameson, Rosie between us, I said to Spike, "This thing really is a hairball."

Spike nodded. "Usually we're able to think a couple moves ahead," he said.

"*We're* able to think a couple moves ahead?" I said.

"Yup," he said. "Me and you, kid. A team. Like Nick and Nora."

It was just one more thing to love about Spike. He loved old *Thin Man* movies as much as I did. A lot of snappy patter and a couple pitchers of martinis before they finally figured out who was responsible for that stiff in the drawing room.

"Let's say that killing Carbone was just a head fake, which is what Frank Belson called it," I said. "Why, though? Whoever's behind this wanted Desmond to know he was closing in on him. He wanted to tighten the noose. Why would he plant the gun on Carbone and do everything except hire a skywriter to make the cops and the rest of us think the thing is over?"

I sipped coffee that tasted more like whiskey than coffee and was lip-smacking good.

"Maybe," Spike said, "it is you he is trying to throw off."

"Why me?"

"Because this person, whomever he is, has clearly done his homework," Spike said. "And if he *has* done his homework, he knows that you may be a bigger threat to him than Desmond or Felix or even the cops, whom he may have surmised aren't kept up at night worrying about bad guys shooting each other up. You should be flattered, if you think about it. All those bad guys and he's worried about a girl."

"I'm convinced a girl started this," I said.

"Say it's Albert," Spike said. "If he waited this long to get even with Desmond over Maria Cataldo, he's got nothing but time now."

"Maybe not," I said. "You hear that cough the other day? It sounded like your basic death rattle. And roll."

"You know what I'm saying," Spike said. "The game of cat and mouse continues."

"Eek," I said.

"Wouldn't Desmond have known if Albert had been one of Maria's potential paramours?" Spike said. "And if he'd done more than lust after her from a distance?"

"Paramours?" I said. "I think that expression was old when Nick and Nora were young."

He toasted me with his coffee cup.

"Look at it this way," Spike said. "If the shooter did pop Carbone as a way to throw everybody off, maybe you've got him on the run and you don't even know it."

"Or maybe we're giving this guy too much credit, and he's out of control in a controlled sort of way, and capable of anything."

"Including making another run at you," Spike said. "Which is why you thought you might have been followed out of Cambridge."

"Yeah," I said.

"I could stay the night," Spike said.

"Nah," I said. "Would make me feel like a girl."

"Can't have that."

"Marry me," I said.

"Right," he said. "Who needs sex?"

I laughed and said, "We do!"

"You decide when you're going to tell Desmond all you know about Maria?"

"No," I said. "I'm holding back for now. But so is he. I just don't know what, or how much."

Spike said he was going to walk home.

He'd recently purchased a new condominium in an area on the other side of the Common that used to be called the Combat Zone but had now been gentrified in a pluperfect way over time.

I put on a short leather jacket, grabbed Rosie's leash off the table along with my .38, and told him I'd walk him as far as Charles Street. Spike leaned over and kissed me on the top of my head.

"This was fun," he said.

"Best. Wingman. Ever," I said.

"You'll figure this out," he said.

"You sure?"

"Always have," Spike said.

"Blah, blah, blah," I said.

"Well," Spike said, "there's the old fighting spirit."

I opened the front door, letting Rosie lead the way. I had the handle of her leash and my keys in my right hand. But as I took my first step outside, I dropped the keys, which fell to the concrete with a clatter that only sounded so loud because the street was so quiet.

"Shit," I said.

Everything happened at once then, me turning just slightly to look down at where the keys had fallen and Spike saying "I'll get 'em" in the split-second before we heard the unmistakable crack of a gun firing from somewhere at close range in front of us and the bullet hitting the front door between us.

FORTY-TWO

Spike rolled over in front of both of us, his gun somehow already cleared.

I held Rosie to me, as low to the ground as I could keep both of us, and could see a man running up River Street in the direction of the Meeting House.

"Stay down," Spike said. "I'm going after him."

"No," I said.

"Yes," he said.

I had my gun out of the side pocket of the leather jacket by now, and could see lights going on all around us.

"Go back inside," Spike said, "and call nine-one-one if somebody hasn't already."

He looked like a sprinter coming out of a crouch now. All the times and all the miles we had run the Half Shell, I knew how fast he was, as big as he was, how quickly he could get himself up to full speed when he wanted to show off.

But as he got near the corner of Charles and River, I saw the retreating figure suddenly stop and turn and get into a crouch himself and fire again.

Spike went down.

I heard a scream from up above me as I ran for him, and then another scream, and Rosie barking as she ran behind me, and a screech of tires somewhere up ahead. Then the street was quiet again until I could hear the first sirens in the distance.

FORTY-THREE

They took Spike by ambulance to the Tufts Medical Center on Washington Street, not terribly far from where he now lived. It turned out to be a flesh wound. The ER doctor said he was lucky. Spike said, "Relative to what?"

"Relative to about a foot closer to the center of your mass," the doctor said.

They had finished working on him. Frank Belson had arrived and was with us, having badged the nurse working the desk and saying, "Friend of the family." The doctor had already informed Spike that there was no reason for him to stay the night, even though they'd already established they had a room for him if needed.

The doctor said he was going to get Spike a sling.

"What color?" Spike said.

"Excuse me?"

The doctor was tall, young-looking, spoke

with a slight Spanish accent. His name tag said "Ramirez."

"I just want something that clashes with the fewest of my outfits," Spike said.

The doctor frowned, said, "I think we go with basic blue here," and left.

"Cute," Spike said. "The doctor. Not the color."

"Really?" Belson said.

"I actually thought he was kind of cute myself, Frank," I said.

"Talk to me," he said.

I told him everything that had happened from the time I opened the front door.

"Shooter was waiting out there," Belson said. "Hard to hang around on your street without somebody noticing."

"You have a pretty good view of my front door for a pretty good distance up River," I said.

"Maybe he was moving around, from corner to corner, and then was in the right place to take his shot when we came out," I said.

"Lucky," Belson said.

"Well, for him," Spike said.

Belson said, "We'll send people over in the morning to canvass the neighborhood."

"If he was out there a long time," I said, "he knew Spike was inside with me. If not, he was there to shoot just me. If there had been people on the street, he could have just walked toward the Public Garden, or past our little dog park toward the river."

"If you hadn't dropped your keys . . ." Belson said.

"Yeah," I said.

"He's back-shot everybody else so far," he said. "This is different."

"Almost more arrogant," I said.

"And he's willing to take a shot at him," Belson said, nodding at Spike, "before he runs off."

"He tried to scare me off once," I said.

"Other than the Burkes and me and the Scarlet Pimpernel here," Belson said, "who knows that you're still on this?"

"Albert Antonioni," I said.

"Now somebody comes right to your front door," Belson said.

"And somehow nobody has yet taken a shot at Desmond Burke," I said, "around whom this whole thing is supposed to revolve."

"Curiouser and fucking curiouser," Frank Belson said.

FORTY-FOUR

Belson sent Spike home in a squad car. He drove me home himself. On the way he asked me for all the information I had previously withheld from him.

"You know pretty much everything I know," I said.

"Bullshit," he said.

"Not sure I can even remember every single thing I've told you so far," I said.

"I can," Belson said.

I honestly couldn't remember everything I'd told him. So I told him now about all the guns going missing all of a sudden. I told him about Desmond and Albert and about Maria Cataldo, and about her dying in Providence and living in Providence for some period of time before that. I told him about my theory that Albert might have been jealous of Desmond and Maria and waited a very long time to get even with him.

"You're telling me this all might have started because this Maria wouldn't go to the prom with Antonioni back in the day?" Belson said. "And went with Desmond instead?"

"It has to be more than that, if Albert is the one behind all this," I said.

"Which we are only surmising that he is."

"Correct."

"When did she go away?" Belson said.

We were sitting in the car in front of the house by then.

"Desmond believes it was April of 1980," I said. "When she was in her early twenties."

"Where'd she go?"

"Unclear," I said. "All I know is that at the other end of her life she ends up in Providence."

"Near Albert," Belson said. "Who buried her. Where was she living when she died?"

"It was on the death certificate," I said. "I don't remember the exact address."

"She own that house?" Belson said.

"Don't know that yet," I said.

"Worth knowing," he said.

"In the morning," I said.

"You think Desmond was aware his long-lost love was living an hour away in Goombah Central?" he said.

"I'd ask him, but Richie said he's out of town for a couple days."

"Where?"

I shrugged. "Maybe stealing more guns."

Belson said, "I'm putting a car out here tonight."

I grinned. "For me?"

"For your old man," he said. "It would fuck up our friendship if you got clipped on my watch."

"You old softie."

"You know who we really need to talk to?" Belson said. "Maria Cataldo."

He waited while I went into the house and got Rosie and walked her halfway up the block and back. His car didn't pull away until an unmarked pulled up in front of the house.

I brushed, washed up, moisturized, put Rosie at the end of my bed and my .38 on the nightstand next to me. Shut off the lights and thought about Maria Cataldo, who'd left and gone away, hey, hey, hey.

In the morning, I called the tax assessor's office in Providence, Rhode Island, and the third person to whom I spoke, a pleasant woman named Mrs. Krummenacher, informed me that the house in which Maria Cataldo was living on Pleasant Valley Park-

way at the time of her death was owned by
Mr. Albert Antonioni.

FORTY-FIVE

I met my father for breakfast at the Taj Café, where he had taken me as a little girl for special occasions when it actually was still the old Ritz. It was another reason why I knew it would always be the old Ritz for me, the way it always would be with Phil Randall. He still called the football field at Boston University, my alma mater, Braves Field.

I had waited until this morning to call and tell him about Spike.

"You could have called last night," he said.

"And had my sainted mother shit a brick?" I said.

"The mouth on you," he said.

Now I was telling him over our late breakfast what I had learned about Albert Antonioni's house on Pleasant Valley Parkway and how, no pun intended, even more roads than ever seemed to keep running through him and Maria. By now he was working on eggs with hash. I had ordered oatmeal.

"I think I may have been going about this all wrong," I said. "I haven't found out as much as I could have, or should have, about this woman."

"If it is about her," he said, "then she has inspired some very deep emotions in some extremely hard men."

"If Albert gave her a house in which to live, he must still have had feelings about her," I said.

"Ones that certainly passed the test of time," my father said. "But this might not be anything more than an enduring friendship, not an enduring love."

"He still might be the one looking to settle a score with Desmond," I said. "You do understand we persist in making several leaps of faith here. Some of them giant ones."

"Faith and hope," he said.

"Or it could be another of Desmond's enemies," I said.

"Who are legion," he said.

"You mind if we get back to Maria for a second?" I said.

"Whatever you want," he said. "You're paying."

"Could she have married in the time after she left Boston?" I said. "Had children? Had a life completely apart from the one she was leading as Vincent Cataldo's femme-fatale daughter?"

"She must have left some kind of footprint between Boston and Providence," he said. "Isn't Big Brother always watching?"

"Him or Facebook," I said. "Or the Russians."

He poured some Tabasco sauce on his hash. He used hot sauce on food only when my mother wasn't around.

"Start with what footprint she may have left in Providence," he said, "and work your way back from there."

"You mean go knock on some doors," I said.

He smiled. "Good girl," he said.

"Long time since I've been that, Daddy," I said.

"Not to your daddy," my father said. "How's Spike, by the way?"

"Says his arm hurts like a bitch," I said. "Said the same thing that Richie said, that getting shot isn't for sissies."

Phil Randall smiled again.

"Was in his case," he said.

FORTY-SIX

I went alone to Providence this time. The only person who knew I was going was my father. He had asked if I wanted him to tag along. I told him that as much as I always welcomed the pleasure of his company, I was going it alone today.

"I know how much you hate baseball expressions," he said. "But you are some tough out."

"For a girl," I said.

"Hey," he said, "nobody's perfect."

It turned out that Albert Antonioni had done well by Maria Cataldo. I had no idea how long Maria had lived on Pleasant Valley Parkway. But according to the Providence recorder of deeds, the two-story brick home with white pillars forming an archway in front had belonged to Albert Antonioni since 1975.

I had no idea if there was still a Mrs. Albert Antonioni. Perhaps he had lived here with Maria. Maybe he moved around, from one property to another, as a way of making himself a moving target. What was the Italian expression for mistress? *Goomara? Goomah?* One of those. Or both. Maybe Maria, when she was back in Albert Antonioni's life, had become his *goomara.*

But there was nothing on this tree-lined street, with obviously expensive homes, that spoke of the Mob. It looked like a street where young professionals could live more cheaply here than they would up in Boston in suburbs like Chestnut Hill or Wellesley. I had read all the stories in the *Globe* about how more and more people were commuting all the way to Boston from neighborhoods in Providence exactly like this.

My father's friend from the Providence cops, Pete Colapietro, had told me over the phone that Pleasant Valley Parkway was just far enough away from Providence College to make it a desirable location.

"You get closer to the college," he said, "you've got these absentee owners and a bunch of triple-deckers where they have loud parties and puke out the windows."

"Kids today," I said.

"Future hedge-funders," he said, "and other white-collar criminals."

I stared up at 140 Pleasant Valley Parkway

279

and thought: *Lot of house for an old woman.*

I went up the front walk and rang the bell, not knowing if anyone still lived there, or had ever lived there with Maria Cataldo. There was no sound from inside, everything about the house as quiet and still as the neighborhood.

I tried the front door. Locked. The shades for the first-floor windows were drawn. I thought about how easy it would probably be to walk around the back and pick a lock and get inside, but then imagined alarms going off and the police coming for me before goons working for Albert Antonioni did.

I turned and looked at what was obviously a well-maintained front lawn. The white pillars on either side of me had been freshly painted. There was no "For Sale" sign, but that didn't mean that Albert didn't have the house on the market. Or was still living here himself.

One more thing I didn't know, added to a long list of things I didn't know, as I continued to wander through a deep, dark forest.

Knock on some doors, my father had said.

I went to the house to the right. No one home. Then to the house to the right of that. No one home. So no chance yet to use the cover story I had created for myself, about a long-lost relative of Maria Cataldo's hiring me to find out as much as I could about her final days.

The third house I tried was one directly across the street from 140. I heard a voice from inside call out "Just a second," and then a tall, attractive woman with silver-blond hair opened the front door. I introduced myself. She introduced herself as Connie Devane.

I quickly provided my cover story in an earnest, friendly way, apologizing for bothering her.

"Could I see some ID?" she said.

I reached into my bag and showed her my license, which had my picture underneath "Bureau of Investigative Services." If Connie Devane knew that you could get one of these from the same people who made up fake IDs for college kids, she did not let on.

"Please come in," she said.

We sat in her sun-splashed living room. She wore jeans and a white button-down shirt and sandals. I told her I would try not to take up too much of her time. She said she had just taken a break from her writing. "Oh," I said, "you're a writer?" She said she was trying to be.

I asked how long she had lived in the neighborhood. She said fifteen years, the last five after her husband was gone.

"Did he pass away?" I said.

She smiled. "Sadly, not yet," she said.

"Oh."

"Are you married, Sunny?"

"Divorced," I said.

"Good divorce or bad?"

"Good," I said.

I knew this was a conversation that could take me all the way down a rabbit hole, but there was no way to politely avoid it if Connie Devane was the ex-wife who wanted to tell me all about it.

"Lucky you," she said.

I smiled back at her. "Maria Cataldo," I said.

Connie Devane said, "I didn't even know that was her last name. The first time I met her she just introduced herself as Maria."

"How long did she live across the street?"

"I can't tell you exactly," she said. "I think it was right before Mr. Wonderful moved out on me. But I never even saw any moving vans. One day she was there, and the lights were on at night. I think the house had been empty for years before that." She put out her hands. "Maybe five years ago?"

"You said you met her."

"I was starting a run one day," she said. "She was working in a small garden on the side of the house. Just to be friendly, I walked up the lawn and introduced myself. Welcome to the neighborhood, blah, blah, blah. Around sixty, maybe? But you could see she must have been some kind of great beauty when she was younger. She was polite but made it clear she had no desire to make a new friend." Connie Devane closed her eyes, as if trying to see Maria Cataldo better. "One thing I remember is that the shovel in her hand was shaking badly, the way her head was," she said. "Remember what Katharine Hepburn was like when she was old?"

"Maria Cataldo died from Parkinson's complications," I said.

"I remember thinking it had to be that at the time," she said. "It was around the time that Muhammad Ali died. He had it, too, right?"

I nodded.

"The last couple years," she said, "I never saw her outside, in the garden or anywhere else."

"Did she ever have visitors?"

"Hey," Connie said, "it's not as if I was on a stakeout."

"Wasn't suggesting that you were," I said. "Just looking for anything that might help."

"My writing room is upstairs," she said,

"facing the street. So, yeah, I did see some people from time to time."

"Can you describe them?"

"An old man would show up every few days," she said, "right up until the end. Town Car. Driver. The whole works. Even a good-looking young guy who'd walk the old man to the front door."

"Like a bodyguard?"

"Not like one," Connie said. *"One."*

"And you say they showed up fairly regularly?"

"They did," she said. "And while I don't want to sound ethnically, ah, insensitive, that they might be Mob guys of some kind. This is Providence, after all. I'm pretty sure people like that have their own baseball cards."

"Always the same man walking him to the door?" I said.

"Yes," she said. "I remember that because occasionally the younger man would come alone at night, carrying what I assumed to be food."

I nodded again. She held up a finger. "Seriously?" she said. "I don't want you to get the idea that all I do is sit and stare out the window at the neighbors."

"It honestly hasn't occurred to me," I said.

284

"Then one day the ambulance came," she said.

She shrugged.

"It was almost as if she'd never been here at all," Connie Devane said.

I had nothing to add to that.

"Maybe people will say the same thing about me someday," she said.

I stood and thanked her for her time.

"I hope I helped," she said.

"More than you know," I said.

There was an air about her that she was sorry to see me go, that she had liked having the company, if even for a few minutes. Divorced woman, observing other people's lives.

That wasn't me someday, I thought, on the way to my car.

That was me *now*.

FORTY-SEVEN

He was leaning against the driver's-side door of my car.

It was one of Antonioni's men who had been with him both times at the Old Canteen. Not the one who I thought was a Richie type. This was the shorter guy with the thicker body, the one I'd decided was meaner, even knowing I was grading him, just on appearances and from a distance, against the curve. But up close the eyes were as mean as I thought they would be. He was wearing a leather bomber jacket that had aged on its own, not fatigued as some kind of fashion strategy. Dark-rinse jeans. Black T-shirt. Black motorcycle boots. My father had spoken of hard old men at breakfast. Here was a younger model.

I took some consolation in the fact, or at least the hope, that he probably didn't plan to shoot me where I stood.

"What are you doing here?" he said.

"Wow," I said. "I was about to ask you the same thing."

"Why are you hanging around this house?" he said.

"Trying to find out a little something about the woman who lived here," I said.

"Why's that?" he said.

"She was a friend of a friend."

"What friend?"

"A client," I said, as if that explained everything except the Big Bang Theory.

"We both know you're lying."

"Not sure our relationship has progressed to that point," I said.

"I could make you tell me the truth," he said.

I smiled. "Maybe you could," I said. "But then again, maybe you couldn't."

"Mr. Antonioni told you to leave this alone."

"I'm having trouble identifying what 'this' is," I said. "Like trying to decide what the definition of 'is' is."

"You're not funny," he said.

"Am, too," I said.

"This," he said, "is whatever the fuck it is keeps bringing you down here and bothering us."

"I wasn't aware I was bothering anybody," I said. "And how did you even know I was

287

in the neighborhood."

"Mr. A. knows what he wants to know in Providence," he said.

"Good for me to know," I said.

"You being smart?"

"It comes to me naturally," I said. "What's your name, by the way?"

He waited, as if debating with himself if it was a good or bad idea to tell me. Then he shrugged.

"Joseph," he said. "Joseph Marchetti."

A car slowly passed us. I moved to my left, but not closer to him. When the car was gone, I took another step back into the street. I wondered if Connie Devane was watching the show from her upstairs window, and what she was thinking.

"Did you used to come visit Maria Cataldo here before she died?" I said.

"You just won't stop fucking with this," he said. "Is that what you want me to tell Mr. A.? That you won't stop fucking with this even after being told to stop?"

"You can tell Mr. Antonioni whatever you like," I said. "I don't see as how I'm bothering him."

"I'm telling you that you are," he said. "And now I'm the one telling you to stop."

"Or what?" I said pleasantly.

"Or you'll get hurt," he said.

288

I smiled and turned slightly away from him, as if I couldn't believe I was having this conversation. And then I did something I had often practiced in front of a mirror at home, and reached into the bag that was over my left shoulder and pulled out my gun with my right, and had the .38 out and the hammer back as Joseph Marchetti was still practicing his death stare and not paying nearly close enough attention.

"What, you're gonna shoot me in the middle of Pleasant Valley Parkway?" he said. "My ass."

"Probably won't shoot you there," I said. "But up to the point when you threatened to hurt me, you'd only been annoying me."

I kept the gun pointed at his nose. After I had pulled it out of my bag, I had made sure to take another step back and keep myself out of his reach, even if he was dumb enough to make a move on me.

"Now please step away from my car, and keep your hands where I can see them as you walk away from me," I said.

"You got no idea how much more trouble you just made for yourself," he said.

"Something else that comes to me naturally," I said. "Now slide along the car and then get moving."

He did that.

"No idea," he said again.

When he was on the sidewalk, he just started walking, not looking back, as if he didn't have a care in the world. When he was twenty-five yards away from me, I said, "Hey, Joseph." I was leaning over the roof of my car, gun still on him, which is why he probably didn't notice that I had my cell phone in my left hand. I had already clicked on the photo icon, so when he turned I was ready to take his picture.

"What," he said.

"Make sure to tell Albert that a girl got the drop on you," I said.

Then he smiled. It did absolutely nothing to soften his features.

"You a good shot?" he said.

"Good enough," I said.

"I'm better," Joseph Marchetti said.

When he had disappeared around the corner, I got behind the wheel of the Prius and started the engine and was thrilled that it didn't blow up.

Then I once again got the hell out of Rhode Island, checking my rearview mirror all the way home.

FORTY-EIGHT

Pete Colapietro, Providence cop, seemed to know where most of the bodies were buried from Narragansett to Woonsocket, both literally and figuratively.

Talking to him was a little bit like talking to Frank Belson, except that Pete was funnier than Frank, not that I would ever tell Frank that.

I called Pete when I got back to Boston and asked him about Joseph Marchetti.

"Told he's worked his way up to midlevel-goon status," Pete said. "Kind of guy Antonioni would use if he wanted to scare somebody he hadn't sufficiently scared himself. But Joe's not like family, if that's what you're asking. By all accounts, though, he *is* supposed to be some shooter."

"I'll keep that in mind," I said.

"Protect and serve," Pete said.

"Does Albert have any other family?" I said. "Wasn't there a son?"

"Allie," Pete said. "Dead, as Casey Stengel used to say, at the present time."

More baseball. I was starting to believe that guys thought about baseball more than sex.

"Natural causes?" I said.

"Considering his line of work and who his old man was, yeah," Pete said, "I guess you could put it that way."

"If Albert wanted somebody to be gotten," I said, "would Marchetti be his man?"

"One of many," Pete said. "But yes."

I thanked him.

"Sunny?" he said before I ended the call. "Just from the little I know, Joe Marchetti is not somebody on whom you put a gun and then he just lets it go."

"Figured."

"They either have eyes on you," he said, "or somebody in the neighborhood made a call."

I thought back to the day I thought I had been followed from Susan Silverman's office.

"Aware of that, too, Pete."

"Maybe you need to have somebody good to have eyes on you, too," Pete Colapietro said.

I told him I would also keep that in mind, thanking him again. Then I texted Connie

Devane the picture of Joseph Marchetti I had taken on my phone. We had exchanged numbers before I'd left her house.

She called me after she got the picture.

I said, "Is that the guy who used to come alone and visit Maria Cataldo?"

"No," she said.

"Shit," I said.

"You want me to keep watching the house for you?" she said. "It would make me feel useful."

"That would make one of us," I said.

FORTY-NINE

Richie and I were having dinner at the Capital Grille on Boylston, next door to the Hynes Auditorium. The restaurant had originally been on Newbury, right before you got to Mass Ave. But they'd decided they needed a bigger space and found it the next block over. Blessedly, the steaks hadn't gotten any smaller, nor the side dishes or desserts. Nor had the big pours for their wine.

Sometimes you just needed red meat and red wine, as diligent as you were about maintaining a girlish figure. Tonight was one of those nights.

"You pulled a gun on this jamoke?" Richie said.

"I did."

"And you thought this was a prudent decision . . . why?"

"There was just something about him that pissed me off," I said. "The casual way he

294

thought he could harass me in broad daylight, and that I was just supposed to take it."

Richie smiled.

"He fucked with the wrong Marine," he said and raised his glass. I touched his with mine. We both drank.

Richie said, "I could tell my father to once again urge Albert Antonioni to leave you alone."

"I think we are well past that," I said. "Albert told me that your father had run out of favors."

"Maybe Desmond still has things that Albert wants."

"You mean business things," I said.

"Who the hell knows?" Richie said.

Garrett, our waiter, brought Caesar salads for both of us. When he was gone, Richie said, "I've been thinking: It's still a possibility that Maria might only turn out to be a side actor in this."

"I know I could be wrong about her," I said. "But I don't think I am. I think she's the star."

"You hate being wrong," he said.

"You're the same way," I said. I smiled sweetly. "Look how angry you were at yourself after so badly remarrying."

"I know you like to play this game," Richie

said. "But I don't."

"Change of subject?"

"If you do, I'll pay the check," he said.

"You're doing that anyway."

He smiled. I liked it when he smiled.

I said, "Your father knows more than he is telling about her."

"I've continued to ask about that in different ways," he said. "To no avail."

"Ask again when you get the chance," I said. "I'm willing to offer sex in return."

Richie Burke smiled then, and I felt the way I did when he smiled at me that way on our first date.

"As if I need to negotiate to get that," he said.

And, as it turned out, he did not.

FIFTY

Before Richie left in the morning I said, "Please do not look for a way to engage with Joseph Marchetti."

"By 'engage,' " he said, "I assume you mean do not go down to Providence and find him and beat the living shit out of him."

"It doesn't get us any closer to an answer," I said.

"It would make me feel better about everything," he said.

"You can't beat up everybody who's mean to me," I said. "It would become a full-time job."

I spent a lot of my morning trying to do another Google search on Maria Cataldo, an even deeper dive than before, hoping there had been something I had missed. But there was not. I called Pete Colapietro, who said I wasn't required to check in with him daily.

"How does somebody disappear from

radar the way she apparently did?" I said. "Before and after the invention of the Internet?"

"She must have had money," he said, "because for the life of me I can't find credit card information on her anywhere. Or a home she ever owned. Or driver's license. Or anything."

"Give me the simple life," I said.

"Must have been a lot of money," he said.

"Mob money is often like that," I said.

"Daddy's money," he said.

"Yes, sir."

"So far what I've mostly got is bupkus," Pete said.

"Join the club," I said.

I made myself more coffee and then fell back on one of my rock-solid foundations for first-rate crime detecting:

I made another list.

I painstakingly wrote it all down again, from the start. No supposition this time. Just facts, in an orderly timeline, as accurate as I could make it. I wrote down all the names, from Richie and Desmond and Felix and the late Peter Burke. Buster. Billy Leonard. Vinnie Morris. Charlie Whitaker. Tony Marcus. A bad sport named Joseph Marchetti.

Albert Antonioni.

Connie Devane.

Maria Cataldo.

Who Desmond had loved and lost. Who maybe Albert Antonioni had loved, too. A girl named Maria: who had lived in a house that Albert owned, and had often been visited by him.

And by a younger man.

Who was that younger man?

I looked at my list, and when the beating I had taken off Exeter Street had occurred. I thought about the recklessness of that, and the further recklessness of coming to my house and trying to shoot me and shooting Spike instead. It reminded me of something I had read in a novel once, *Baja Oklahoma* by Dan Jenkins. It was a book I'd picked up in college, one about a spunky waitress who dreamed of making it as a country songwriter, and who wouldn't allow herself to ever believe she couldn't do that in a man's world.

A woman who wouldn't take any shit from anybody.

In it there had been a list of the Ten Stages of Drunkenness, and I'd always thought the last two were the best:

Invisible.

Bulletproof.

Maybe that's where our shooter was now.

Maybe he thought nobody could catch him, or touch him.

But he was wrong.

I was going to catch him.

I just needed a little boost.

So I called the best booster I knew, Ghost Garrity, a thief who could disable any alarm and who could pick a lock while wearing oven mitts, and asked if he wanted to make a run down to Providence with me.

There was the brief feeling that perhaps I was the one thinking she was invisible, and bulletproof.

Fortunately, the feeling passed.

FIFTY-ONE

Ghost Garrity had a bad toupee, which presupposed the notion that there were actually good toupees. He usually walked around in sports jackets and ties that seemed to be the color of various sorbets. He was small and whippet-thin and jittery, except when he wanted to steal something, or execute a successful break-in. Tonight he wore a black nylon windbreaker and black jeans and a black ball cap with the "G" logo for The Gap on the front.

"Ghost," I said, "you shop at The Gap?"

"Lifted it," he said.

We had waited until dark and parked a block away from Maria Cataldo's house on an adjacent street.

"Tell me again what we're looking for here," Ghost said.

"Something."

"That narrows it down," he said. "You

never told me who owns the place, by the way."

We were making our way across the backyard. I told him who owned the house. Ghost stopped.

"The fuck," he said. "You want me to filch a house belongs to Albert Antonioni?"

"I do," I said.

Ghost said, "The price I gave you? Double it."

"If we live," I said.

"You're not funny."

"Am, too," I said.

We made our way across the rest of the backyard to the back door. Ghost gently tried it, just in case. Locked. Then he reached into his gym bag and came out with two pairs of night goggles that looked as if they'd been borrowed — or lifted — from Navy SEALs.

"Put these on when we get inside," Ghost said, "unless you want the whole freaking neighborhood to see the lights go on."

Before he picked the lock, he held up what looked like an over-sized version of an iPhone and tapped it a few times with his finger and finally said, "Deactivated the alarm."

"You were able to do it with that thing?" I said.

"You wouldn't believe how many of these alarm companies use wireless," Ghost said. "Takes the challenge out of this shit."

"Now what?"

"Now I work my magic on the door," he said. "Want to time me?"

Even with a dead bolt, it took him about a minute, and then we were inside, putting on the goggles, Ghost going around the kitchen and closing the levered blinds, the room now weirdly lit by the night vision, as if we really were Navy SEALs about to go room to room hunting for bin Laden.

"You want to do this together?" Ghost said. "Or you take one room and I take another."

"We separate," I said.

"And I'm looking for something, I just don't know what," he said.

"Anything she might have left behind," I said. "Anything that might tell me more about who she was."

"She was somebody living at Albert Fucking Antonioni's house," Ghost said, "that's who she was."

"Nobody likes a whiner," I said.

It seemed that all that had been left was the furniture. No paintings on the wall, no photographs, no books in the wall shelves, nothing on the antique coffee table in the spacious front room, nothing on the mantel above the fireplace. No clothes in the master bedroom upstairs, nothing in the drawers of the nightstand next to the old four-poster bed. No toiletries left behind in the bathroom. The two spare bedrooms were the same. It was as Connie Devane had suggested to me, as if Maria Cataldo had never been here at all.

The goggles were uncomfortable, too tight around my eyes, as I carefully searched the closets and the shelves in them and under the beds, looking for any trace of her. But it seemed every trace of her was gone, the way she was.

I quietly made my way downstairs.

Ghost said, "I checked the basement. It's so clean it's like they're fixing to sell."

"It's like they didn't just clean out everything except the furniture," I said. "It's like he had somebody sweep the place."

"I'll take one more look upstairs," he said, " 'case you missed something."

He went silently up the stairs. It occurred to me, and not for the first time, that they didn't call him Ghost for nothing.

There was a den next to the main living room that I had already checked, with a huge vintage desk with brass handles on the drawers. I pulled them out again, one by one, and checked underneath them, feeling like an idiot to even think that the old woman had taped something to one of the drawers, or had some kind of secret compartment. The desk was pressed up against a side window. It was a bear to move it away from the wall, but with some work I managed to at least move it forward a couple of inches.

When I did, I heard something gently fall to the carpet.

And there it was.

It was easy to see how anybody who had cleaned out the house could have missed it. How even Ghost had missed it. It must have fallen halfway down behind the desk and just stayed there, until now.

A small, slender picture frame.

With a color photograph inside, slightly faded, of a beautiful, dark-haired woman who I assumed was a younger version of Maria Cataldo.

She was smiling, and had her hand on the shoulder of a boy who looked to be about nine or ten, in front of a sign for the Grand Canyon National Park.

A boy who looked amazingly like a young Richie Burke.

FIFTY-TWO

When we were back in Boston I dropped Ghost on Tremont Street. He said it was close enough to his apartment. I had pointed out to him, more than once, that I was a private detective by trade and could find out where he lived if I really wanted to. But this was the way we'd always done it, just as I'd always paid him in cash.

He said he had to get out of his cat-burglar clothes and get dressed up to go out.

"One of the jackets from your Fontaine-bleau collection?" I said.

"What's that supposed to mean?" he said.

I smiled and thanked him again for doing me a solid.

On the sidewalk he shook his head and said, "I just knocked over Albert Antonio-ni's house."

"But you didn't steal anything."

"Yeah," Ghost said, "that'll get me over if

he ever finds out it was me did it."

It was a little after eleven. I called Richie from the car and asked if he might want to come over.

"Is this about romance?"

"Not tonight, dear," I said. "Too tired."

"Shit, I was afraid of that," he said, and said he was on his way.

"Cute kid," Richie said. "But it's not me."

"He looks just like you," I said. "And didn't you tell me you went to Arizona when you were a boy?"

Richie nodded.

"Felix took me," Richie said. "My father had promised me a spring-break trip. Then something came up, the way it always seemed to. But Felix didn't want to disappoint me, so we did go to Arizona. But not to the Grand Canyon. We went to Sedona. We hiked the red rocks and rode horses. I liked the riding better than the hiking. Made me feel like a cowboy."

"You never went to the Grand Canyon?" I said.

"Good Christ," he said. "Just how stuck are you on this?"

"He looks just like you," I said.

"But he," Richie said, "is *not me.*"

He took in some air, let it out.

"My father and my uncle may lie to you," he said. "I do not."

He had always exhibited an almost eerie self-control. I had told him once that he was a good sport until he wasn't. But when he did stop being a good sport, no matter what the setting or the circumstances, something would change. In his eyes, mostly. It had always reminded me of the flash of lightning.

It wasn't happening now. But it was clear that my line of questioning about the photograph was beginning to annoy him.

"I had to ask," I said. "I'm not looking for a fight."

"Gee," he said, "there's good news."

"I'm guessing that we could probably find a lot of pictures of a lot of dark-haired kids that age who look like that, too," he said. "But they'd remember the goddamn Grand Canyon, and so would I."

"Well, maybe you got me there," I said.

"Let me get this straight," he said. "It was about to be a working theory of yours that Uncle Felix and me just happened to run into my father's long-lost love at one of the most famous landmarks in America? And that he wanted to have a picture of the two of us so, what, he could put it in a scrapbook when we got back to Boston? Am I missing anything?"

We were drinking Bushmills tonight. We both sipped some. I didn't like it as much as Jameson, but I knew Richie liked it a little more. He scratched Rosie behind an ear as he drank. I sensed in the moment that he liked her better than he liked me.

"Okay," I said. "Let's take you out of the picture."

"Thanks," Richie said.

"You're welcome," I said.

He raised his glass in a mock toast.

"At the very least," I said, "this picture could mean Maria had a son that no one, at least no one back here, knew about."

"Finally you make some sense," he said.

"Just spitballing here, big boy."

"And Sunny Randall's first rule of spitballing is that you can't be afraid to hold back a cockeyed idea."

"Correct."

"Even if it happens to be an *especially* cockeyed idea, like me having posed for a photograph with Maria Cataldo, someone I never met, at a place I never visited."

I finished my drink. He finished his and abruptly stood up.

"Gonna head out," he said.

"Don't be mad," I said.

"I'm not," he said. "Now I'm the one

who's tired."

"Okay," I said.

"Maria could have just been visiting Arizona the way Felix and I did," Richie said.

"She and Little Richard also could have lived there," I said, "and it was just a day trip."

"Little Richard," he said, sadly shaking his head.

"Couldn't help myself," I said.

We kissed lightly on the lips. He put his arms around me. I felt the same rush of excitement I always did when we were this close. I knew he knew, as I put my head on his shoulder.

When I finally pulled back I looked up at him and said, "So I'm going to assume, once and for all, that my theory about you and Felix running into Maria in Arizona is a big old no-can-do?"

Richie leaned down now and said to Rosie, "You deal with her."

He left. I looked out the window and saw his car pull away, and then the one I knew had Desmond's men inside pull out behind him. I briefly wondered why they didn't just carpool.

I rinsed our glasses, stuck my .38 in the zippered pocket of my favorite Eileen Fisher vest. Rosie and I went outside. She did her business quickly, dear girl.

We went back inside. I set the dead bolt, not thrilled with how easily Ghost had vanquished the one on Pleasant Valley Parkway, and set the alarm. Wireless. Remembering how quickly Ghost had disarmed the wireless alarm at Maria's house, I made a mental note to get a better one installed. Went through my nightly process with my ridiculously expensive face wash and cream, brushing and flossing. Put the gun on the table next to my bed, shut off the bedroom lights, having left the door ajar just enough that some light from the hallway snuck into the bedroom.

I wasn't afraid of the dark.

Well, maybe a little bit.

I didn't fall asleep right away. Sometimes whiskey helped, sometimes it did not. Maybe tonight was one of the nights when it really was a stimulant.

I got up out of bed and went back to the living room and picked up the photograph of Maria Cataldo and the little boy, brought it back with me into the bedroom.

Rosie was snoring slightly at the end of the bed, but I knew she secretly wanted to talk after I switched on the lamp next to my gun.

"That little boy and Richie could be brothers," I said.

Rosie didn't stir, or respond. But she didn't have to. I knew my girl was thinking right along with me.

"Maybe," I said, "because they are."

FIFTY-THREE

The next morning I met Spike at Spike's for coffee. He was no longer wearing his sling.

"Are you better?" I said.

"No," he said. "But the sling kept getting in the way."

"Of what?"

"Things," he said, winking at me.

"Things plural?" I said.

"Don't be coarse," he said.

He had made the coffee. It was dark and strong and delicious. I described it to him in those words. "Like me," he said.

I took out the photograph of Maria Cataldo and the boy. I placed it on the table in front of him, next to one of Richie I had found in a scrapbook I began to keep after we had gotten married. Felix Burke had helped me get photographs from Richie's childhood and teenage years and college.

"They could be twins," Spike said.

"Tell me about it," I said.

"You think the little boy in the picture is Desmond's," he said.

He made no attempt to make it sound like a question.

"I have no proof," I said. "But, yeah, let's say the idea is trending."

Spike was staring down at the two photographs.

"You do this with Richie yet?" he said.

"No," I said. "But he's too smart not to be thinking the same thing."

"You think if she was pregnant with Desmond's child she would have told him?" Spike said.

"If she did, and Desmond has known about this kid all along, we've established who our greatest living actor is," I said.

Spike sipped some coffee and remarked that, damn, I was right, he did make a damned fine cup of coffee.

"So Richie may have a half-brother," he said.

"That is what I am positing, yes," I said.

Spike said, "And you think this boy, all grown up, has now come out of the past to avenge his mother's honor, like, oh, shit, I can't believe I'm even saying this, some evil twin?"

"I keep wondering if Desmond knew and

is lying his ass off," I said.

"Look," Spike said. "This is a man who's made a career out of playing things close to the vest. You told me one time he didn't actually tell Richie what the real family business was till he was graduating high school."

"But if Desmond has secretly been in the kid's life all along," I said, "then why is the kid coming for him now?"

"Beats the hell out of me," Spike said.

"If this is her son, and Desmond's son, I need to find him," I said. "And maybe get the chance to ask him all the questions I'll never get the chance to ask his mother."

"Maybe Albert knows and Desmond doesn't," Spike said. "About the boy."

"Or maybe they both know and they've *both* been lying their asses off to me the whole time," I said.

"Are you suggesting there is no honor among thieves?" Spike said.

"Really?" I said.

Spike shrugged.

"Low-hanging fruit," he said.

FIFTY-FOUR

Before I attempted to meet with Desmond Burke, I called Nathan Epstein, who, despite recent tumult at the FBI that seemed to involve all his superiors past and present, remained the field agent in charge of their Miami office, after having served for years in the same capacity in Boston.

"How have you managed to survive?" I said on the phone. "In the Bureau, I mean."

"By pretending I don't know who the president is," he said.

"You're aware that the rest of us don't have that luxury," I said.

"You don't have years of training as a dedicated civil servant," he said.

He asked where I was.

"Boston," I said. "Where else?"

"Where in Boston?"

"Wait a minute," I said. "Where are you?"

"Just because I now have a 305 area code doesn't mean I'm always there," he said. "I happen to be here."

"Why?"

"Business," he said. "I don't mean to get too technical with you, but I classify it as bad-guy business."

"Oh," I said. "That."

"So where are you at the moment?" Epstein said.

I told him I'd just had coffee at Spike's on Marshall Street. He asked if I could stand to drink one more cup. I told him I'd still be looking to have one more cup of coffee when I was dead. He said he could meet me near the statue of Red Auerbach in the Faneuil Hall marketplace in fifteen minutes.

Now we were sitting on a bench across from the statue, both of us drinking Starbucks coffee. Epstein looked as I remembered him: small, balding, tiny round wire-rimmed glasses. He had always reminded me more of a career public accountant than a G-Man. But I knew him well enough by now, and knew enough about him, not to underestimate his toughness.

Better yet, he owed me a favor, or at least said he did, because of a case on which I'd helped him out a little over a year ago right before he left for Miami, one that saved the Bureau some embarrassment and took a rogue agent off the books. This, I had informed him, was that favor.

"Catch me up," he said.

I told him, bumper-sticker-style. When I finished he said, "To use a clinical expression, this sounds like a hot mess."

I asked if he could find out whatever there was to find out about Maria Cataldo.

"She ever have a job that you know about?"

I shook my head.

"Got a Social Security Number for her?" he said.

"Nope."

"She ever have a driver's license anywhere?"

"Not that the cops have been able to determine."

"Credit cards?"

I shook my head again.

"Internet?"

"No email, no Facebook, no Instagram, no nothing," I said.

"Imagine that," Epstein said. "Married?"

"I got nothing," I said.

"Takes a big person to admit that," he said.

Epstein might have smiled. It was hard to tell with him, just because life in general so often seemed to amuse him.

"She own property?"

"Albert Antonioni owns the last house in which she lived," I said.

"Well, this sounds like a piece of cake for an experienced Fed like myself," Epstein said.

He stood up.

"There's one other thing," I said. "Unrelated to Ms. Cataldo."

"I give and give and give," he said.

"Have you guys noticed the uptick in movement of illegal guns around here?" I said.

"By 'you guys' I assume you're referring to the Federal Bureau of Investigation and the Department of Justice?"

"Them," I said.

"ATF," he said, as if that solved all of the mysteries of the universe.

"I know that you know what they know," I said. "But I don't have a personal relationship with big shots there the way I do with you."

"Right," he said.

"If you get the chance," I said, "would you mind terribly asking around on that, as well? I think Desmond and Albert might be in some dick-swinging thing involving guns."

"If you ask for anything else," Epstein said, "I may have to start using vacation time."

"I should have called you sooner," I said.

Now Epstein did smile.

"No shit, Sherlock," he said.

FIFTY-FIVE

I was sitting in Desmond's living room in Charlestown with him and Felix and Richie.

I was well aware that Desmond would never have agreed to see me on his own. I knew Richie had brought some sort of force to bear.

"The thing of it is this," I said to Desmond. "We've gone over this before. I don't believe in coincidence, and neither does Richie and neither do you."

"Who does?" Felix said.

Now the pictures of Maria Cataldo and the boy and a young Richie Burke were on the stump coffee table in front of the Burkes.

"This proves nothing," Desmond said.

"Dad," Richie said.

"It is my unproven assertion that the boy in the picture with Maria is her son," I said. "And yours."

"Goddamn it, now you're just being ridiculous!" Felix Burke said to me, with surprising force.

"Ridiculous," Desmond said, "because of an unfounded theory."

"Working on that," I said. "The unproven part."

"Why won't you leave this be?" Desmond said.

He stared at me with eyes as dark as coal. He did not look angry. Just terribly old. As old as all of this.

As old as the photographs on the table.

"I don't leave things be," I said.

"This family is no longer your family," Desmond said.

"But he is," I said, nodding at Richie.

"Dad," Richie said, sounding tired himself. "You have to admit that it is possible that Maria left when she did and the way she did because she was pregnant with your child."

"Many things are possible," Desmond said, "but turn out not to be so."

"But if she was pregnant," I said, "you are telling us you didn't know?"

"I did not," he said. "But would I have wanted to know? Of course."

Felix Burke said, "Sunny, you think that somehow the boy in that picture is the one who has come after us this way?"

Felix looked older, too, except for his

slicked-back black hair, which remained forever young.

"It is the only thing that makes sense," I said.

"For what reason?" Desmond said.

"I plan to ask him that when I find him," I said.

"It is now my turn to ask you to walk away from this," Felix Burke said. "I know you will never walk away from Richard. But walk away from Desmond and me. I've never asked you for anything, Sunny. I'm asking you now. Give it up."

"I can't," I said.

Then I told him and told Desmond about Maria having been back in Providence for years, living in a house owned by Albert Antonioni.

Desmond looked at Richie. "You knew this?"

Richie nodded.

"And didn't tell me?"

"I promised Sunny I wouldn't," Richie said. "And I was raised to keep my word."

"I'm your father," Desmond said.

"And I'm your son," Richie said, "sometimes in ways I'm not sure even I fully comprehend."

We all sat there. It occurred to me how much of my life had been spent in the company of hard men like these. Sunny and the boys.

I asked Desmond again when Maria had left Boston. He told me. Richie said, "The boy in that picture would be about my age."

To no one Desmond said, "All this time, she was an hour away."

"But gone now," Felix said, as if putting out a fire that had not yet begun. "Another reason it is time for all of us to let go. We live in the past enough, Desmond, you and me."

"But it means he knows things about her that I do not," Desmond said.

He looked at me, perhaps because I was the only woman in the room.

"If she came back," he said, "why would she come back to him?"

"I'm going to ask this again," I said. "When Albert and Maria were younger, could they have had a relationship that she kept from you?"

"No," he said. He spit out the word. "In those days, when we were together, she just used to joke that I better treat her right, because if I were out of the picture, she would not lack for attention."

He closed his eyes. "But I did treat her right," he said.

When he opened his eyes finally, he was

once again staring at me.

"You honestly think he might be the one trying to kill me?" Desmond said.

No one said anything until Richie said, "Our father."

Fifty-Six

The next day Epstein and I were once again sitting across from Red Auerbach.

"I feel like we're sneaking out to the malt shop," I said.

"It's best that you not come to my office when I am engaged in what I like to think of as off-the-books activities," he said.

"But you're one of the good guys," I said.

"So I constantly remind myself."

"You said you had stuff for me," I said.

"Actually," he said, "I do."

Seven months or so from when Desmond thought Maria had left Boston in the spring of 1980, she had married a man named Samuel Tomasi in Prescott, Arizona. A month after that, Epstein said, she gave birth to a son named Robert.

"Prematurely?" I said.

Epstein shook his head. "Even for us it can be a bear getting hospital records," he said. "But it was a long time ago. This time we managed."

"So she *was* pregnant when she left Boston," I said.

"So it appears."

"Robert Tomasi has to be Desmond's kid," I said.

"So it appears," Nathan Epstein said.

Maria divorced Samuel Tomasi a few months later. I asked Epstein what had become of Tomasi. He said he had no idea, that Tomasi went off the grid at that point and so did Maria Cataldo.

"You can still do that in the modern world?" I said to Epstein. "Go off the grid?"

"It was the eighties, remember, before everybody knew everything about everybody," he said. "If it is your intent to disappear, if you don't have a job or own a home and didn't establish an Internet presence later, yes, it can be done."

"It sounds as if Samuel Tomasi's only job was to give the child a father, at least on the birth certificate," I said.

"Before our Maria, as they say in the crime shows on television, was in the wind," Epstein said.

"Maybe her father sent her out to Arizona to give the boy a name," Epstein said. "And then sent him somewhere else to keep this Maria's secret."

"So what became of young Robert To-masi?" I said.

"His last known presence was public high school in Prescott," Epstein said. "He had a few brushes with the law. Fighting mostly. Never made it to his senior year. Then . . . *poof.*"

"Poof?"

"It's a complicated law enforcement expression," he said. "But we just went over this. If it is your intent not to be found, you can sometimes hide in plain sight. Especially if no one is really looking for you."

Until now, I thought.

"Could he have died young?"

Epstein said, "If he did, the selfish bastard did it without telling anybody."

He sipped his coffee and frowned. "You think they lie when they tell you they're giving you an extra shot of espresso?"

"To a G-Man?" I said.

"Are we even now?" he said.

"Hell, no," I said.

He sighed.

"I will keep poking around on this and see if I can determine what happened to the son," he said.

"You're making America great again," I said.

Epstein sighed more loudly than before. "Somebody has to," he said.

FIFTY-SEVEN

Epstein left. I stayed where I was, finishing my own coffee. My father had known Red Auerbach slightly, and had always told me that Red was just one of those guys who was, in Phil Randall's words, smarter than all the other guys.

I wanted to walk across the marketplace now and sit next to Red on his bench and ask him if he thought the young guy visiting Maria Cataldo at the house in Providence was her son.

And if it wasn't Robert Tomasi, or whatever Robert Tomasi might be calling himself, then who was he?

I had been pulling at threads since the night Richie had been shot. Along the way, someone had shot Spike and taken a shot at me. And while pulling at threads, I had without question poked a bear in the form of Albert Antonioni, who had threatened me in person and by proxy in the person of one Joseph Marchetti. Thread-pulling. Bear-poking. Could you even have them both in the same conversation?

If Red Auerbach didn't know, perhaps Susan Silverman would when I saw her later.

I had established the connection between Albert and Maria. But that didn't mean there was a connection between Albert and the shooter. Except that the guy in the alley had said, "We keep fucking with him because we can." Meaning Desmond.

So who was "we"?

I took my phone out of my bag and called the Providence Police Department and was connected to Pete Colapietro and told him about what I'd learned from Nathan Epstein and what I now wanted to do.

"You're shitting," he said.

"No, sir."

"Let me make some calls and get back to you," he said.

"If I'm right about this, which you have to say would be a pleasant change of pace, the guy I'm looking for might have been right in front of us all along," I said.

I watched the parade of tourists across what I had always thought of as one of the main plazas of the city. Over in front of The Black Dog, an old man I recognized from the day before fed pigeons. There was a long-haired young woman off to my right, wearing a Black Dog T-shirt and distressed jeans and playing the guitar rather well, her guitar case open for contributions.

"We go through with this," Pete Colapietro said, "it might be the two of us who might want to think about hiding."

"Don't be a girl," I said.

"So," Susan Silverman said, "it appears the game's afoot."

"Excuse me?" I said.

She offered the tiniest of smiles.

"It's something else the man of my dreams likes to say," she said.

Considering how little I knew of her life outside this office, even an admission like that made me feel as if she had suddenly spilled her guts to me.

We were in her office at five in the afternoon. Even at this hour, the latest I knew she scheduled her appointments unless there was some kind of emergency, there was the palpable sense about her that her day was really just beginning, and that her focus and energy were as quietly intense as ever.

She wore gray pants today and a black cotton turtleneck sweater with a simple strand of pearls. By now, and even in her understated way, I knew her appearance was as important to her as mine was to me. And, being a vain and at least somewhat of an attractive woman myself, I knew that it took a hell of a lot of time and effort to make her beauty look as effortless and natural as it did.

We had been talking about the case. I sometimes did that with her. Sometimes she was able to help organize my thoughts just sitting across her desk from me. Which, I supposed, was part of the job description.

"I don't know if I'm right about this," I said. "But my gut tells me I am."

"It has often served you well in the past," she said. "Your gut."

"I'm aware that your goal here is not primarily to help me solve complicated cases," I said.

"Full service," she said.

"This person, whoever he is, has killed at least two people that I know of, and perhaps one more," I said. "So if he's not technically a serial killer, he's getting there."

She waited.

"He shot Richie and shot Spike and tried to shoot me and even shot up a house," I said.

"And while the logic of all this," she said,

"may seem at least somewhat random to you, even erratic, it makes perfect sense to him. Even doing something as reckless as coming to your house and nearly revealing himself. With him, there is a hidden, interior logic at work."

"If it is the missing son, could he be avenging some perceived injustice against his mother?" I said. "Would that fit his interior logic?"

"Only if you can discover what the injustice is," she said. "Whether perceived or quite real."

"If I can find him, maybe I can find that out," I said. "Before he kills anybody else."

"But," Susan Silverman said, "you are proceeding on the assumption that the son remained in her life until she died."

"Call it a working theory," I said.

"Or more gut instinct," she said.

She may have smiled again.

Or not.

"Yes," I said.

"It lies not in our power to love or hate," she said. "For will in us is overruled by fate."

"Christopher Marlowe," I said.

"My boyfriend also likes poetry," Susan Silverman said.

"If this guy feels as if his mother, whom he loved, was somehow wronged by Desmond Burke, his hatred of Desmond could consume him," I said.

"Beyond the point of obsession," she said. "And compulsion."

"As he proceeds toward what he considers the logical end to his plan," I said.

We sat in silence. A robin landed on the windowsill behind her, stared at me briefly, then flew away. I knew our time was almost up.

"One more thing," I said. "Would you mind terribly dropping all your other clients for a couple weeks and focusing solely on this case?"

Susan Silverman did smile now, rather brilliantly.

"Even full service has its limits," she said.

FIFTY-EIGHT

I was sitting with Pete Colapietro in the front seat of his car. It was our plan to spend the next several hours following Albert Antonioni around, as long as Albert began this day the way Pete said he began most days, with an espresso and a pastry at Constantino's Venda Ravioli in DePasquale Plaza.

We were up the block, with a good view of the front entrance.

Pete had been telling me about how Albert Antonioni had a rather complicated home life, according to some checking he had done with Police Intelligence and Organized Crime. Turned out, he said, that despite the fact that Albert was the legal owner of the house in which Maria Cataldo had lived and he had frequently visited, he had at least three other homes in Providence in the names of various business associates.

Pete had put air quotes around "business associates."

"One is the guy who's listed as the CEO of Albert's vending-machine business," Pete said. "The other two are top lieutenants in his less legitimate enterprises: Tommy Marchi, Ed Schembri, Matt Connors."

"Matt Connors?" I said.

"He must be trying to be inclusive," Pete said.

Then he touched me on the arm and pointed and said, "Showtime."

An SUV had just pulled up in front of Constantino's Venda Ravioli and Antonioni had gotten out. There were two men in the car with him. They got out as well. The one from the passenger seat opened the door for Albert. He walked between them into Constantino's, to what Pete said would be his regular table, a round marble one in the back near the freezer.

One of the troopers stayed in the car, the other stood to the side of the front door.

"You recognize either one of those guys?" Pete said.

"I think they both might have been in the room at the Old Canteen," I said. "But neither one of them is who I'm looking for. The driver is too blond, and the guy by the door is too old and too fat."

I showed him the copy of the picture of

Maria and the little boy I'd brought with me.

"I'm looking for the grown-up version of him," I said.

"Because you think he's the one doing all this."

I nodded. "Now I just have to find a way to prove it." I sighed and shook my head. "The things I can prove don't help me enough. But the things I can't prove, I know I'm right about."

"I actually think I followed that," he said.

"I feel like I've been some kind of drone from the start," I said. "Just being operated by a kid on a sugar high."

"I got one of those," Pete said, "you can have him, you want him."

Albert stayed inside for an hour, came back outside with another old man, hugged the other old man, kissed him on the cheek, got back into the SUV.

"Tallyho," Pete said.

"You're not worried they'll make us?"

"Ho ho ho," he said.

Besides, Pete said, Albert being the creature of habit that his friends at Organized Crime said he was, he was fairly confident where his next stop was going to be. Pete was right. A few minutes later the SUV pulled up to the Acorn Social Club on

Acorn Street.

"You've heard of the Ravenite Social Club in New York, right?" Pete said. "Gotti's old hangout?"

"I have."

"This is the Providence version of that," he said.

He said he'd been in there, and it was pretty much everything he'd expected, a windowless front room, old men playing cards, a couple television screens, one showing horse races from various tracks around the country, the other showing the security feed from the camera above the front door.

"They let you inside?" I said.

"The *goombahs* think it's funny, having a lively exchange of ideas with cops sometimes," he said.

He grinned.

"Last time I was there one of them was bitching that he had to go get some cash from an ATM nearby and bail his son out on a DUI," he said. "I asked him how old his son was. Guy said, 'Fifty-seven, going on fifty-eight.' "

This time Albert Antonioni stayed inside two hours. When he came out, the SUV was still there, but he got into a different car, a black Town Car. Before he got in, he turned and waved at a Crown Vic parked up Acorn Street.

"Who's he waving at?" I said.

"Couple guys from Organized Crime," Pete said.

"They know you're following him around today, too?" I said.

"More the merrier in Goombahville," he said.

"Ours is a glamorous lot."

"Ain't it?" he said.

The next stop, as predicted by Pete, was at the Palomino Vending Company, which Pete said was actually a legitimate business, and one with which Albert had always done pretty well, even though he left the hands-on running of it to others.

"That way he can focus on his real passion," Pete said. "Doing really bad shit to people."

It was past four o'clock when Albert Antonioni finally came out of the Palomino Vending Company. I was past hungry by then, and needed to pee.

The Town Car was long gone. The SUV was still there. But now a black Lincoln Navigator pulled up, only the driver inside.

The driver got out, came around and hugged Albert Antonioni, gave a quick survey to the street, opened the back door, and helped Albert into the backseat. Came back around the front of the car.

I had already pulled the long-lens camera out of my bag, one I'd brought along just in case I needed it.

"Shazam," I said.

I kept snapping away until the guy got back behind the wheel of the Navigator and drove away.

"We got a winner?"

"Think so," I said.

"You know him?"

"And had forgotten him," I said. "He was there at the Old Canteen, both times. I remember thinking the first day that he reminded me a little bit of my ex-husband."

"Shazam, shazam, shazam," Pete Colapietro said.

And put our car into gear.

"We gonna stay on Albert?" Pete said.

"I think of it as staying on Little Richard," I said.

FIFTY-NINE

Pete said he didn't recognize the driver but trusted that somebody at Organized Crime would.

"You think it's our guy?" Pete said.

"Has to be," I said.

"Just off what he looks like?" he said.

"Just because it has to be him," I said.

"My wife always boxes me in with logic like that," he said.

We followed the car to a big house in what Pete Colapietro said was the Mount Pleasant section of Providence. It looked even richer and more elegant than the street on which Maria Cataldo had lived, bigger, older houses set even farther back from the road.

"This is Mount Pleasant," I said to Pete. "Maria lived on Pleasant Valley Parkway. As a detective, I'm detecting a trend here."

"What can I tell you," he said. "We're a very pleasant city."

We passed the Triggs golf course, Pete pointing out that back in the sixties there had been a famous Mob hit there by a couple bookies named Rudy Marfeo and Anthony Melei. I told him that was good to know. He said he had a lot of fun facts like that.

Antonioni and his driver went into the house together. The driver did not come back outside. Pete drove past the house and parked on a side street a block away.

"If this is one of Albert's houses, it wasn't on my list," Pete said.

"Worth repeating that this is an old man," I said, "who hasn't lasted this long by throwing caution to the wind. Much the same as his old friend Desmond Burke."

"Now what?" Pete said.

"We wait."

"Maybe the one you called Little Richard lives there with him," Pete said. "Like a live-in bodyguard."

"Something else that would be good to know," I said.

Pete turned on the car so he could turn on the radio. "You mind if I listen to the Sox?" he said.

I grinned. "Yes."

"You come from Boston and you don't like the Sox?" he said.

343

It came out "Sawx," as if that was the way it was supposed to.

"I liked going to games with my dad when I was a little girl," I said. "And I'd go with Richie once in a while if we had good seats and the weather was nice. But I just never thought there was enough going on."

"Part of the appeal," he said.

"So I've been told. Repeatedly."

"I'm feeling the urge for beer and peanuts just listening," he said.

"It'll pass," I said.

We sat and he listened to the game, but as he did, we talked about his job. We talked about how I saw the job when I was still with the cops. He talked about his family, and how you couldn't do better with a cop wife than he'd done. I told some stories about my dad, some of which he'd heard, starting with the one about my dad and I and the day the Spare Change killer died.

Two hours later Little Richard was still inside the house. I told Pete we could call it a night and he could drive me back to where I'd parked my car on Federal Hill and thanked him again for everything he'd done, that it was above and beyond. He said he didn't mind waiting a little longer, if I wanted to. I said I was fine, that we knew where Antonioni lived now, or at least lived part of the time.

Pete asked if I planned to circle back here myself before I went back to Boston.

I grinned again. "Maybe I will, maybe I won't," I said.

"You gotta keep reminding yourself of something," he said. "This isn't just my turf. It's his."

"I'm going to head back," I said. "I got a lot today, pictures and this address and the fact that Little Richard and Albert might be living under the same roof."

"Okay, then," Pete said.

"Okay," I said.

He drove me back to Federal Hill. As soon as his car pulled away, I drove straight back to Mount Pleasant. The Navigator was still parked in the driveway. Then I drove home. I called Spike from 95, asking him if he'd remembered to take Rosie out the way I'd asked him.

"I'm insulted that you even felt the need to ask," he said.

"Sorry."

"How did it go?"

"I got a lot today," I said, and told him about the driver and the house and the pictures I'd taken. Then I said, "All I need now is a plan."

"Well," Spike said, "ask yourself something: Who the hell doesn't?"

SIXTY

Pete had shown the pictures I sent him to his buddies at Organized Crime, and was informed that the driver's name was Bobby Toms.

"Short for Bobby Tomasi," I said.

"Would be the way I'd bet."

"What's his story?" I said.

"That's the weird part," Pete said. "He has none. Isn't in the system as Bobby Tomasi or Robert Tomasi or Robert Toms or Bobby Toms. They say that all of a sudden, and nobody can remember exactly when, he was a fast-tracker with Albert. Who, they say, treats him like a son."

"Maria's son," I said.

"Who you now think is the one trying to start a Mob war with the Burkes," Pete said.

"Hard to believe he could do that without Albert knowing," I said. "Or without Albert's say-so."

"But if he wants to take out Desmond, or

347

he and Albert want him to take out Desmond, why not just do it without all this fucking around?"

"Maybe the fucking around is part of it," I said.

Pete said he'd call if he found out any more fun facts from Goombahville. I told him I'd been meaning to ask if it was politically correct for one Italian to call another one a *goombah*. He said he was pretty sure there were rules in the handbook that covered it.

What I really needed to do was find a way to talk to Bobby Toms. I imagined myself driving back down to Providence, walking up to Albert's front door, ringing the bell if somebody hadn't already shot me, and hoping Bobby answered the door.

"Hi," I could say in a cheerful voice, "I'm conducting a survey about your mother," and see how things went from there if he didn't try to shoot me in the eye.

"Oh, and by the way, you sonofabitch," I could say, "are you the one who shot my ex-husband in the back and smacked me around on Exeter Street that time?"

I was close now. I could feel it. Bobby Toms had to be the son and Desmond Burke had to be his father, because nothing else made sense and because as a boy he really did look like Richie's twin, evil or otherwise.

But what could Desmond Burke have possibly done to Maria Cataldo to make their son start shooting up Boston this way?

And how did guns somehow figure in to all of this?

The only way to get all the answers I wanted and needed was to close this case. Which I told myself I would. Because I always had in the past. Maybe if I did, I could go back to working on a case that would actually pay me a living wage.

I was so lost in the fog and the moment and all the questions I still had that I didn't hear the ring of my cell phone right away.

I looked at the caller ID. "Richie."

"Hey, you," I said when I answered.

"Desmond's been taken," he said.

SIXTY-ONE

I met Richie at Felix's now-repaired home at the marina in Charlestown.

"The boys were waiting to drive him to Mass," Felix said. "My brother is always ready at ten minutes to seven. He's one of those. Thinks even being a minute late is a mortal sin. When I'm a few minutes late, he looks at me like he wants to give me a good smack."

"And the house had been watched all night," I said.

"Yes," Richie said.

"But when they finally went inside to check on where he was, he was gone," I said.

"Yes," Richie said.

There were three Dunkin' Donuts cups on the table in front of us. Felix picked up his and drank some of his coffee. I could see his ruined boxer's hands shaking as he did.

"They use the key they have," Felix said,

"and go inside and call out to him. But like Richie said. He's gone."

"Didn't he set the alarm at night?" I said.

Felix looked at Richie, then back at me.

"Sometimes he does," Felix said. "Sometimes he doesn't." He shrugged. "We're old. We forget."

"The one who took him could have come from the water side," Richie said. "And in through the back somehow."

I thought of how easily Ghost Garrity had gotten inside Maria Cataldo's house, and how the gadget he'd brought disarmed what had been her alarm. How easy he said it was to disarm them in general.

"This is war now, Richard," Felix said. "If that fuck Antonioni is the one who ordered this, I will kill him with my own hands."

"It could be one of his people who took Desmond," Richie said.

"I think I know which one," I said, and told them both everything I had learned about Bobby Toms, and how Pete Colapietro and I had followed him to the house in Mount Pleasant. Richie looked at me. "You were going to tell me this when?" he said. I told him I was about to call him when he called to tell me about his father.

"Albert knows," Felix said. "That's the way it would work with us. That's the way it would work with them."

Us. Them. To the death.

"Is there anything you've not told us?" Richie said to his uncle.

It took a longer time than I would have liked for Felix Burke to say that he had not.

"Uncle Felix," Richie said, as if talking to a child.

"Have I ever lied to you, Richard?" he said.

"Often," Richie said.

"About anything important?" Felix said.

"Less often," Richie said.

I sipped coffee that had gone cold. Even cold was better than none.

"Desmond's alive," I said. "I'm sure of it."

"You can't be sure," Felix said.

"This ends the way it started with me," Richie said. "If the guy wanted him dead, he'd be dead. Come into the house with a silencer and do it and leave, maybe even by boat."

I looked at Felix Burke. I couldn't remember a time when I had ever seen him scared. But he was scared now, and it showed. It had always been him and Desmond against the world. Their other brothers were gone. Now Desmond had been taken.

"You don't know," Felix said again.

"I do," I said. "So much of this has been an elaborate production. He wanted to torture Desmond and, as a by-product, the rest of us. I believe he's known the endgame from the beginning. But ultimately this is something between him and Desmond. I believe he wants to kill him. But wants it to be a slow death. He might even want an audience."

"I could go down there and take that fuck Antonioni," Felix said, as if it were the old days, as if he were young and not afraid of anything or anybody.

"And get yourself killed in the process," Richie said.

"We have men, too," Felix said.

"Who didn't help us a whole hell of a lot today," Richie said.

"You know the resources I have," Felix said. "You remember the time I found a killer for you."

"Tommy Noon," I said. "I remember."

He had been the killer in a case on which I had once worked for a young woman named Sarah Markham, who had hired me to find out who her birth parents were.

"We may need those resources before we're through, Uncle Felix," Richie said. "But let us handle this for now."

" 'Us'?" he said.

353

"Sunny and me," Richie said.

I looked at him.

"Sunny and I will find him," Richie said.

"Yes," I said. "We will."

SIXTY-TWO

Richie and I went back to River Street Place. I changed into a black T-shirt and one of my pairs of preferred white jeans. I knew it was getting a little late in the year for white jeans, but I looked damn good in them. And I knew that Richie thought I looked damn good in them.

When I came down the stairs, Rosie was next to him on the couch. There were two glasses of red wine on the table in front of them. I knew he noticed the jeans. He always did. And I always noticed him noticing.

We both drank some wine.

"You honestly believe he's not dead already?" Richie said.

"We're getting to the end of foreplay," I said. "But I honestly think it's still foreplay."

"If he is dead," Richie said, "Felix will take an army down to Providence and kill them all and let God sort things out."

"I know," I said. "But you have to keep him under control for the time being. Let me do my job."

"Our job," Richie said.

We drank more wine.

"I feel as if we should be doing something right now," he said.

"Tomorrow," I said.

"First thing," he said.

I nodded.

"You have a plan," he said, staring at me.

I nodded again. Rosie rolled over and let Richie rub her belly.

"Dr. Silverman says that in the shooter's mind, everything makes perfect sense," I said.

"So how do we find where he's taken him?" Richie said.

"The only thing that makes sense is that it's another property of Antonioni's," I said.

"How do we find out which one?" Richie said.

I smiled at him.

"Forget about your uncle," I said. "How about if we take Albert?"

SIXTY-THREE

Richie said he was going back to Charlestown to spend the night at his uncle Felix's. He called it babysitting. I told him I wouldn't necessarily refer to it that way in front of Felix.

"Felix is used to dealing from strength," Richie said. "Being in charge. This is different. We do something wrong here, Desmond dies."

I had explained by then that I didn't exactly want to take Albert Antonioni, I just wanted to borrow him for a little while. And then reason with him.

"Tell me how," Richie said.

"Let me work on my plan a little more," I said, and then told him what he needed to find out from his uncle.

"Promise me you won't set anything in motion without telling me," he said.

"Have I ever lied to you?" I said.

"Often," he said.

"But about things that matter?" I said.

"Less often," he said.

He kissed me hard. I kissed him back. When Richie was gone, and the two men watching him were gone, I called Spike and told him my plan.

Then made two more calls after that.

I met Tony Marcus in his office at Buddy's Fox at noon the next day. Junior was there, as was Ty Bop. Tony was behind his desk, wearing a charcoal suit with wide pinstripes and slightly wider lapels than were the current fashion, dressed for a big night on the town even in the middle of the day.

Always my relationship with him had been transactional. So was it now.

I got right to it, explaining what I wanted to happen and hoped would happen as quickly as possible. For once he did not interrupt, just nodded and listened, as if I were his stockbroker bringing him up to date on his portfolio.

"It would just be a part of the diversification project into Rhode Island you've been talking about," I said.

"Think I couldn't have come up with this on my own, if I'd've thought of it first?" he said.

"I'm sure you could have figured out

something on the girls," I said. "Having guns to bargain with just makes it easier."

"You pretty cocky, girl, thinking you can produce those guns," he said.

"I can't," I said. "But I believe Felix Burke can. And will be highly motivated to do so."

"Where the guns at?"

"Somewhere," I said.

"And you think Felix just gonna tell you where they at?"

"If it means saving his brother's life he will," I said. "I'd bet my own life on that."

"You think Albert been the one calling the shots on this war on the Burkes all along?" Tony said.

"He's the only one who could have set it all in motion," I said.

"What's in it for him?"

I said, "This is nothing more than a working theory. But I think he set this whole thing up to take Desmond's guns, and then take out Desmond once and for all."

"Lot of moving pieces," Tony said. He smiled. "So to speak."

"Still are," I said. "Why I'm here."

Tony made a steeple with his fingers. I wanted to ask him where he had his nails done, because I was convinced his manicurist was way better than my own.

"You get something you want, Albert gets

Desmond's guns, Felix gets what he wants most in the world," I said. "He gets his brother back."

"If that old fuck still be alive."

"If he is," I said, "we need to move on this."

"And you're telling me all's I got to do is set up the meet," Tony Marcus said.

"Uh-huh," I said. "Sooner rather than later."

"And then I got to just do a little acting job when you show up and try to find out what you lookin' to find out," he said.

"Who better than you to play you?" I said. "The part you were born to play."

He smiled.

"I love it when you blow smoke up my ass," he said, "you come here wanting something bad enough. Most girls be willin' to fuck me to get something they want that bad."

"You should know by now," I said to Tony Marcus, "that I'm not most girls."

His fingers were still steepled. He closed his eyes in thought. Finally he said, "Rewards here do seem to outweigh the risk."

"Uh-huh," I said again.

"I'll set up the meet," he said.

"Nice doing business with you," I said.

Tony's smile was as white as what I could

see of his white shirt.

"The balls on you," he said.

I said, "That's what they all say."

SIXTY-FOUR

Tony had already managed to set up the meeting for that night at a diner on the outskirts of Taunton, not far from the Rhode Island line, not exactly halfway between him and Albert Antonioni but close enough.

I had suggested Taunton to Tony, out of the same sense of compromise that had once brought Desmond Burke and Albert Antonioni there for the sit-down I had attended during the Millicent Patton case. Desmond had been there that day to provide support for me and to have my back. If everything went as planned, though hardly anything ever did, tomorrow I would now have his.

Richie and I were on the couch in the living room after I returned from Buddy's Fox. We had gone over my plan, and were now going back over everything that had happened since he had been shot, one last time. We knew that everything that could be set in motion for tomorrow had been set in motion, despite all the loose ends that I knew still existed and all the questions I had that still needed answers, including the one about who had shot Dominic Carbone.

"That one still doesn't fit," I said.

"Unless Bobby Toms wanted to throw us off," Richie said, "and didn't care how he did it."

"Remember, Susan Silverman says that what might seem like a pathology to us likely makes perfect sense to him," I said.

"The avenger," Richie said.

"But avenging *what*?" I said.

We had circled all the way back there.

Richie drank some of the coffee I had made for us. When he put his cup down, he seemed to be at rest. I knew better. Knew him well enough to know how fiercely he was fighting to maintain composure. He was Desmond Burke's son, as much as he had been kept separate from the family business. He was Felix Burke's nephew. As different as he was from them, he was of them.

He blew out some air, unclenched his fists, and gently rubbed Rosie's head.

"This will work," he said.

"Yes," I said.

"You're convinced Albert knows where

Desmond is being held and that Desmond really is still alive," Richie said.

"Yes," I said.

"Felix didn't even attempt to deny he had the guns," Richie said.

"He say where?"

" 'In a creative place' is all he said. And said he would tell us where when Desmond was safe."

"But his word is good on turning them over?"

Richie nodded.

"Good," I said.

"Obviously your father knows where they are, too," I said.

"They would have to kill him before he'd tell," Richie said.

"Because he won't give them the satisfaction?" I said.

"Because he's Desmond Fucking Burke," Richie said.

There was another silence between us. We both drank whiskey. Finally Richie said, "I very much want you to be right about all of this."

"I am," I said.

"And you still believe that we can rescue my father before it is too late?"

"Who better than us?" I said.

Sixty-Five

The diner, a dive called Jake's, was up the road from a sports bar on Bay Street called Home Plate.

It served a breakfast and lunch crowd and was generally closed, we had learned, by four in the afternoon at the latest. The original Jake was an old Providence friend of Albert Antonioni's. The family still ran it but were long gone by the time the principals and their seconds arrived at a little after nine o'clock. That part of the deal had quickly been brokered by Antonioni's people.

Pete Colapietro had called the Taunton cops and told them to ignore lights inside if they were passing by, telling them there was a meeting taking place that might help him close the books on what he told them was some major shit.

"I am taking it on trust," he'd told me, "that this isn't going to turn into *Gunfight at the O.K. Corral.*"

"Okay," I'd said.

"Okay meaning it won't," Pete had said, "or that you're hoping it won't?"

"Little of both."

"What I was afraid of."

Richie and I were in one of the two cars parked up Bay Street. Tony had brought Ty Bop and Junior with him. Albert had brought two of his own troopers. That was the deal.

Tony had chuckled speaking to me from his car and said, "I know that old man tougher than a cheap steak. But he don't know that even though the sides look even, they not."

"What do you know about cheap steaks?" I said.

"You forget, Sunny Randall," he said. "I wasn't always slicker than shit."

He knew that he had about half an hour to conclude his business and then we were coming in. Albert Antonioni had once told me that if I wanted to take him on, I needed to bring an army. So I had brought a small one.

At a quarter to ten o'clock, Richie and I walked through the front door of Jake's at the same moment that Spike and Vinnie Morris came through the door from the kitchen, both with guns in their hands. Vinnie had a .44. Spike had a Smith & Wesson nine-millimeter that I was fairly certain was new.

Junior and Ty Bop and Albert's men looked at Spike and Vinnie. Tony Marcus and Albert looked at Richie and me.

"Don't," Vinnie said to the other shooters in the room.

"We need to talk," I said to Tony and Albert, but Tony knew I really only wanted to talk to Albert.

Tony spoke first.

"You just made a whole lot of fucking trouble for yourself, girl," Tony Marcus said, playing it as well as Denzel would have.

"Well, yeah," I said. "But let's face it, that's not the first time you've told me that."

"This wasn't part of no deal," Tony said.

"You're a businessman, Tony," I said. "Did you think I was going to let Felix Burke cut you in on this gun deal and get nothing in return?"

"Why isn't Felix here?" Tony said.

"Because I am," Richie said.

Albert looked across the booth at Tony.

"You didn't tell me she was in this," he said.

"All due respect, Albert," Tony said. "Just 'cause we about to do business don't mean

I got to tell you all my business."

Richie and I stood in the middle of the room. Richie had said nothing. By instinct I looked over at where Ty Bop was standing near the counter. I knew that he knew how much of this was show. But I also knew that he had the jangled nerves and attention span of a hummingbird. So I was hopeful that he was still processing that in the moment Richie and Spike and Vinnie and his boss — and me — were all on the same team.

"Deal's off," Albert said, and started to slide out of the booth.

"Don't," Vinnie said again.

"I know who you are," Albert said.

"So don't," Vinnie said.

"What," Albert Antonioni said to me, "you just gonna hold us here?"

"I just think of this as an extension of the negotiations that I assume you and Tony have now concluded," I said.

"This ain't your business," Tony said, still acting, and still selling it like a champion.

"Think of this as my commission," I said. "As I understand it, you are getting a whole new territory for your prostitution business, a territory you say you have sought for some time. In return, Albert is about to make a killing, so to speak, on the biggest bulk shipment of illegal guns ever to make its way into New England. My ex-husband and I want nothing to do with any of that. But we do want a little somethin' somethin' in return."

I looked at Albert. "I'm curious about something," I said. "If you wanted Desmond and Felix's guns so badly, why didn't you just take them, and not go after the Burke family this way?"

There was something completely reptilian now in Albert's eyes as he stared at me.

"The first time I ever met you was during that thing with Brock Patton and his daughter, remember?" he said. "You and your husband and Desmond and me. I never told you, because it wasn't shit you needed to know, it was between Desmond and me. But there was a price tag came with me leaving you alone. He never talked about it with anybody else. I never talked about it with anybody else. But the price tag was that Desmond would leave the gun business to me."

I looked at Richie. He shook his head, like it was news to him, too.

"We had an understanding," Albert said. "Now all this time later, he breaks it. I couldn't let that stand."

"I get that," I said. "But why wait this long?"

The old man shrugged. "I figured that I'd let him do the work and then take what should've been mine all along."

"Street justice," Tony said. "Gotta respect that."

"So what do you want from me?" Albert Antonioni said to me.

"You need to tell us where we can find Desmond and Bobby Toms," I said.

"I got no fucking idea what you are talking about," he said. He looked at Tony, as if for backup. "You got any idea what she's talking about?"

Tony made a helpless gesture with his hands.

Albert turned back to me. "You better kill me," he said. "Because if you don't, you're the one's dead once I get out of here."

"I don't think so," I said.

He started to say something. I held up a finger.

"Here's why," I said. "Because Felix Burke believes you are up to your eyeballs in this. He believes you had at least prior knowledge of the harm having been done to his brothers and his family. It was his intent to come here tonight and kill you and your men. Richie convinced him otherwise. Felix has given us his word that if you help him get his brother back, you get his guns and your money. And you're the one who doesn't end up dead."

"Fuck you," Albert said.

"Beautifully put," I said.

"You think I'm still afraid of the Burkes?" he said. "Fuck them, too."

"Take the deal, Albert," I said. "Take the guns, give us Desmond. Because I have the feeling that whatever happens now, Tony is going to get his girls, anyway."

Tony shrugged and smiled and said to Albert, "The heart wants what the heart wants."

I was trying to appear, and remain, calm, even though I was the opposite of that, even though I was once again in a room in the company of men, some as dangerous as men could be. Including, in this moment, Richie Burke.

"I don't know how much of this you have had a hand in, Albert," I said. "But I refuse to believe that you don't know where Bobby Toms has Desmond. I refuse to believe you didn't set this whole thing in motion. So tell us where they are. There are other things I wish to know, but, again, this is not the time, which is now being wasted."

"Say you're right," Albert Antonioni said

finally. "Say I do know. What makes you think I don't call him and warn him the minute you walk out that door?"

Spike said, "We're just gonna hang out here while they do their thing, Albert."

"You think the two of you can just keep us here?" Tony said.

Spike smiled.

"Well, kind of," he said.

I knew they could, mostly because I knew Ty Bop and Junior weren't going to try them. And I knew that two of the guys from Vinnie's crew were now posted outside, one at the front door, one the back.

I looked at Albert.

"He's her son, isn't he?" I said.

He slowly nodded his head.

"And Desmond's?" I said.

He nodded again, as if he had a nice, slow rhythm going for him with his nods.

"Take the deal, Albert," Tony said.

"Where are they?" I said to Albert Antonioni.

He looked around the room, at Spike and Vinnie, at Richie, at his own men, finally at me. It was as if he was working out a math problem.

He nodded one last time.

"The beach house," he said.

SIXTY-SIX

Narragansett, Richie informed me on the ride there, was called Providence South. And was where Mob guys went to the beach.

"How do you know that?" I said.

"Desmond and Felix thought Cape Cod was too fancy for them when I was a boy," he said. "We used to come down here. Their form of reverse snobbery."

Over time, Richie said, some sleazy developers tied to Antonioni had paid off enough politicians, some of whom had ended up in prison for taking kickbacks, and gotten enough permits to build big, vulgar beach homes on bluffs that had once belonged to a nature preserve.

"The area to which we are headed," Richie said, "is now called Black Point."

The very last house at Black Point, once belonging to the late Allie Antonioni, was set apart from the rest overlooking the bay, as if at land's end. We parked about a half-mile away, having passed summer homes now shuttered, hardly any lights on either side of the road for as far as we could see. We walked from there. There was the chance that Bobby Toms, who had provided security for Albert Antonioni, had security for himself out here. But we had decided we just had to risk it, having run out of time.

When we got close to the driveway that fed down to Antonioni's house, we could see lights on the ground floor. There was a big, bright moon on this night, far too bright to suit me, so we could look down the shore to a crescent of sand jutting into Narragansett Bay, and some lights actually still lit from what Richie said was the Bonnet Shore Beach Club.

Richie was wearing a black hoodie and black jeans. As was I. I had a Glock in my hand and a smaller Kel-Tec gun strapped into an ankle holster. Richie carried a Colt in his right hand.

We stood at the foot of the driveway that led down to a house that looked as if it had once been a classic saltbox and then had simply grown into some sort of Mob Mc-Mansion.

"Security cameras?" Richie said.

"If there are, there are," I said.

"We're going in," he said.

"We are," I said. "There has to be a way to get to the back of the house from the beach. You don't own a house like this without beach access."

"Say there is," Richie said. "Say we get to the backyard. What happens if we trip something and all the lights go on?"

"We improvise," I said.

There was a neighbor's house closer to the Bonnet Shore Beach Club, maybe a quarter-mile from Antonioni's, another that was completely dark. We made our way in that direction, through that front yard, down the bluffs to the narrow beach. Up ahead, lit by the moon, we could see a stairway leading down from Antonioni's to the water.

"We can't use the steps," I said. "Let's climb up through the bluffs if we can."

So we did that. I stumbled a few times and went down into the sand. Not Richie. There had always been an amazing grace about him. He was one of those who could walk through a crowded room and somehow not make contact with anyone.

We finally reached the top, and the small backyard where Antonioni said that Bobby Toms was holding Desmond Burke.

"Now what?" Richie whispered.

"Now we make our way to the front and

see what we can see and hope the fucker's alone and we've got him outnumbered," I said.

I could hear my breathing. And his. And the sound of the water below us, and what wind there was in the night. We made our way along the side of the house. No floodlights were lit. There were no other sounds as we tried to creep noiselessly along the house until we came to one of the side windows on the ground floor, draperies partially drawn.

I took a deep breath and inched forward enough to see in.

There, tied to a chair, face bruised and swollen, sat Desmond Burke.

It was then that we heard the click of the hammer behind us and a voice I recognized say, "Either of you move, I shoot her first."

Joseph Marchetti then told us to drop our own weapons. We did.

"Want to take my picture now?" he said.

SIXTY-SEVEN

Bobby Toms sat us on a couch in front of the side window across from Desmond after Joseph Marchetti had walked us inside. The ankle gun was still well hidden by the black Chelsea boots I was wearing. Maybe Marchetti had been so swept away feeling me up that he stopped before he got down there. So at least I still had a weapon, if a small one, when the balloon went up.

"Let them go," Desmond Burke said through swollen lips. "It's me you want."

"Shut up, old man," Bobby Toms said, and asked Joseph Marchetti to go back outside in case Richie and I hadn't come alone.

Years after the photograph of him and his mother had been taken at the Grand Canyon, Bobby Toms's resemblance to Richie wasn't as vivid. But was still there. Maybe because he wore black as well tonight, black leather jacket, black T-shirt underneath.

The gun in his hand was a Sig Sauer.

In a low voice, barely above a whisper, Richie said, "If you're going to kill us all, at least tell us what this is about before you do."

Bobby Toms nodded at Desmond. "Ask him," he said. "We've had a good long talk about the old days."

Desmond looked at Richie and me. He seemed to be summoning all the strength he had just to keep his head up.

"I keep telling him," Desmond said through swollen lips. "I didn't know she was pregnant. I never knew he even existed. I never saw her after she left Boston."

"After you raped her," Bobby Toms said.

"I did not rape her!" Desmond shouted at him. *"How many times do I have to tell you that? I loved her!"*

"Liar!" Bobby Toms shouted back, and took two steps closer to him and gave Desmond a hard, open-palm slap to the side of his head, snapping it back.

I sensed Richie leaning forward slightly on the couch and put a hand on his arm.

Bobby Toms turned and put his gun on Richie and said, "Don't even fucking think about it."

Then he was pacing back and forth in front of us.

"I didn't even know it was you until she died," he said to Desmond. "She told me I belonged to him. Tomasi. She said he died right after I was born. Who the fuck knows where he went or how he died? But she was the one who was dying a little bit at a time, my whole life. Not just because of the Parkinson's. Like she was dying of being sad. Doing volunteer work at the church the whole time I was growing up. Like she was the one paying for her sins."

"I would have tried to help her," Desmond said.

"Mr. Antonioni helped her!" Bobby Toms said, shouting again. "He was the one who loved her. He was the one who took care of her."

"Who told you that Desmond raped her?" I said, already knowing the answer.

"Mr. Antonioni," he said. "Told me that he raped her when she told him she planned to leave him for good."

He turned back to Desmond.

"Now he's going to admit it to me and in front of you," Bobby Toms said. "Or he can watch me do the two of you before I do him."

"I didn't rape her," Desmond said, head hanging again. Bobby walked over and hit him harder than he had before.

I needed time.

I said to Bobby Toms, "Why did you kill Peter?"

Keep him talking.

"Why not?" he said. "I called him and told him I knew who had shot him."

He pointed his gun at Richie.

"Told him to meet me out there in Chestnut Hill," he said. "Who shoots anybody in Chestnut Hill? I told him it was about Maria Cataldo. You know what he did? He laughed. And called her Desmond's *brasser.*"

Even I knew that was the Irish slang for *whore.*

"So I shot him," Bobby said. "And then I shot up the other old man's house to let him know I could. And I shot the mook bodyguard to let him" — he nodded at Desmond — "know I could get as close to him as I fuckin' well wanted."

He smiled, his eyes too big and too bright.

"I even shot one of my own," he said.

There it was.

"Dominic Carbone," I said.

"Thought I could buy myself a little more time," he said. "Buy Mr. A. some time while we looked for those guns. Said he'd cut me in when it was over." He looked at Desmond. "Now you two are gonna tell me where the guns are, because this old fuck won't."

"Albert already knows where they are," I said.

Not technically true. But close enough. "We just made a deal with him tonight. The guns for Desmond."

If Bobby Toms was faking his surprise at that news, he was doing an excellent job of it. But I didn't care whether we'd surprised him or not.

Keep them talking, like Phil Randall said.

Somehow it was as if Richie was thinking right along with me.

"Why didn't Albert tell you sooner?" Richie said. "About Desmond being your father?"

"She made him promise," Bobby said. "But then she was gone. So he told me. Told me that Desmond had never paid for what he did to her, and that maybe it was time. And maybe we could make him pay in all kinds of ways."

He shrugged and said, "So I made him pay a little bit at a time. Gotta tell you, this has been some fun shit."

In the distance there was the sudden crack of what was clearly a gunshot, and then another. Two minutes later, the front door opened and the blond guy shoved Felix

Burke into the room ahead of him.

"Gang's all here," Marchetti said.

Joseph Marchetti went into the kitchen, came back with a chair, then shoved Felix Burke down onto it.

"He shot Padraig," Felix said to Desmond.

Padraig Flynn was one of Felix's body men, and had been for as long as I had known him.

"How did you find us?" Richie said to his uncle.

"Tony told me about the meeting at the diner," Felix said. "I told you I would stand down. I lied, but it was about something important this time."

He smiled a sad smile.

"You thought you were looking out for me," Felix said. "I was looking out for you."

I casually crossed my right leg, the one that had the gun underneath the boot, over my left.

"What is this about?" Felix said, as if talking to everyone in the room.

"Ask him," Bobby Toms said again, pointing his gun at Desmond. "Ask him what he did to my mother. How he started killing her a long time ago."

And then I saw fully all the steel and the

rope in Desmond Burke, everything in him that had taken him off the streets of Southie and had separated him from all the others who wanted what he wanted, all the ones who thought they'd end up kings of the hill. Saw everything in him that had enabled Desmond Burke to outlast and outlive them all.

"You can shoot me where I sit, boy," he said. "You can fucking well shoot all of us. But I will never admit to the lie you were told about me and the lie you are telling. I never forced myself on a woman in my life, and I certainly did not force myself on your mother."

Bobby Toms walked back over to him and put the gun above the bridge of his nose and said, "For the last time, you stop lying to me."

"He's not," Felix Burke said then.

Turned and looked at his brother, something profoundly sad behind his eyes, and then looked up at Bobby Toms and said, "You're pointing your gun at the wrong one."

"What the fuck are you talking about?" Bobby said.

"He's not your father," Felix said. "I am."

SIXTY-EIGHT

Joseph Marchetti continued to point his gun at Richie and me, which gave me no opening or opportunity to reach for my own, as Felix Burke seemed to be talking to himself as much as he was talking to his brother, or to the rest of us.

"It wasn't just Albert who loved her," Felix said. "So did I."

I remembered the night in his brother's living room now, when he had practically begged me to walk away from it all. I remembered the photographs I had seen about how much Desmond and Felix had looked alike when they were younger.

In this room now, Felix could no longer hold his brother's gaze and so stared out the window closest to him instead, at the night or the water or the dark nowhere.

"It was just the one time, that spring," he said to Desmond. "The two of you had broken it off. She called me, hysterical, already a little drunk, to tell me she was leaving Boston forever. She came over to my apartment. And I swear on your own son's head that it was my intent to console. But then more drink was taken, by both of us." He ran out of words then.

"And you betrayed me," Desmond said, finishing the thought for his brother. "The both of you."

"I loved her first," Felix said.

I wondered what Desmond would have done in the moment if his hands were not bound behind him.

"She called me a few months later, without telling me where she was," Felix said. "She told me she was pregnant, and that it had to be my child, and that her father was making arrangements. I didn't ask what the arrangements were, and she didn't tell me. What she did tell me was that she never wanted to see me, or you, ever again."

"You're all lying!" Bobby Toms shouted now.

"I'm not," Felix said.

In a much quieter voice, Bobby Toms, talking only to himself now, said, "Fuck it. Time to end this."

"Yeah," Joseph Marchetti said, and turned away from Richie and me and shot Bobby Toms in the forehead.

Marchetti took a step back then, slightly away from the window, so he could see us all at once and said, "The old man told me to tie up as many loose ends as I had to." He grinned. "Starting with the loose cannon."

He looked at Desmond and Felix and said, "Now who wants it first?"

Then everything seemed to happen at once, Joseph Marchetti pointing his gun at Desmond and Felix throwing himself and his chair sideways to put himself in the line of fire, in the instant before Marchetti pulled the trigger. Then I was clearing my own gun and rolling off the couch as the window behind Marchetti and behind Richie and me shattered, and a bullet from outside hit Marchetti in the back of his head and he went down next to Bobby Toms.

Richie was already across the room, kneeling next to his uncle Felix, the one who'd raised him more than his own father had, the one who'd just taken a bullet intended for Desmond Burke in the back.

Then Vinnie Morris was kicking in what was left of the shattered side window and stepping through it, saying, "I didn't have a clear shot because the two of you were in the way, but I figured I couldn't wait no longer. Then the guy moved just enough."

Richie was holding his uncle Felix in his arms. I went and got a kitchen knife and cut loose the rope tying Desmond's hands, and then Desmond was lying next to his brother on the floor, saying something that I could not hear and feared Felix could not hear.

Blood was blood.

I called 911, and then Pete Colapietro.

SIXTY-NINE

Richie and Desmond rode in the ambulance with Felix on the way to Rhode Island Hospital, the same one in which Maria Cataldo had died.

Then it was just Vinnie Morris and me. Before Richie and I had left Jake's, I had told Vinnie that if he didn't hear from us within an hour after we left him and Spike at the diner that he needed to come after us.

Spike had asked why I didn't want him to be the one to come after us.

"Because Vinnie is a better shot than you," I'd said.

"Better than anybody," Vinnie had said.

Before he left, Vinnie had apologized again for not getting a clear enough shot before Marchetti shot Bobby. I told him that it had finally become a moment, as embarrassed as I was to say it, when he needed to shoot first and ask questions later.

"Yeah," he said. Then he said, "That expression you always use about the balloon going up? That fucker had gone up."

"There was more I wanted to know," I said.

"It was them or you," he said. "And Richie."

I knew it hadn't been an ethical choice for Vinnie, even though I knew he operated by a code he had constructed for himself, one where he wasn't a criminal, just the people who hired him. And Vinnie knew when I had enlisted him to help tonight that I wanted Bobby Toms arrested, not shot. But what had ended in this room, Bobby is the one who had started it all. Until it had been him or us.

Then Vinnie was gone, almost as if he hadn't been there at all, on his way back to Jake's to pick up the men from his crew with whom he had originally driven down from Boston. Somewhere between Jake's and his bowling alley, I knew his long gun would disappear forever.

Pete Colapietro lived close enough to Black Point that he managed to beat what seemed half of the Providence Police Department to the scene. When he arrived I told him that Bobby Toms, likely with the assistance of Joseph Marchetti, had kidnapped Desmond Burke and brought him here. That Marchetti had walked Richie and me into this room. That shortly thereafter, shooting had commenced.

Colapietro listened. By now I knew he was the kind of cop Belson was. And my father had been. He would be able to pretty much remember what I was telling him, word for word.

"So Marchetti shot Bobby Toms first," Pete said.

"Yes."

"Pretty much at the same time that another shot came from outside and put down Marchetti," he said.

I could hear the first sirens in the distance.

"Must have been a sniper," I said.

He gave me a long look. "You know I like you, Sunny," he said. "I've been pulling some strings for you. I kept the Taunton cops away from that diner tonight. I rode around with you the other day on my own time. But I'm a cop. And a goddamn good one. And even both of us knowing that a couple of no-good guys came off the books tonight, I know there's a lot of shit you're not telling me here. Starting with who the outside shooter was who shot Antonioni's shooter."

The sirens were getting louder.

Pete nodded at the window.

"Guy who could make that kind of shot in the night, from a distance," he said.

"Maybe Albert thought these guys were making too much trouble for him," I said. "Maybe he hired somebody. Who can know these things?"

He gave me another long look. "You know anybody who can make a shot like that?" he said.

"Only heard of them," I said.

"Yeah," he said. "Me, too."

"I just got caught up in the middle of a Mob war," I said. "All the way to the end."

"That's your story," Pete Colapietro said.

"And I'm sticking to it," I said.

Pete said, "I'm gonna need you to come to the station and make a statement. And answer some questions that I might not be the only one asking."

I told him Richie and I had left the car up the road a bit.

"We'll go now," Pete said.

"Understood," I said.

By now the cavalry had arrived, lights flashing, cars making plenty of noise on the gravel driveway. Pete badged everyone in sight, telling them that I was with him. We got into his car. He drove me to my car.

On the way to downtown Providence

Richie called and told me that Felix Burke had died not long after they'd gotten him inside the hospital.

Sins of the father, I thought.

Felix being the father.

SEVENTY

We had sat up long into the night after Felix Burke's funeral, Desmond, Richie, me. We had been drinking whiskey for some time. Irish, appropriately enough. Midleton Very Rare. Desmond was finally ready to tell some of the things Bobby Toms had told him after Bobby had taken him from this house in the night, things about his mother and the life they had shared in Arizona, in a house in the name of one of Vincent Cataldo's shell companies, about how when the money she had inherited from her father had finally run out, she had decided to call Albert Antonioni.

"Somehow Albert had convinced him that he was the only one who had ever truly loved his mother," Desmond said. "There had been something between them before we took up together. She honestly did never tell me. In the world in which we existed, she clearly thought there was enough bad blood, and did not want to be responsible for more."

He looked at Richie and said, "I've always known how much Albert hated me. I just did not know how much he loved her."

He drank. We all did.

"Why do you suppose Albert pointed him at you?" Richie said.

"Maybe someday," Desmond said, "I will get to ask him that myself."

Desmond took in some air slowly, and held it, and then let it out as slowly as he had taken it in. Then drank more Irish whiskey. I had watched him drink a lot. And show no signs of being drunk in any way.

"He had always wanted to beat me, in everything," Desmond said. "Now he saw a chance to take my guns and so take my money, and tell himself he didn't have to be the one to kill me in order to beat me."

"Blood money," Richie said.

"Felix's blood," Desmond said.

"Do you think Albert ever suspected that Bobby might be Felix's son?" I said.

"Maybe I can ask him that, too," Desmond said, "if the occasion arises."

Public lives, I thought, *private lives.*
Secret lives.

Two weeks later, there were two stories

played on the same page of *The Boston Globe,* as if of a piece.

One was about the body of Albert Antonioni, described as a notorious Rhode Island crime boss, found floating in the water of Narragansett Bay, between Antonioni's own home at Black Point and the Bonnet Shore Beach Club, two bullet holes in him, one in the forehead, one more in the back for good measure. Providence police, the story said, had been notified that the body was there by an anonymous call made to their Crimestoppers tip line.

The other story was about two Cranston, Rhode Island, warehouses filled with illegal guns — most of them automatic weapons — being raided by ATF agents. The estimate for the value of the guns was two million dollars. The story said it was the biggest raid of its kind in the history of New England. The warehouses, now abandoned, had once been owned by the Palomino Vending Company, owned by the late Albert Antonioni.

It was, I knew, the interesting place where Felix had stored their guns.

I was still at the kitchen table reading my *Globe* and drinking my coffee and occasionally feeding Rosie some of my blueberry scone from Starbucks when my phone rang.

I saw the name come up and so was smiling as I answered.

"You're welcome," I said to Charlie Whitaker.

SEVENTY-ONE

Richie and Rosie and I had walked along the river for a bit and were now sitting on the dock facing Cambridge. It was the second week of October, an Indian-summer afternoon, and the scene across the Charles looked pretty enough to paint. Maybe even by me someday. Just not until I finished, finally, my small stone cottage from Concord. I was close now, and happy with it. Just not totally happy. So it went.

"For the last time," I said, "do you believe Desmond somehow shot Albert himself?"

"The last time?" Richie said. "You promise?"

"Well, maybe last time today," I said.

Before he answered he fed Rosie a treat from his pocket. She was on a leash but at rest between Richie and me. Because of the treats. And because she liked being between Richie and me.

"I think he did it," Richie said. "I don't

know how he got to him. I don't want to know. But yes, I believe he would do it himself. His own sense of justice, and vengeance."

"Always been a lot about him you didn't want to know," I said.

"And look what it got me," Richie said. "Now I know more about him than I ever wanted to." He paused and said, "About both of them."

"You miss Felix," I said.

An answer, not a question.

"It's odd, if you think about it," Richie said. "I looked up to him the way he always looked up to Desmond."

He fed Rosie another treat. We had been discussing where to have dinner. I had even promised to watch a Red Sox playoff game with him later. I had suggested cooking dinner myself. Richie had smiled when I made the offer and said, "No, thank you."

"Desmond loved her," I said now.

"Probably more than he loved my mother," Richie said. "But that's something he'll probably only admit to God. If he even admits it to Him."

"And Felix loved her," I said.

"Maybe more than Desmond did."

"Albert loved her," I said.

"She must have really been something."

He turned to look at me. "Like you."

"Taking care of her at the end may have been Albert's one true thing," I said.

"Won't be enough to get the old bastard into heaven," Richie said.

"How Catholic of you."

"Comes and goes," he said.

"The ironic part of this," I said, "if irony even applies here, is that Albert wanted Bobby to take out Desmond. But in the end, Albert and Bobby really ended up taking out each other."

Rosie roused herself, briefly, having noticed another dog, a pug on a leash being walked by a pretty young redheaded woman. But we both knew Rosie was only bluffing. If she didn't know there were more treats, she sensed it.

Richie said, "It's interesting, what Bobby told my father about Maria working at the church."

"I wonder if she saw her greatest sin as having gotten pregnant outside of marriage," I said, "or that Felix was the one who'd gotten her pregnant."

"Maybe both," Richie said.

"Powerful force, guilt."

"That and grudges," Richie said.

"Make the world go 'round," I said.

He reached over and took my hand and

held it in his.

"Dr. Silverman," I said, "thinks that in a vastly complicated way Albert convinced himself that not directly punishing Desmond himself was a form of respect, even if a subordinate did the shooting and the killing."

"I think it just makes him a coward," Richie said. "Who fucking well got what he deserved."

The Burke in him coming out, the way it did sometimes.

"There's so much we'll never know," I said.

"That bother you?"

"No," I said.

"Liar," he said, and squeezed my hand.

"So what *do you* want to eat tonight?" I said.

He turned to look at me again. "Not Italian," he said.

We held hands and stared at the water.

I received the first of two phone calls then, one right after another, by sheer chance.

Or not.

The small screen read "Desmond."

I stood, held up a finger to Richie, and walked about twenty yards away, out of his earshot.

There were no salutations.

400

"You told the coppers where to find my guns," he said. "That wasn't part of our deal."

"We had no deal," I said, "other than me keeping you alive."

"Those were my guns," he said.

"I probably never mentioned it before," I said. "But I hate illegal guns. *Hate* them. Especially the fast-shooting kind that shoot schoolchildren."

And ended the call.

Before my phone was in my back pocket, it started buzzing again.

This time the screen read "Unknown Caller."

I stayed where I was, almost certain of who the unknown caller was.

Women's intuition.

"Sunny Randall!" I said in a cheerful, receptionist's voice.

"You fucked me over," Tony Marcus said, not sounding cheerful at all.

"Well, hello yourself, Tony," I said.

I saw Richie staring at me. I smiled and waved.

"Once Albert was gone," he said, "those guns should've reverted back to me."

"I don't think so."

"Who gives a rat's ass what you think?"

he said. "I'm *tellin'* you how it is. And what it is."

"It may be a fine point," I said. "But since we don't know when exactly Albert died, we may be dealing with a chicken-and-egg thing here."

"You tipped off the goddamn Feds, didn't you?" he said.

No reason to tell one last lie. Or keep secrets.

"As a matter of fact, I did."

"What's Desmond think about that?" he said. "Maybe he thinks those guns were more his than mine, even if I did make a deal with his brother."

"I don't care what he thinks," I said. "And I'll tell you why, Tony. I get that guns are a part of my world. Part of my own family business, if you think about it. But if I just took a shitload of them off the street, and off you, well, hooray for me."

"Just so you know?" Tony said. "We got a brand-new grudge going now, girl. So you take care watchin' your back."

"So it goes," I said.

I hung up on him and walked back over to Richie. He asked to whom I'd been speaking.

"The usual," I said. "Bad guys."

"You'll tell me which ones later?" he said.

"If you can somehow manage to charm the information out of me," I said.

I smiled at him.

"Give me an honest answer," I said. "Do you think I'm looking older?"

Richie smiled back.

"I'll tell you when we get back home," he said. "Provided you can charm *that* information out of me."

I kissed him on the lips and then the three of us walked back over the bridge to River Street Place. I still didn't think of it as home, and didn't know if I ever would. But it would do for now.

ACKNOWLEDGMENTS

One more time, I would like to thank the real Mike Stanton, my tour guide in Providence.

I would also like to thank three dear friends who were generous with counsel and support in the writing of this book:

David Koepp, Harlan Coben, and Raymond Kelly, former Police Commissioner of the City of New York.

And finally, David and Daniel Parker, Ivan Held, Sara Minnich: Who gave me the chance to come play with the cool kids.

ABOUT THE AUTHOR

Mike Lupica is a prominent sports journalist and the *New York Times*-bestselling author of more than forty works of fiction and nonfiction. A longtime friend to Robert B. Parker, he was selected by the Parker estate to continue the Sunny Randall series.

The employees of Thorndike Press hope you have enjoyed this Large Print book. All our Thorndike, Wheeler, and Kennebec Large Print titles are designed for easy reading, and all our books are made to last. Other Thorndike Press Large Print books are available at your library, through selected bookstores, or directly from us.

For information about titles, please call:
(800) 223-1244

or visit our website at:
gale.com/thorndike

To share your comments, please write:
Publisher
Thorndike Press
10 Water St., Suite 310
Waterville, ME 04901